The Accardi Job

The Accardi Job

RYDER LIM

This book takes place in a time when terms and attitudes which might be considered offensive by modern readers were common.

This is a work of fiction. Names, characters, places, and incidents are products of the author's imagination or are used fictitiously and are not to be construed as real. Any resemblance to events, locales, organizations, or persons, living or dead, is entirely coincidental unless clearly meant to reflect historic events.

Chapter 1

A Mysterious Man

New York City, nineteen forty-seven. The rain poured from the heavens, and the tall, dim lamps shone onto the streets. Stray cats, shattered glass, and piles of shit filled desolate road. Bobby Davinson, a man with little money, respect, and dignity left in his miserable life, lived in a small apartment on Bathgate Street. Bobby's apartment had only a taped-up couch, a leaking roof, and rats crawling through the darkness. He awoke quickly, tossing his head side to side. He rubbed his rough palm gently over his face and eyes, then groaned with despair, looking at the clock. It read one fifteen a.m.

Bobby lay still, staring at the endless rain through the cracked windows. He then reached over to grab a bottle of whiskey lying on the weathered floor. His thirst was never quenched, however, for he found nothing but emptiness upon angling down the bottle. The groggy man stood up and slowly stepped over to his fridge, only to find it too was empty. So, Bobby decided to go out.

Bobby was a black man with short hair and a sturdy jawline. He wore a drenched coat in the light rain, a roughed-up top hat, some poor boots, and pants about to split in half. Nearly tripping over curbs, Bobby strolled down the damp street and continued walking until he was about fifteen feet away from the nearby bar. He then promptly paused, hearing loud chattering and laughing coming from within. A group of proud white boys toppled out of this nearby bar, meeting the half-opened eyes of Bobby.

The boys were all drunk as could be, no older than nineteen and no more than five of them, all in tight-collared shirts and nice pants. They continued laughing for a good minute before they looked ahead and finally cleared their minds enough to notice the black man who stood before them. Suddenly, their laughs turned sinister as they all looked up to stare at Bobby, yelling with booze down their throats and tequila in their heads, "You lost, pal?"

"Just heading to the bar," Bobby answered, slowly.

"This town doesn't want you colored folk around here. So why don't you skedaddle on back home to where you belong," said the boy.

"Please, I don't want any trouble."

The front boy slowly stepped closer until Bobby was able to smell his stenchful breath. He looked Bobby dead in the eye, still drunk, and said, "Maybe you didn't hear me right. Go on home before we bust your nigger ass up!"

Bobby nodded his head and started to turn around. Suddenly, however, Bobby sprung around and jabbed the boy right in the face. The kid, as drunk as could be, went flying down onto the puddled ground, and with a voice of rage, he then shouted, "GET 'EM!"

Bobby swiftly turned once again and started running away. The boys chased after him. Bobby ran faster and faster down the dark streets, until he came into a glum alleyway behind a couple of abandoned buildings. With the lights flickering and the mud crawling with opossums, Bobby ran to the end of the alley only to find a tall, barricaded fence. He turned to find the white boys right behind him. The kids slowed down as they approached him, yelling, "Who do you think you are, nigger?!"

The boy then rushed on Bobby, pushing him down to the ground. "Get up! Get up nigger!" The boys screamed and screamed at the man until they pulled him up themselves. They started beating Bobby. They punched and kicked at the poor man until he was covered in his own blood. Moments later, a policeman in a short vehicle strolled down the road, and hearing the faint sounds of agony, he turned the wheel to slowly drive toward the alleyway. He inched up more and more and saw the group of white boys beating on poor Bobby. The boys stopped and turned in slight fear, but that fear soon vanished as the cop gave a slight nod, turned his head and drove off, noticing who Bobby was.

Bobby tried fighting back; grabbing a bottle, he hit one of the kids with it, but it only made matters worse. "Take that!" they yelled. "Nigger!" they called him. The front boy of the group grabbed the bottle that lay on the floor and smashed it atop Bobby's fragile head.

The bar down the street held an old colored bartender, who was making himself busy as he heard laughs and chants coming from a pack outside. The bartender looked through the big glass windows across from him to see outside no more than five young white boys walking past his bar, laughing and babbling. About four minutes later, the bartender looked up again at the bell's ring to see who came in—it was Bobby, looking around at the green walling and the dimly lit lights as he slowly walked over to the counter, where he made his seat.

"I'll take the usual," Bobby said in an aching tone. The bartender stared at him for a minute, glancing at his wounds and bloodied face before he leaned over to him and said with a grin, "Yu' got it bad this time. Yu' gotta stop aggravating these white boys, or one of these days yu' going to end up killin' yu'self."

Bobby breathed in as he softly stated, "Yeah, well, I never back down from a fight."

The bartender, who placed a drink in front of the bloodied man, replied, "Well, then maybe stop starting 'em?"

The broken and blood-soaked man looked down at the countertop as he closed his eyes roughly, allowing no unwanted tears to pass through.

Ding, the bell rang. The door to the front of the bar opened and then closed as a mysterious figure walked in. This mysterious man was also of color. He had a short black mustache running thinly across his lips; he wore a dark pork pie hat, a semi-expensive pair of pants, hard, thick boots with rough souls, and a dark blue sweater underneath that of a nicely made leather jacket. The man walked over to the counter where he took his seat.

"Scotch if you will," the man uttered to the bartender.

The working man put a glass on the counter and poured into it before softly pushing the glass to his left, placing it in front of the mysterious man, who tossed the drink down his throat briskly, before looking to his left. Upon seeing Bobby, the mysterious man pulled out a white piece of cloth and said, "Here boy, take this."

Bobby slowly looked up and stared at the man as he reached out his arm and grabbed the cloth. "Th-thank you," he said.

"No problem. Those white boys ruffed you up pretty bad, huh? I saw them, on my way to the bar," the man replied, looking down at Bobby's arm and around his body, which was as red as an apple, covered with blood and bruises.

Bobby looked at the mysterious figure and said, "Nothing I haven't handled before. Nice to meet you. My name is Bobby Dav…"

"Bobby Davinson," the mysterious man interrupted.

"How did you…"

"Born August fifth, nineteen oh one in Saint Thomas, attended Harvard Medical School, dropped out though cause you had to care for your mother who was ill at the time, but went back after her demise. Spent five years as a surgeon, two as an entrepreneur, and one as a cab driver. You got a gambling addiction and only stopped when you owed ten grand to the Savelli family, which you said you would pay off but now you're not so sure, and these days you spend your time at home reading cheap novels or drinking what liquor you can find all day long. Occasionally you get roughed up by some white boys for simply the color of your skin, but you don't let it get to you."

"How… how do you… How do you know all that? Do you work for Melassy? Cuz I told him I-I would get the money, I just need a little more time."

"I do not work for Melassy, or Cleo, or any family under Accardi."

"Then who are you?"

"You can call me Jones," the man said in a small, although serious voice.

4

"I'm sorry, I'm still confused. I—"

"How would you like to pay off your debt and earn a whole lot of money in the process?" Jones interrupted again. "Cause I've got a job, a high-paying job, and I need more sets of hands. If you're interested, come to this address tomorrow at eight a.m. on the dot, don't be late."

Placing a well-printed business card directly in front of Bobby, Jones got up from the counter and started for the door.

"Wait!" Bobby called out as Jones slowly turned back, facing him. "Wh-wh-wha-when-uh... Why me?" the bewildered man asked.

"Cause you have nothing left to lose," Jones said, looking back into Bobby's eyes. Walking out into the foggy night, Jones softly remarked once more, "Eight a.m." And just like that, he was gone.

II

Back to nineteen forty-three, David Cockspy and his brother Arnom Cockspy were enlisted into the second World War. In Western Alaska, the two brothers made busy, playing cards with other soldiers in the small, compact base hidden along the foothills of the mountains. Everyone wore hard, hot, itchy uniforms and had long rifles on them at all times. The air was filled with screaming crows, tired soldiers, and a smell that even the devil himself would have nightmares about. In some spots, there were tents where people would eat, cook, and sleep. Beyond the base was always gloomy and dark, even midday.

David Cockspy had a wife back home, and though he had been gone for six months, he maintained a connection with his wife by constantly writing to her. With him shipping out to new places, it was rare to receive a card from his wife promptly, but every night David would look up at the stars and remember his loving Charlotte back home and count the minutes till he could see her again.

"Hah! Trip aces! I win!" one of the soldiers exclaimed, slamming his cards down on the tiny crate being used as a table. David, his brother, Arnom, and the other soldiers looked up at each other, exchanging sarcastic grins with the game winner.

Shuffling the cards, a soldier said, "Yeah, I can't wait to get back home to my two little girls. I'd give anything just to make it home to them, cook their favorite chicken dish, and cuddle with my darling wife. What about you Arnom, you got a woman back home?"

"I'm afraid not. I guess I just haven't found the right gal yet," said Arnom.

"Screw that! You ain't need no 'right gal'! I'll tell yuh' what, next time we go to a bar together, I'll patch you up with just the woman, trust me."

"I don't know, I don't care for emotionless sex," Arnom said.

"That's about the stupidest thing I've ever heard," another conversed.

"Well, we all have our differences."

"I bet he's still a virgin," one of them said, causing the other men to laugh.

The general was marching along the grounds when he saw the group of soldiers playing cards. "What do you dogfaces think you're doing!?" he shouted, fierce in tone.

The men all rose and saluted their general as David replied, "Playing cards general!"

The general looked at the men and shouted in a fierce tone, "Get off your lousy asses and get to patrol or the next lot of you will be bubble dancing for the rest of the week!"

"Sir, with all due respect, there is no action, and we have already patrolled for the past sixteen hours. I honestly don't think we'll get visitors soon," said clever Arnom.

"LOOKOUT!"

BAM!

"EVERYONE to their stations NOW!"

With a sharp grin, the general said calmly, "Looks like we have visitors."

The troops rallied and stormed to the edges of the mountainous hills, tossing their bodies against the stony slants, their rifles directly in front of them. Shooting began and the battle was grave. Landmines blew up by the dozen, as hundreds of enemy soldiers charged toward the Americans, all firing their own weapons. David saw a huge man with a giant rifle close to the hills. Looking through the scope and placing the red center directly on the zoomed in image of the soldier's head, David aimed his rustic rifle. But suddenly everything slowed down. All David could hear were screams, shots, explosives detonating, and the sound of his stiff breath. He had a clear shot on the approaching enemy, but he was completely frozen in place, stuck in time.

David's pointer finger, which leaned against the trigger, was shaking. His breath kept getting louder and louder until it became the only thing he could hear. He could not move, he could not think, he was just standing there, staring at the troop he laid his pupils on. David's eyes widened as he saw the huge trooper slow down and toss up his rifle. The shaking man still could not move and still could not pull the trigger, all while the enemy soldier slowed to a full stop. As at least forty other enemy troops ran past him, the large man aimed his firearm up to the tops of the hills. David knew someone was about to die if he didn't pull the trigger. His dirt-covered eyes wouldn't blink, and he was shaking so hard it looked as if he was having a seizure.

Breathing a hundred miles per hour, David's heart was about to shoot out of his chest, his eardrums about to shatter. But then everything went silent. David stared at the soldier and heard one loud shot. The enemy's gun tossed out a metal bullet capsule that sprung at a motionless David.

Swiftly turning to his left, David's heart fell as he saw his only brother, Arnom, shot in the head. At the impact of the bullet, a small burst of blood spurted out of Arnom's forehead, and then the blood slowly poured out, David's dear brother falling backwards, dropping his rifle. David dropped to the ground to catch his brother. Everything went cold in Arnom's body, and his veins just vanished. The glimmer in his eyes slowly faded to black as his tongue crept out of his mouth.

"No no no no no! Arnom!" David shouted. Tears flooding his face as David watched as his brother let out a small groan, crying out in

7

great agony. "No no no no no no no no no! NOOO! I'm sorry! I am so so sorry!" David sobbed again and again.

With his mind crumbling, and his face collapsing, his heart shattering, David awoke.

"GET UP! Get up you slopes!" the guard yelled, banging on the cell door. David flashed his eyes open and sprung up out of his small bed. He slowly breathed in and out, gasping from the memory he had relived. He put both his hands on his face and looked at the walls, waking from his dream. The walls were made of concrete, and the single window was smaller than a pillow. He looked to his right at a giant metal door with a small mail slip-like hole for the guards to look through. "Get up fathead!" the guard shouted, thrusting open the metal door.

David slowly looked down as he saw the gray cloth outfit he had on and remembered the present.

"Let's go! It's breakfast time!" the guard yelled. David marched out of his cell and followed the line of prisoners down to the cafeteria to receive breakfast. At the long metal table in the cafeteria, David couldn't stop thinking about his dream. The horrifying memory circled his mind enough to where he didn't realize the pack of angry men approaching him. A couple of inmates went up to David and said with angry tones, "What you think you doin'?"

"What does it look like? I'm eating," David said, sarcastic and soft.

"Yeah, well, you see here fella, this is our table, and that seat you're sitting in, that's my seat."

"Sorry, but I don't see your name on it," David replied.

"Think you're funny huh?"

The large inmate grabbed David by the ends of his shoulders, and hearing the chants and laughter from the men behind him, the inmate lifted David off the ground. The giant beast-like man stared into David's eyes before he tossed him across the cafeteria. "Not so funny now, huh, funny guy?" the inmate said, proud and loud. David's slick brown hair and his short dark beard shriveled as he was kicked in the stomach repeatedly by the inmate's friends.

The guards all around the cafeteria simply ignored the situation. As the inmates walked away to their food, David started coughing until he threw up. The stinky smell of baby food mixed with burnt pasta flew through the acid of his stomach as it was spurred out. The guard walked over to David and said with a serious tone, "You better clean that up."

So David, by order, dropped a saggy, wet mop on the floor but moments later, still aching all over with bruises. He struck the mop side to side when the large inmate who had hassled him earlier dropped his food-filled tray on the floor right in front of David as he walked off. "Oops! My bad," the bald, tattooed man said, chuckling whilst David stood sad and depressed.

"Cockspy! You have a visitor!" a guard yelled from across the empty cafeteria. David rotated back, glaring at the guard, giving him a confused and suspicious look. He rested the mop on the wall and followed the guard. The rusted door that stood in front of David minutes later was opened promptly, with David's escort fashionably pushing him into the secluded room and locking the door behind him. Inside the room, a mysterious man sat, looking down at the metal table in front of him. As David drew nearer, the man slowly lifted his head, revealing more of his hat-covered face. This was a dark man, with a small, tight mustache, a blue sweater under a bruised, brown leather jacket, and a dark pork pie hat.

"Who the hell are you?" David asked, somewhat scared.

"Why hello, my name is Jones."

"Jones? Th-that's it, just Jones. No first name, last name, middle name. Just Jones? Ok, Jones, who are you, and what do you want with me?"

"You've been here, for how long? Two, no... almost three years. Wow! Almost three years! Is that right?"

"What of it?!"

"That's a long time to be shut out of the world."

"Who are you!" David asked, now in a louder tone, angered by the mysterious man's riddling remarks.

"I'm a businessman. I have been watching you for quite some time and what I have found is greatly fascinating. You're in here for arson. Correct?" David angrily slammed his hands on the table, saying aggressively, "Who the hell are you! I don't want any trouble so just leave me alone!"

Looking at David, seeing the scared little boy inside of him, Jones replied, "I am here to give you a choice. Now, would you like to keep moping around like a depressed donkey or would you like to take a seat and listen to my offer?" David looked at him with a curious grin and slowly fell into the chair.

"The way I see it, you have two options. You can sit in this hellhole for the next three years or you can get out of here, earn back your freedom, and make a whole lotta money while doing it."

"What do I need to do?"

Jones rose from his seat, tossing a card in front of David, saying, "This address, tomorrow, eight a.m. Now if you will excuse me, I have breakfast reservations." Jones then walked away from David, leaving him with a shocked and confused expression. On his way out, Jones slightly nodded at the guard outside the room, while the guard did the same. As David looked at the card, the guard walked over and said, "David Cockspy, you have been released."

David sprung back toward the guard and said in shock, "What!?"

It was a bright, sunny morning outside of the prison. A sharp jacket over a tailored collared shirt with khakis and polished shoes was what David now wore. He walked out to the street, took a deep breath in, hardly believing what his eyes were telling him, and started moving his legs. Off he was—somehow, a free man.

III

A nice car pulled up to the back alleyway behind an old parlor shop. The door to the car opened and one foot at a time, a man got out. This was a large white man with bolder eyes and an overly tight blue suit. He had a very nice dark fedora hat on. It looked as expensive as the rest of his outfit, including his shoes which were nicely polished and tightly worn. The large man shut the car door behind him with a loud slam and began looking around. Just then, from out of the shadows crept a squirmy little man. This was a short man, about five foot four.

A well-kept man with a small, skinny mustache, the squirmy Greek man was. With a polite yet sinister voice, he wore a dark brown suit with light stripes down them. He carried with him a briefcase as well. "Yoohoo," the man yodeled from behind. The big man turned around and jumped up with his arms, saying, "Ah, Sylvester. Good to see you, my friend!"

Sylvester Erellio was a thieving con man who was wanted in various states for small crimes like petty theft, and sometimes larger crimes like bank heists.

"Have you brought what I asked for, Sylvester?" the big man asked.

"Have you ever known me not to, Cleo? Do you have my money?" Sylvester responded with a jolly voice.

Cleo the Cow was his name; he was the nephew of the head of the family Maleté, one of the four crime families serving under the Accardis. Cleo snapped his puffy fingers, and his bodyguard approached the stubby Italian man with a metal briefcase. Cleo opened the briefcase and inside were rows of stacked cash. Sylvester followed and placed his own briefcase on the car, snapping up the hinges before slowly opening it, revealing five beautifully cut diamonds. The diamonds were very rare, and worth quite a lot; they held crystals inside the crystals and were pierced with glazing blue beams. Cleo slowly walked over to the diamonds with a big smile on his face. He felt the diamonds with the tips of his fingers and said, very amused, "Just like Grandmama's. Well, let's let Augusta make sure the diamonds are legit, then I'll give you your money and we'll all be happily on our way." Sylvester nodded with a gracious but ominous look.

Augusta, the diamond analyzer, leaned forward to the diamonds as he pulled out a small telescope-like device. He looked into the glass and carefully examined the diamonds. He continued looking very carefully until he leaned back out and wiped the lens of the small device with a piece of cloth. "They're real," he said surely.

"Ah, great!" Cleo said joyfully before he gladly handed Sylvester the case of cash, saying, "Pleasure doing business with you as always. Prego my friend." Sylvester, with a large smile, turned and slowly walked away as Cleo walked over to his new diamonds. Grabbing the edges of the briefcase and slowly pulling them down, Cleo suddenly stopped. Staring at the diamonds he reopened the case and leaned forward. He analyzed the diamonds as he drew a big, hate-filled frown on his face.

His bodyguard opened the car door for him and said, "Sir?"

But Cleo took his face out of the case and turned around to scream, "Sylvester!"

Sylvester quickly turned and asked, "Yes, is something the matter?"

"You tiny little GRIFTER!" Cleo screamed angrily. "When I was a wee boy my grandmama had diamonds just like these around her neck. I could never forget the sparkle and sizzle in those diamonds, and supposedly these are the same type of diamonds, yet I do not see that same light and sparkle. They're FAKE!"

As Cleo slammed the briefcase of diamonds on the ground, Sylvester knew it was over and made a run for it. Cleo ran to get inside the car, yelling at the driver, "Don't let him get away!" As Cleo slammed the door and the car started to chase after Sylvester, Cleo, in the back seat of the car, looked to his left at the diamond analyzer and said, "Addio amico mio." Cleo then pulled out his twenty-two and shot the traitorous man right in the center of his neck. "Oh, mèrda! Now I have blood on my jacket," the big man exclaimed with a frustrated tone.

Sylvester sprinted as fast as he could down the streets of Brooklyn. Bumping into every man and woman there was, he never stopped for one single breath. Quickly looking back, Sylvester saw

Cleo's car chasing after him. He kept running and running away from the man he had ripped off. He soon, however, came across a road rushing with cars. He looked side to side, gaining a worried grin on his face before he leapt into traffic and ran across the street. He kept stopping and running and walking and jumping, but he finally got across the street. He continued to run to the end of the following street until he saw a nearby candy store. Running into the shop like a madman and jumping over the counter, whilst clutching the briefcase full of cash, Sylvester looked up at the cashier who stood next to him.

"Hey! What do you think you're..."

"Sh, sh, sh!" Sylvester interrupted, placing his finger vertically against his lips. He looked at the young candy man and said with a frightened screech, "Please." The man nodded his head, somehow feeling sorry for Sylvester, and looked up. Sylvester let out a big breath of ease at this.

BANG! BANG! BANG! Sylvester heard as Cleo fired his Tommy gun, spitting bullets through the store windows. Smashing through the glass, all the tiny bullets came crashing into the walls of jellybean jars and the shelves of chocolate bars, making them come flying down. The women screamed and the men ran away at the obliteration of the shop, while the candy man froze in terror.

BAM! BAM! BAM! the young candy man heard as bullets bounced into his chest, making him flop backward onto the extirpated shelves. The man's body slid down to the ground, landing right next to Sylvester, who looked at a near back door, and, thinking of his own life, he wondered if he could make it out.

"I know you're in there you one-eyed gopher!" Cleo screamed. Sylvester quickly got up, ducked down, and ran toward the back door. Upon seeing Sylvester, Cleo fired his Tommy gun once again. With roaring shots and blazing slugs, Cleo shot to kill. Sylvester jumped through the door onto the ground, barely making it out alive. He instantly stood up and continued running through the back of the store. Cleo looked at his men and waved them in to follow the escaping man. The men gave Cleo a slight nod and ran into the store, guns raised.

Sylvester heard the men coming behind him. He pushed over a cart of gumballs and then ran straight out the door into the back alleyway. The men running after him immediately slid and fell backwards. Sylvester paused for a moment in the back alleyway as he took a deep breath in. The men were now pissed off, and they fired in the air, warning Sylvester that he was about to get the beating of his life. Hearing this suddenly, Sylvester jumped back on the run and flung himself down the next street.

Passing through the nearby market, Sylvester grabbed and chucked up bags, beads, shirts, and anything he saw to get in the men's way. Cleo's men simply pushed it out of their way and continued to run after the man, as they held out their arms and fired. Shot after shot they were close, but Sylvester's skin never bled, for he was fast, clever, and kept causing distractions for the chasing men. As they shot, the civilians screamed and ran away. The men were further down behind Sylvester's trail, who up ahead took a pause for breath, as he also gasped at seeing the swooshing traffic in front of him.

Sylvester turned around to see Cleo's men catching up to him. He flipped around again and once more jumped through the moving traffic. He zig-zagged through the road until he hastily jumped past a speeding car. Upon dropping his cash-filled briefcase, Silvester swiftly looked back, but Cleo's men drew near and raised their arms toward the thieving man. He decided to run off, leaving the money behind.

Jumping onto the sidewalk and continuing to run, Sylvester went on dodging the shots of the following men. With Cleo's men close behind him, the endangered man looked around for shelter. He saw a small café just to his left and decided to run in to hide. Zipping past the door, making the bell ring, Sylvester jumped inside. He looked around at the packed room to see but one open seat in a booth. He cursorily ran toward it, and, tossing himself into the booth, ducking down, he looked out the window. Waiting no less than thirty seconds, Sylvester saw the chasing men pass the café in which he hid. It was at that moment he knew he was safe. He took a deep breath in and had a moment of relief, until he heard a mysterious voice.

"That was some chase. Of course, you did take track all through middle school, but then you sadly quit when you dropped out of high school in your sophomore year. Shame, I believe you would have made it to nationals."

Sylvester slowly lifted his eyes up to see a man sitting across from him in the same booth. He stared at the mysterious man in shock of his wise words and wondered who he was. He was a medium-sized black man, with a pork pie hat and a dark leather jacket over a blue sweater.

"It is a pleasure to finally meet you, Sylvester. My name is Jones," the mysterious man said. He looked down slightly and slowly passed over a cup of coffee. "Dark espresso with a hint of whipped cream, just the way you like it," Jones said in a sinisterly cheerful voice. Sylvester could barely get the words out and quietly tried to reach for the knife on the napkin beside him.

"I wouldn't do that if I were you," Jones remarked.

"Why's that?" Sylvester asked, intimidated.

"Because then you wouldn't be able to hear about the amazing offer I'm about to make you."

Sylvester put down his arm and sat upright. He looked slightly intrigued as he stared at Jones. "How do you know all that stuff about me?" he asked.

"As I said, my name is Jones, and I am a simple businessman."

"A simple businessman doesn't know what a stranger did in middle school."

"I suppose so. I have been admiring your work for quite a while. The famed Sylvester Erellio. It isn't every day you meet a celebrity now, is it?"

"I'm no celebrity."

"To me, you are, and to answer your earlier question, I am here to hire you."

"Thanks, but I'm good."

"You have an average salary of thirteen grand. I can bump that number to a height you can't even see. So, you have a choice. You can continue this sad life of low, pathetic scams and cons, or you can do a job with me and never have to work or worry again. The choice is yours."

Jones stood up and began walking away. As he left, he dropped a card with a location and time on the table, saying, "If you are interested, meet me at this address tomorrow at eight a.m. sharp, and don't be late." Jones walked out of the diner.

Sylvester picked up the card and started sipping the espresso, worried, confused, bewildered, and most of all, intrigued.

IV

The disco moved in circles and a jazz band played on stage. Strippers, dealers, hotshots, and kingpins were having their fun in an array of ways. The Devil's Pit, they called it—the biggest nightclub and mob spot in town. If you were a criminal who wanted to party, that's where you would go. Even the low-life drug heads went to the dark side of the club. There was a bar in the center of the giant room, one filled with all sorts of the finest liquors. The rest of the room was filled with strip poles, gambling games, and many booths toward the sides where the top gangsters would often speak about their business.

One booth in the back had six people sitting in it, five of which were wearing lovely black and white suits, smoking vintage cigars. The first one was old and wise looking. The second man was younger and skinnier and had his hair greased back. Sitting next to the second man was a shorter woman with blond hair. She had on a sparkling pink dress with a fur scarf around her neck. The third man was large, with a mustache and a big hat. The fourth man was a little younger than the rest, with brown hair and blue eyes. The final man sitting all the way to the right was the oldest. He was bald and had on a black hat, glasses and polished shoes.

The fifth man was drinking and smoking simultaneously as he said, "Jessica, darling, why don't you run along and get us some more drinks." The woman looked at her date to the right, who nodded his head. She left the table and the men began conversing. "Did you hear that Cleo the Cow got scammed by a low-level cutthroat this morning," the third man exclaimed, laughing.

"What are you talking about?" the first man asked.

"He was at an exchange and got duped with fake diamonds," the third man said, the table erupting in laughter.

"That dumbass is as stupid as a rat's tail, yet he is one of the highest authorities in town. It's the biggest joke!"

"But the grifter wasn't all that smart either. Wait till you hear this... the cutthroat lost the money! The fool dropped it on the street, and it got crumpled by traffic!"

"Cleo, that dumbass, is running his family's house into the ground," the first man remarked at the table of hysterical men.

"Ey Starc, how's the business going?" the fourth man asked.

"It's going great. We got confidential info on the governor and now he's helping us bring in more shipments through the station. I've got a train coming in tomorrow. Fifteen crates of the good stuff," the third man rejoiced.

"What did you have on the governor?" the fourth man asked, quite curious.

"Boring tax fraud or something like that, not that interesting, but sure would hurt his upcoming campaign."

"What about you, Terrance?" the fourth man asked.

"My boy was snatched by the pd... so I had one of my men shoot him, right in the stomach," he replied.

"And you, Rocco?" the fourth man inquired.

"It's good, it's good. I had a debtor try to skip town. He owed me five grand, so I had my men go hunting when he didn't turn up. They brought him back to me in essentially one piece."

"What did you do to him?"

"What would any man do?" the gangster replied, chuckling.

"Enough of this!" the fifth man interrupted, angered. "Let's talk business! The docks had over fifty shipments coming in last Thursday, all of which were apprehended by the G-men. Now I have some guys on the inside who are going to get us back as many of those shipments as possible."

"We are aware of this, sir, but why are you bringing it up?" the second man asked.

"Because that was top secret information. Information only the five of us had," the fifth man said as armed guards walked over. The four men shriveled in suspenseful angst, looking back and forth at each other with glaring suspicion.

"So… which one of you is the nasty, craven bastard who I'm gonna shoot in the head?" the fifth man asked with a very calm and serious tone. The table sat in fear, whilst the fourth man acted as calm as possible, slowly reaching into his pocket. Out of his pocket, he took a small beeper device. He pressed this device twice and it started beeping a small green light. The fifth man noticed a hint of the light. "What is that!" he yelled with a fierce voice. The guards moved over the table to see the beeper, and as they looked up, they aimed their pistols. Suddenly, the giant thud of a door being smashed through crowded the nightclub. About twelve armored NYPD boys came in and aimed their arms.

"Hands in the air, you're all under arrest," they shouted. The women screamed and ducked down whilst the men froze in question. As the five men continued to smoke and drink in angst, the fourth man stood up from the table, pulling out a badge. "Sorry to ruin your night boys," the undercover cop said, smiling at the four men.

Downtown, at the station, officer Jefferson Williams, who just returned from his cover as the fourth man, walked past four glass windows. Inside the windows were officers interrogating the men he had just earlier conversed with. The officer continued to stroll down the hall till he arrived at the elevator. On his way up, the elevator stopped on the third floor, and into the enclosed space came a tall brunette, with high heels, a tight blue blouse and rosy lips. Jeff sneakily looked up and down at the beautiful woman before he said, "Excuse me, miss…?"

"Clark. Barbara Clark."

"Ah, well Ms. Clark, excuse me for asking but, are you new here?"

"Why yes, I just moved here from Atlanta in fact."

"Ah! A glorious city it is."

"Yes, I did love it, why do you ask?"

"Oh well, I just think that I would have remembered seeing a woman as beautiful as you."

Chuckling and blushing, the woman exclaimed, "Well sir! You and I have only just met."

"So? Is it a crime for me to notice a woman's beauty?"

"I suppose not. You are quite handsome yourself."

"Oh well, my oh my! Ms. Clark, we have only just met!" the man joked. "My name is Jeff, Jeff Williams."

"Well, it is a pleasure to meet you Mr. Williams," the woman replied, shaking the man's hand.

"Forgive me for my bluntness, but I would most like to take you out to dinner sometime, and after all, since you have just moved here, I'm sure you would be most interested in trying some of New York's finest restaurants."

"Well, I am keen on trying new things."

"Excellent!" Jeff exclaimed as the elevator door opened.

"This is me," the woman said. "You may find me at Detective Manster's office."

"Wonderful! I will be most looking forward to our dinner Ms. Clark!" Jeff exclaimed as the beautiful woman stepped away.

Upstairs, on the ninth floor, Jeff straightened his tie, pulled on his suit, and took a deep breath in with a wide smile. The door to the elevator opened and he walked out with pride. Jeff passed his co-workers with a boastful stride before the deputy stopped him. "Williams!" he yelled at the accomplished man. The deputy smiled and laughed as he walked over to Jeff. "I'm very proud of you son! We apprehended four of the biggest members of the Geoguffri family, and just two hours ago, we intercepted the train containing all of Starc's incoming shipments, all thanks to you! Now the public and everyone else thinks the kingpins of crime in this city are these little people like Costello, Luciano and Anasgasia, but the real fight is with Accardi and the four main families under him. Now Accardi may have the public fooled, thinking they're just some kind of philanthropic business, but hopefully, these guys can prove he's one of the biggest mob bosses the country's ever seen, and now we are starting to make progress! We gotta do to these guys what we did to Al Capone. The man thought he was the big boss then BAM! Now I know…"

Suddenly, a small woman with a plum dress walked over to Jeff. "Mr. Williams, the chief would like to see you in his office, immediately," the woman interrupted in a strict yet quiet voice. Jeff turned to the deputy and shook his hand, then took off, trying to get away from the blabbermouth. On the tenth floor, Jeff walked into the office directly at the end of the hall. "Come in Williams," the chief said as Jeff slowly creeped open the door. "Please have a seat," he said with a disappointed tone. "How's your day going Jeff?"

"It's going well. I just made a big bust only a few hours ago."

"I heard, very impressive! So how have things been with you?" the chief further inquired.

"It's good," Jeff replied.

"Ah, I remember the old days, when we took on the city side by side."

"When you say 'took on the city' in the good old days you mean pulling all-nighters on paperwork," said Jeff as the two chuckled.

"Look, you know that I admire your work, and we are great friends; hell, we used to be partners, and it… it was hard for me to demote you for all that uptown business. But hey! You somehow became more efficient when it happened. Jeff, look I don't want to be doing this, trust me but… but uh, well my intelligence has recently informed me that your father is Marc Winger, the man who is currently serving life in prison for the Spearville incident in Kansas. Is this true?"

Jeff, confused and frustrated, replied, "Yes sir, it is."

"Why didn't you tell me?" the chief asked in disappointment.

"Because I have no relation to my father other than blood. I haven't seen him since I was five, we don't share a name or a title and I

20

have nothing but a small recollection of what he looks like. It simply is not important to any account, especially on a professional level."

"Jeff, you are a head officer and a great one at that, but this city has had so many terrible things happen to it over the years, one of those including corrupt cops."

"I can assure you that I am not corrupt."

"I know Jeff... I know. But as you know, we cannot afford another public outbreak. So in that manner, it is in my deepest pain to relieve you of your duty and service to the NYPD. Your father killed over thirteen people and even though you are a good man, the community cannot handle it, and it is also not policy to keep you employed. I am sorry Jeff."

After heated words, and a hard fight, Jeff went home that night with a small box of his personal possessions. As he walked over to his kitchen and poured himself a cup of hot tea in his cozy home, he started to have a rush of anger. He slowly walked into his closet and scrambled through his clobber until he found an old, framed photo of his teenage dad. He held the photo up in madness and started trembling to the point where he screamed. In anger, he cried out and chucked the photo on the ground, shattering it into pieces. The glass went everywhere, including on his feet.

"AH!" Jeff screamed in pain. As the angered man bled from a large cut on the bottom of his foot, he stepped in agony back to the kitchen, where he scrounged for his medkit. He went through the cabinet until he found the box, plopped it on the table and lifted his foot. He added the disinfectants but then realized that he had nothing to wrap his bare foot with. With slow suffering and unbearable pain, Jeff put on his shoes. The despairing man had to walk all the way across the street to the drugstore. As he tripped on an old, glass bottle on the way, tears began to pour down his face one by one as he screamed once more. His eyes slowly filled with water, and his foot bled through his shoes.

Jeff thought to himself, the only thing his life was good for was being a cop, and now he had lost that. After a march of suffering, Jeff made it inside the drugstore and went to the aisle to the immediate right.

21

He slowly walked in pain down the aisle until he found the bandages he needed, then stepped softly to the checkout counter. He placed the bandages on the table, the cashier saying, "That's gonna be twenty-five cents."

The man nodded as he reached into his pockets. However, nothing came out. He patted his pants all around and looked up to the sky in madness. The suffering man looked at the cashier, putting on a big smile. "Hey… uh… how about we call this a gift? From you to me?"

"Twenty-five cents!" she replied in a high-pitched tone. Jeff looked down in painful misery, his face glum and sorrow.

"I'll pay for it," a mysterious man exclaimed, slamming a quarter on the counter. Jeff slowly turned to his left, shocked and relieved. The stranger he looked at was a medium-sized man of color. This mysterious man wore a dark blue sweater under a brown leather jacket. He held a small, compact mustache and a pork pie hat. "Let's take a walk," the man said softly as he grabbed the bandages, handing them to Jeff. Out on the streets, the two men spoke as they strolled. "Thank you for that. I'll pay you back when I get back to my apartment," Jeff said with a thankful yet awkward tone.

"No need," the man said. "It's on me." Sitting down at a nearby bench, Jeff lifted up his foot and began wrapping it with the bandages.

"Who are you?" he asked.

"You can call me Jones."

"Pleasure to meet you, Jones," Jeff replied, annoyed though grateful. "My name is Jeff."

"Haha! Yes, I know. I know a lot about you Mr. Williams," Jones said whilst joyfully smiling. "You're five foot nine, you were born and raised in Kansas until your mother had to move out here to get away from the acts of your father. You were a decorated lieutenant who was about to be promoted to captain until you decided to turn off your radio and go to bed with a woman while on duty. You were five minutes away from a burning motel that every other cop in the city was thirty minutes away from and so… two people died, because of you. So they demoted you, until today they found out who your father was and decided to do more than demote you."

With confusion-caused anger, Jeff paused on bandaging, slowly saying with his eyes large, "How… how do you…"

"Let's just say that I have connections," Jones interrupted.

"Who the hell are you? What do you want from me?"

"No no no, not from you… for you. You have just been fired and coincidentally… I have one more slot I need to fill for a job."

"What kind of job?"

"The kind of job where you get paid a whole lot of money." Jones tossed a small white business card on the bench where Jeff sat, as he himself stood tall. "Meet me at this address tomorrow at eight a.m. sharp. Don't be late."

"What if I don't want to?"

"What else do you have to do Mr. Williams?" Whilst the injured man was left in frustrated confusion, Jones walked off into the darkness of the night.

<h2 style="text-align:center">V</h2>

Morning came with a scintillating sun, and the four men chosen for the job were on edge. Each of them had to decide whether or not to go to the meet. They didn't trust the man and didn't trust the job, but even though they were doubtful, they still ended up in taxis on the way to the address. The four cabs pulled up minutes after the next. The first cab dropped David off. Then five minutes later another taxi came, dropping off Sylvester. The address led to a giant warehouse surrounded by the sea. The old, rusty warehouse was out by a couple of molded docs and a small rocky shoreline. Connected to the warehouse was a small pool house/bar, made of marble floors and a nicely-tiled roof. Sylvester walked up to David, who stood waiting at the pool house door.

"Who are you?" David asked.

"Sylvester Erellio. And you are?"

"David Cockspy," David said as the two shook hands.

"What are you waiting for?" Sylvester asked.

"The doors are locked."

"Oh, really?" Sylvester asked sarcastically. The man bent down and opened up a small black cloth kit. He next pulled out two thin, long silver sticks to pick the lock and open the door. David watched with curiosity until he saw the bronze lock fall to the ground. The giant red door then was pushed open. Inside was the pool house. It had a large pool in the center, with no roof above, a bar to the right under red roofing, and to the left laid outdoor furniture surrounded by a chimney. Looking at the neighboring fellow, David asked, "Are you sure this is where we're supposed to be?"

Sylvester pulled out the card Jones gave him. He showed it to David, who then pulled out the same card.

"This looks a little too nice," David said with distrust.

"Well, that doesn't look as nice," Sylvester spoke, looking at the large gray door that laid at the end of the pool house and seemed to lead to inside the warehouse. Sylvester and David walked up to it and without surprise, learned it too was locked, this time from the inside, which Sylvester couldn't pick. "What do we do now?" Sylvester asked.

"Wait for Jones to show up, I guess."

"What do we do in the meantime?"

"Drink?" David said, walking to the bar.

About six minutes later, another taxi drove up to the warehouse, and out came a very dark man with rusty old clothes. He walked briskly and opened the pool house door promptly to see two men laughing and drinking. As he entered, the two men faced him. "Got a card, huh?" Sylvester asked.

The man said, "Why yes" as he pulled out the same exact card from Jones as the others.

Sylvester walked up to the new man and handed him a glass. "My name is Sylvester Erellio and this is yet another man who has received a card," Sylvester explained, pointing to David.

"What's your name?" the dark man asked.

"The name's David Cockspy, and yours is…?"

"Robert, Robert Davinson, but people call me Bobby. So, you all just waiting here till that guy gets here?"

"Basically," David exclaimed. Four minutes later, the final man pushed open the pool door to hear the now three men laughing. As he walked into the pool house, the other men stopped laughing and looked toward him. "Card?" Sylvester asked.

"Yep," the new man said, holding the card up in the air.

"Come, have a drink while we wait. My name is David Cockspy, this is Sylvester Erellio and Bobby Davinson," David spoke, pointing to each of his new companions.

"Pleasure to meet you but forgive me if I do not wish to get sauced at eight in the morning," said a loud and sarcastic Jeff.

"Nothing wrong with a couple small drinks."

"I suppose, but you all look like you're having a bit more than a couple," Jeff responded.

"And you? what would your name be?" David asked.

"Jeff, Jeff Williams," he stated, loud and proud. Over twenty minutes passed as the four men continued to talk, wait, and get shicker.

"So, does anyone know what this supposed job is?" Bobby asked.

"Something probably illegal, I know that much," said Sylvester.

"If that's true then why would he hire a man like Jeff, a cop?" David asked, recalling Jeff's earlier statement about being in the NYPD.

"Former cop," Jeff interrupted abruptly. "So David, what did you used to do?"

"I was a dentist for a while," David said as the other men began to laugh.

"Of course you were a dentist, Cockspy. Haha!" the men went off.

"How did you end up in jail?" Jeff asked, quite rudely.

"That's a story for another time. How did you get fired?" David fired back at Jeff.

"The station figured out who my father was and weren't comfortable with it, I guess."

"Who was your father?"

"Marc Winger," Jeff replied. The other men paused and ran their brains, finding the name slightly familiar.

Bobby, a sucker for news, looked up at Jeff, exclaiming, "Marc Winger? As in the man behind Spearville?"

"Yes," said Jeff. "My father left when I was eight and my mother paid the price for his actions. I can assure you, whatever hatred or disgust you have toward the name of my father, know it is only a chunk of the way I feel toward him. Hey Sylvester! I think I'd heard a story about you yesterday."

"Really? Not surprising; the cops have admired my work for years and have many times tried to arrest me. But no one can catch this cat."

"Um no, actually, I have never heard of you at the station. I heard that you hilariously dropped the money you stole from Cleo the Cow yesterday morning in the middle of a traffic-filled street where it was pummeled by cars and grabbed by bystanders." Sylvester's smugness quickly faded into embarrassment, and the men once again cried out in laughter.

"So, any of you have a lady?" asked Bobby.

"I had a wife once; her name was Charlotte. She was blonde and slim and kind and beautiful. But she left me after I went to prison," David said, again getting a bit too personal.

"I don't, I used to have a redhead but I broke up with her after she became too clingy," Sylvester said, trying to be a part of the conversation.

"Me, I've always been a multiple-woman kind of guy," Jeff explained.

"Sure you have, paid women maybe," David joked, the men giggling and chuckling yet again.

"Where is this guy!?" Bobby asked, frustration evident in his tone.

"Relax, he'll be here."

"No! Bobby is right. He said eight a.m. sharp and yet it's a quarter till nine, with still no sign of him."

"Maybe this is all a sham."

"Not everything is a con, Sylvester."

"Yeah? How do you know?" Sylvester argued. "You were in the military, David, where you could trust everyone, it was law, but me? No, no, I on the other hand lived in the dark corners of the city where you couldn't trust a puppy. People can do mind-bending things. I say we call it quits and go home!"

"Go home, yeah, to where though? Shall we go to Jeff's place, which he is about to be evicted from, or Bobby's rat-infested, leaking apartment, or your nice home, that's surely surrounded by bloodthirsty gangsters, or perhaps you all could be like me, and be homeless! Guess what! We are all broke, with nowhere to go and no one to turn to! I don't know about you, but I trust this man. He got me out of prison. A man doesn't simply do that just for shits and giggles!"

"Think about this David, you had two and a half years left in your sentence. It's not like the man saved your life! We can't trust him!"

"Fine! Then you leave, but I for one am going to wait to hear what this job is before I turn away the chance to get rich."

Bobby grew tired of David and Sylvester's bickering. He looked at the warehouse door and wondered what was inside. He knew the door was locked but figured there was a back door of some sort, so Bobby left the pool house to investigate. "Where is he going?" Jeff asked.

"He's probably leaving like a smart man!"

"If you want to leave so badly then just leave!"

"Maybe I will!" Sylvester argued, his voice larger.

Bobby continued to walk around the side of the warehouse. He saw some old bird nests in the windows and rust pouring off the roof. The dumpsters stunk of mildew and the ground was soggy. The only pleasurable thing about the warehouse was the ocean beside it, and the breeze and noise it brought. Bobby walked around the building until he found the backdoor. He tried to open it, but it was again locked from the inside. The curious man slammed himself against the door multiple times, trying to break down the door, until he faced the wrong way and his elbow hit the edge of the doorknob. The direct impact hurt badly, so he stopped running toward the door. He took several steps back and looked up at the warehouse, then looked back down the side of the warehouse which he walked from. He raised his head and eyes until he saw an opened window about twenty feet above the ground. Bobby was relentless.

He pushed the dumpsters together and grabbed all the things he could find. He stood on a cooler that stood on a broken fridge that stood on a big green dumpster. Even though he was standing on everything he could find, he was still a good five feet away. Bobby, the dimwitted man, looked around in attempt until he saw on the ground an old rope about forty feet long. He tied the rope to another, smaller cooler and threw it up, and it went through the window. The man then grabbed the rope by the end and rested one foot on the brick wall. He inhaled a deep breath in and took another step onto the wall. He continued until he arrived at the window and was able to climb through. Jumping down onto a small, wooden loft, Bobby peered out into the large warehouse he had now entered and saw a kitchen directly below him, next to some couches. Behind him lay multiple rooms, most likely a few bedrooms and a bathroom.

The inside of the warehouse wasn't so bad as the outside and looked a little cozy. Bobby slowly walked down to the table in the center of the oppositely facing couches, seeing something of interest. He glared at the papers sitting on the table. Bank notices, truck rentals, and the NYPD handbook were some of the many things that rested on the wooden board, but all of those were tiny compared to four packets of paper that laid in the center, each containing a picture. The pictures that were on the papers were of the four men. One packet was for David, one for Sylvester, one for Jeff and one for dear Bobby, who slowly reached over to pick up his profile and flip through it. Inside, he found everything about him: information that he didn't know anyone besides himself knew. He was in complete shock.

"Find anything interesting?" Bobby quickly dropped the file in fear as he turned toward Jones.

"What is all this?"

"I told you I know a lot about you, that is how."

"How did you get this?"

"I have connections."

"Have you just been in here the whole time?!"

"No. I just got back from breakfast."

"It's eight-fifty! You said eight o'clock sharp."

"No. I said for *you* to be here at eight o'clock sharp, I never talked about what time I was going to get here. Come on, let's bring the others inside."

Jones put away the files and then walked up to the big door leading out of the warehouse and unlocked it. He opened it to find Sylvester and David shouting at each other, as Jeff sat by the poolside. Quickly, they all stopped what they were doing and stared at the man. "Why the hell are you here so late!?" David pressed with a heavy tone.

"I was getting breakfast," Jones said with a slight smirk. The three men scoffed angrily and followed Jones inside.

"Sit down, please," said Jones. The four men sat down on the red sofas as they watched Jones bring over a drawing board. They looked around the warehouse and were very impressed by it but made sure to keep that to themselves. Jones stepped over in front of the couches with a big chalkboard as if he was about to present a school project.

"You're all probably wondering why you're here, and the fact that you are all here means that you are all at least curious," Jones uttered. "I have had my eye on you for quite a while, all of you." Jones chucked their files on the table, sending the men into a frenzy. They looked through the files to find every secret about them, every dirty deed, every good gesture, everything they had ever done.

"What is this?" Sylvester growled.

"As I have stated, I have connections."

"I'm done with this! You've done nothing but stalk us and try to trick us into doing whatever this is!" Sylvester shouted angrily, jumping up out of his seat.

"I am not trying to trick anyone."

"Says you! I for one have had enough of this. You bring us out here in the middle of nowhere just to keep us waiting for an hour and then show us that you've been stalking spying on and us. I for one will not have it. I am out of here! Have a wonderful life!"

"If you walk away now then you will never get a chance to be as rich as God," Jones stated in a small manner toward Sylvester, who was marching away.

Sylvester stopped marching and slowly looked back. "Fine! I'll listen to what you have to say... for now. But if anything else comes up, I'm out."

"Good, then let's continue. You have all been carefully selected by yours truly, to pull off the biggest heist of the century. You all have a role to play. We will need a combination of cons, strength, endurance and acting, all to form one large... heist."

"Great, so we are stealing something," David muttered in a disappointed tone.

"Yes, my dear friend. The only chance any of you have at making a happy, nice and wealthy life for yourselves is right here, right now."

"So what exactly is this job?" Bobby inquired with an interested glare.

"In a little over a month, the annual Mericorn Horse Race will take place. Mericorn is one of the biggest companies in the country. As I'm sure you all know; it's a business that has many aspects to it, such as the biggest construction company in the city, and is home to over twenty fine restaurants around the states. But really and truthfully, it is the front company for one of the largest crime families in the world... Geoguffri, Savelli, Maleté, Barone, and of course... Accardi."

The men froze in realization. They all looked at Jones with open eyes and tinted frowns. Sylvester quickly rose again from the cushion he'd just sat and cried, "Are you mad? You will try to steal from the head of the four crime families, and Giovanni Accardi himself, the newest in the greatest line of criminal masterminds this city has ever seen! You are mad! This man has more security than you do hairs. I have seen people cut down for a drop of a simple penny."

"There's always something with you. You're impatient," Jones slowly replied.

"Maybe I am a little impatient, but at least I'm not a fathead!"

"Last I checked you were willing to listen to what I had to say. Am I correct? Because I am not done and you are not sitting," stated Jones, heavy in tone. Ill-mannered, Sylvester slid back into his seat, silencing his own lips with a detested expression.

"We will not be stealing from Giovanni Accardi himself, we will simply be... taking it," Jones continued.

"That is stealing!" Jeff exclaimed.

"We will be stealing from the business and the horse race but not from Accardi directly," explained Jones. "Because of this, insurance will give the company back all that it loses. We steal and insurance repays. Accardi won't care because he will have lost nothing."

"Maybe so but I can tell you from experience, these types of men don't just take back what's theirs; they make sure the ones who did it don't ever try it again, because they cannot weaken their title, and their greedy palms often are filled with vengeful taste," Sylvester argued.

"Yes, but there is one thing you're not incorporating into your reasoning."

"And what's that?" Sylvester asked.

"Accardi will never know who did it to him, because we are going to steal it right from under his nose, and by the time he figures out the money is gone, we will be gone, without a trace of evidence as to who we are or where we went."

"Still, it's too risky. How much money could even be in that vault?" Sylvester said sarcastically. Jones looked him in the eye with the slightest smirk and simply stated softly, "Eight million dollars."

The men looked at Jones in shock, speechless. In the men's heads, eight million dollars was more money than any king ever amounted to. The money was irresistible, but the fear of messing with the biggest crime family in the country was too frightening to bear. "It's impossible," Sylvester said as he walked out. One by one, each of the men followed and slowly walked away, out of the warehouse, all while Jones watched, batting not an eye.

Still having not shifted a muscle, Jones confidently exclaimed, "When you change your mind, I'll be right here, waiting."

With slight hesitation, the four men exited. The mysterious man lifted his watch and set a timer just then, saying to himself, "Let's see how long they take."

Bobby's Recollection

I knew I could use the money, especially that much. I mean hell, it would change my life! But alas, Sylvester was right; the Accardis are indeed the biggest mob in the city, perhaps the country, and every soul from the bottom of nasty streets to the top of fancy towers in the Big Apple knew not to mess with any one of the major crime families, least of all the Accardis. I returned to my substandard home that morning and hastened on my work apparel before heading out the door. Though I was late, which was nothing new, my boss not only didn't mind, but I don't even think he seemed to notice me, if anyone ever did, that is. Eddie, my best friend in the whole factory, was helping me work the mill on some decks. "So, I went by me uncle's place this morning," Eddie spoke, "he 'old me dat yuh' gotchuhself in a fight wit sum' dem' white boys. Yuh' can't keep getin' intuh' so much trouble! One dese' days yuh' gonna get yuh'self knocked!" Not unbothered, I replied to my dear friend, "I know Eddie, but you should have seen those boys. I mean they were out to get me, even if I hadn't thrown first, they still would've beaten the crap out of me!" Eddie didn't seem too amused with that last remark and growled at me, "Yuh' don't know dat! For all yuh' know dey coulda jut' walkt' away! Speakin' of walkin' away, looks like Mista' Lang comin' dis way! Dis yuh' chance, Bobby! Go tell him yuh' big idea! He gotta hear yuh' out it's so good!" I was nervous, for I had been trying to talk to my boss for days now about using a new system with the mills to increase productivity on the engine blocks. I knew it was a fantastic system though, so when Mr. Lang was walking by with his secretary and the manufacturing director, I left Eddie to the mill and ran up to him. "Mr. Lang! Mr. Lang!" I called out. He turned swiftly, looking no more amused than his two companions. "Hello, Mr. Lang, it is a pleasure. I'm Bobby Davinson, one of the workers here, and I just wondered if I could run a new idea by you and our manufacturing director? Just an idea on increasing productivity in our engine block manufacturing." He looked annoyed, yet I received a grin. I think he thought it was funny that a colored man wanted to give input on such a complex subject, and to a guy like him. He said, in a sort of funny tone, "Sure fella, go ahead and give us your 'new idea'. I would like to hear it." Both his secretary and the manufacturing director gave a chuckle, but I took his diminishing reply as an opportunity to speak. "Mr. Lang, Mr. Grant," I addressed, "it takes a long time to make one engine block, and the time increases with less men, for over a quarter of the men are moving, cleaning, cooling and melting the supplies for use, before we can even begin to use the mill machines. But, if we begin to purchase such companies as Renter's Junk, or Holly's Parts, we will be able to use a handful of their unneeded supplies to recycle for use in making more engine blocks. If we had more men focused on making the engine blocks rather than preparing the metals to use, it would increase productivity, and recycling such car parts could be used for all sorts of things elsewhere in the company. Of course there is a lot of detail to be discoursed on, but the general idea is that we collect unneeded and disregarded metals that have been thrown out to reforge into new parts for our cars, making faster production time and saving money on new materials which take the workers forever to craft from the beginning. I know this seems sort of simple, but I can assure you I have many complex details to discuss, as well as a better way to make use of our assembly lines." I finished, and with blank faces, all three members of my audience went silent for a long moment. But then Mr. Lang invited me up to his office for drinks. We talked for hours about my plan, and I showed them every benefit, detail, investment, etc. They loved my idea fully, and when they began to speak about next steps, Mr. Lang walked up to me and handed me a nice bottle of whiskey, saying, "Here you go Mr. Davidson, take this as a thank you for your helpful insight on our supply line!" With a happy face, he joyously escorted me out of his office and sent me back to work at the mills. Eddie tried to console me, but I wasn't sad, disappointed, nor in grief, I was furious! If I were a white man and gave such impactful intakes, I would be head of the company in months! But alas, I am a negro, and though I am well educated, quite unusually for others of my race around here, no one cares! I bet that fat bastard was just gonna pass off all my thoughts as his own! Growing up, I had a friend from the library named Andrew. Andrew was white and rich, and his family was quite peculiar. They had me and my family over for dinner, they took me to white parks and white pools, and they were so rich and charitable that no one gave me a nasty look. Andrew even helped me get into medical school. I tried at it, but that malpractice lawsuit ruined everything for me. I loved Andrew, and when I was growing up it was hard for me to understand racism. Any place I went where normally there would be stares and nasty looks, there wasn't, because I was with Andrew. But as I got older I understood it now. Even if you wanted to you couldn't be seen giving a black man decent respect, or you would regret it. Sometimes I wish Andrew had never met me. When I was a medical practitioner, a couple of my white coworkers tried to get me fired with a fake lawsuit that their friend filed. Andrew got me a lawyer and said, "I got you through medical school for you to give up with one bad week?" he said. "No! We will fight this thing!" Andrew was always with me, but God, I never thought that there could be such horror. He and his "Black loving" wife were burned alive in their own home a week before the trial, thus my lawyer, later threatened by the same coworkers, who were no strangers to the KKK, made him sell my trial. I got sloppy, lazy after that, diving into drugs, alcohol, and gambling. I tried to start up my own business, but that went to shit, all because I was careless, and lazy! Here I am, truly trying for the first time in a while, like Andrew would have wanted, but the only black man any wealthy white will ever like or respect is fictitious Jim Crow! Andrew left me his car in his will, and though I would sell it for the money, I need it to get to work, for there aren't any colored buses close enough to where I would be on time to work. Then again, I'm rarely on time. Shortly after Mr. Lang kicked me out of his office, I left, driving on the road to get as far away as I could from that godforsaken place! I guess I got a little too angry though and put too much pressure on the gas. The cop who pulled me over was no teddy bear. He saw my bottle of whiskey in the front seat and said, "What is a negro like you doing with such a fine bottle of whiskey?" I told him my boss gave it to me, but he didn't believe me, or rather, he didn't care. I reached for the bottle to show him, as he requested, but then he grabbed my shoulders and pulled me out of my car. "Are you trying to attack me with that bottle!?" he yelled. "I bet you stole this car too!" he continued to shout. It

didn't matter what I said; I would've ended up handcuffed in the back of
his car if I was Frederick Douglass himself. Either way, I was on my way
to jail, with my car towed and my whiskey stolen. There was another
man handcuffed in the back seat with me, colored, of course. He was nice
and also eye-opening in a weird way. He sounded well educated,
speaking with proper grammar and great vocabulary. I asked him where
he had his studies, to which he replied, "I attended Harvard Law in fact."
So we conversed on the way back a lot about that, since I attended there
too, of course, at least Harvard Medical. We talked about my life for a
moment, but then he began to speak of his own tale, and it was…
interesting. "After Harvard, I tried to be an attorney, but no matter what I
did, every case I ever had I lost, and then the Klan bombed my office, so
I gave up my practice. I was lost, emotionally speaking, and one day I
had a case for this guy on trial, who, once he got to know me, told me his
brother was an art thief, and he could change my life forever if I helped
him out, getting some file or something. I said no, not wanting to get into
any trouble, but here I was, drunk, in debt, wishing I had taken him up on
that offer. I heard about him recently. The client who I decided not to
work for lost his trial and went to jail, but his now opulent brother got
him out. They now reside in London and are extremely wealthy, living
life care-free. Even if something had gone wrong, I truly don't see the
difference between me rotting in a cell and me rotting in this hellhole we
call a society." His sorrows intrigued me and moreover concerned me.
For the few hours I lay in jail, I pondered… Did I make the right call?
Did I pass up on a life-changing opportunity? I could clear my debts,
move somewhere nice, perhaps in Europe. Perhaps I could be treated like

a white man, perhaps not fully, but being rich I suppose gives you more freedom than anything else. I got my friend Joe to bail me out pretty quickly. *Great, now I owe more money,* I thought to myself. When Joe was driving me back to my place in his beaten-down car, we passed by this particular nightclub. It seemed new, with bright lights and fantastical music. It took me a second to unfog my brain of the beauty of the many bedazzling women, but when I did, I saw Short Tony, smoking a cigar and resting his arms on two of the women I had stared upon. I quickly bent down like a briefcase being shut. Joe looked down as we passed the nightclub, and he's not stupid. "Bobby, how much doe' yous owe to all these guys?" he asked. I waited until we turned the corner to answer him, for speaking at the angle I was perched at was quite uncomfortable. "Eh I don't know, a lot I guess," I said. "Bobby, yous have got to get a hold of yourself man! Everywhere yous goes yous gets beat ons by white men, yous are always in the debts, and one dese' days yous gonna getchyuh'self killed." He kept lecturing for a moment, and once he finished, I responded, "You ever wondered what's out there in our universe? A long time ago I read *The War of the Worlds*. A delightful little book about nasty aliens. Got me thinking, what if there was life outside this place? We already know there are other planets. Sometimes I wonder what it would be like. Maybe there's a world out there where they don't have money, just aliens, aliens of all shapes, sizes, and colors working together in a great society. A society where if you do something bad, you get a second chance. A society where everyone is naturally kind, considerate, and gives you the benefit of the doubt. What a world that would be to see. Now I am no genius, and I don't know what's out there, but I know what we got down here. This world is all that matters to us, and if we let it, it will smush us to the ground and turn us to dust. For too long I've tried to be a part of the system in order to change the system. I put in my hours, I follow the stupid laws, I pay my dues, I work the hours, and what do I get? This world just isn't setup for guys like you and me, Joe. People look at us and all they see are illiterate troublemakers, the government looks at us and all they see are more wallets to grab hold of, and society looks at us and all they see are a bunch of little nobodies that they can do with as they please. Well, this may not be an alien planet, but I'll be damned if I let these entitled people's beliefs be truth and law. I'm done playing these rich, white men's games. It's high time I play the game the way the world does." Joe didn't understand half the words I said; sometimes nobody does. My neighborhood, my friends, and most people I work with never had access to the same level of education I had. In fact, most of them spent their early days working to get food for their families, rather than going to school. But my kids would never have to do that! By supper time, I knew I was gonna go back to Jones, but he said he needed all four of us. I didn't know where to find Sylvester or David, but I did hear Jeff talk about this nice little diner earlier. Perhaps I'd go by there and see if he could use some level-heading like I'd had today.

Chapter 2

The Job

I

A man named Jimmy Green made busy, preparing himself a sandwich for delight. He spread the nice, silky peanut butter on a piece of sliced bread and smacked it onto the other slice, which was covered in jelly. This man had a small beard, brown hair and wore a bright, orange robe, dazzled with blinding red swirls. The man picked up his finished sandwich and carried it to his nearby chair, where he then sat, tossing up the latest newspaper to read. This man called Jimmy was living life without a worry, but then he heard the thumpy *KNOCK KNOCK!*

Jimmy smacked down his newspaper and turned his cool smile into a dark glare. He took three deep breaths, lifted his newspaper again, and continued on his read, ignoring the knock. He took another bite of his sandwich and sipped on his water. KNOCK KNOCK, the door went for the second time. The man took five more deep breaths in and then continued to read once more.

KNOCK KNOCK, the door went for the third time. "AH!" Jimmy shouted in anger, slamming his newspaper on the table beside him and jumping up from his chair. He paced across the room in contained fury and stepped over to the door, where he tugged it open like a man pulling an ax out of a log. His face quickly turned from anger to small frustration and annoyance as he saw his dear old cousin, David Cockspy.

"Hey cuz," David whispered with a frightened, guilty, funny tone.

"I thought you had another three years left?" Jimmy said, bewildered.

"Two and a half, and it's a long story."

Jimmy paused, looking down in grievance before he said straight, "You can sleep on the couch."

"Thank you," David said gratefully as he walked into the house. "This is a very nice place, cousin. Marble kitchen, tall ceiling, all these nice paintings and pieces of furniture. How do you afford this?"

"I'm an attorney, which you would know if you ever visited."

"I'm sorry cuz, but I've been a little preoccupied, you know, being in prison and all."

"You wouldn't be in prison if you weren't a careless idiot."

"I'm sorry Jim, I'm sorry. You have no idea…"

"NO! You have no idea!" Jimmy hastily interrupted, shaking with temper. "I had to be the one. Do you have any idea what you put me through? Put this family through? Dave, you killed two people! With you gone, I had to step up and take your place! I was the one… I was the one who took care of YOUR mother when she fell ill… I was the one who stood by her and paid for her medical bills… I had to defend you because you're my cousin, even though I KNOW… I KNOW that you deserve what you got!"

"Jim," David said, slow and soft.

Interrupting again with a low, loud voice, Jimmy shouted, "NO! If it were up to me, you would be rotting in prison for a lot longer, and you would come to regret what you did."

"What? You don't think I regret it? It ruined my life! I lost everything because of what happened!"

"Exactly! There it is! Still, all you can think of is what YOU lost, and what happened to YOU! I know you didn't mean to cause what actually happened, but you were so careless, and so wrapped up in your own drama, that innocent people died, and your family had to pay the price, literally and figuratively. I'm going to let you stay here until you get back on your feet, but… Dave, you may have lost a brother, but your mother lost a son, and then instead of looking after her or your own family, you took the coward's way out, and you left everyone."

The two cousins had a moment of silence and a long pause as they both calmed. David slowly tilted his head upward, saying lightly, "Thank you. For everything." Jimmy nodded as he sluggishly turned around, walking back to his chair. "I'm gonna head out," continued David. "I'll uh, be back later. Uh th-thank you again, Jim."

Before he walked out, however, David paused for a moment at the door and looked back to softly utter, "Jim, you've never been to war, you don't know what it does to a man." David left feeling oh so sorry for himself, as usual, and leaving his cousin feeling the same.

Stepping back onto the slick streets David had grown up in, he realized the city had changed very little since he had last seen it. The windows were still growing flowers and the roofs still carried birds atop them. The man took a deep breath of the fresh city air that he had so long been without. Looking upon banks, houses, restaurants and a few hotels, David felt he was out for good and ready to remodel his life. At that moment, he promised himself he would build a new life for himself, one where he would be happy. His hopes and dreams of happiness about his new, free life, however, suddenly shriveled to oblivion as he stared up at a tall white and red building. He paused for a moment, frightened, but then walked into the tall building with slight hesitation. Passing by him were many old folks—people in wheelchairs, crying babies, and tired nurses. David, as he walked, also began to notice the ill. There was coughing and screaming and sneezing and pure agony all around.

David stepped carefully through the open lobby, and as he walked up to the receptionist's desk, he gave a big frown. "Welcome to Roosevelt Hospital," the woman in white, sitting at the front desk, said. "What can I help you with sir?"

"I... I'm uh, here to see a patient. Her name is Dorothy Cockspy."

The woman scoured through some papers in a drawer for a brief moment, until she exclaimed, "Here it is! She will be in room sixty-five."

"Thank you." David began to walk and made his way with a full heart to the room. As he stood in front of the wooden door, the man took a deep breath in and entered. The room was painted solid white, it had a smell of medicine and a whiff of tragicness. Filled with guilt and great sadness, David trembled like a lost puppy over to the patient, who lay on a flat white bed. The patient woke, and David made his appearance known. "Huh? D-D... David," the woman stuttered softly. She began to cough, and David kneeled down, saying whole-heartedly, "Yes mother. It's me."

"H-how?" his mother asked, starting to drench in her own tears.

"They let me out of prison. Mom, what happened?"

"I've got the cancer, Davie. The doctors say I've got a couple of months left, at best." With tears flowing down his grizzled cheeks, David looked down to the ground, and with a tragic tone, he said softly, "I'm sorry, I am so, so sorry Mom. I wish I was here for you when it happened."

Simply glad he was there, David's mother reached over, and calmly grazed his face with her hand, wiping off one of the many tears that dripped from his eyes. "Oh Davie, I have had plenty of help. I'm just glad I got to see you before I went away. I know the pain you have carried with you these past years. Your brother's death was not your fault, and as for the other thing... well, we all make mistakes, and we all have to live with them for the rest of our lives. We have to learn to live with them, somehow."

"I know, I know, but I can't get it out of my mind that if I had just pulled the trigger, Arnom would still be here today, and maybe I wouldn't have made any mistakes and I could've been here with you when you fell ill."

"I love you, Davie, I will always love you, no matter what." David looked up, his water-filled eyes meetinghis mother's, and let out a slight smile. The bawling man then leaned in toward his mother and tapped his lips gently upon the top of her forehead. "Love you Mom," he said before he made his way out the room, tears pouring out.

"Ninety-seven Hendrickson Street," David exclaimed, entering a cab. He took a big sigh and thought to himself there was one place left he needed to go. A little later, the taxi pulled up to the house, and breathing like a dog, David sluggishly stomped his heavy feet on the ground. He took it step by step until he reached the door of the place he once had called home. Again, taking a deep breath in preparation, David trembled when he knocked.

Charlotte Cuttman was a fairly young, pretty, blonde-haired woman with sparkling green eyes, a slender body, and the mother to a six-year-old daughter. Charlotte was piecing together tacos for dinner when she heard the knock on the door. She put down the tacos and hurried to open it, where she then gasped with shock. Her eyes opened wide, and her breath began to weigh. Her lips and hands began to tremble. She quickly slammed the door back, and David took a big sigh, knocking again. He continued to knock until Charlotte answered.

"Go away!" the woman yelled, quickly tossing the door open again.

"May I come in?" David asked quietly. Charlotte was shaking as she turned her back and went into the kitchen, continuing to assemble the taco shells. David walked in behind her and closed the door. "How did you get out?" she asked.

"A friend got me out."

"Really? Do you have friends?"

"Yes, I do. How uh... how have you been?"

"Oh no oh no, you can't just walk in here after three years and knock on the door thirty-five times just to start a conversation!"

With a saddened tone, David said, "You never visited."

"Why would I?"

"Because you are my wife."

"I was your wife, or did you not get the papers?"

"I got them," David bitterly replied. "I came here to say... I'm sorry."

"You're sorry? You came here after three years and after all the shit you have put me through, put your daughter through, you just say

44

sorry? David, You owe so much to all of us for all that you have caused. My daughter has not had a father half of her life because of you. I've had to be a single mother, because of you!"

"I... I didn't mean for any of this to happen."

"Well, what did you expect would happen? You purposely left our family because of your shit, and I know how hard it was after your deployment, but you just decided to walk away from everything, not caring about what it would do to your family. You didn't even bother to leave a note! Did you even think, for a second, about what it would do to us, what it would do to your daughter, what it would do to me?"

"I wasn't thinking clearly."

"It doesn't matter. You were in an awful place, I understand that, but what you did was inconsiderate, inhumane, and plain selfish."

"I know. Where is she?"

"Who? Samantha? You won't be seeing her any time soon!"

"She's my daughter!"

"No, she's not your daughter; you lost your daughter the day you decided to leave her."

"Where is she?"

"She's at day camp. Now listen, maybe we can work something out, but you can't just drop in on your daughter who has had to deal with not having a father for three years! These things take time and Samantha, she's just not ready to see you."

David nodded his head slightly and said quietly, "How is she doing?"

"Good, she's got a lot of friends."

"That's good, that's good," he said, a tear of joy dropping out his eye. "And you?"

"Things have been tough David. I have to work double shifts at my new job now just to pay rent."

"What job?"

"I'm a nurse," she replied.

"A nurse? Good. That's what you always wanted to be."

"Yeah, I guess we both got what we deserved."

David and Charlotte turned, hearing the slight groans of a working bus. David teared up as he drew closer and closer to the window, releasing a tragic sigh whilst staring at the camp bus. "You need to leave!" Charlotte exclaimed.

David spun around with tears in his eyes, crying, "Please. Don't do this."

Charlotte, with a hint of aggression said, "Go out the back door!"

"No. I'm staying here. I want to see her!"

"You need to leave right now!" she quietly shouted. Charlotte looked past David to the bus door opening, and as David turned to see his daughter step off the bus, he said slow, "Or what?"

"Or I call the cops. I'm sure whoever got you out of prison didn't do it strictly legally."

David spun back around again at her in bitterness. "When can I see her?" he sobbed.

"Get a job, help out with the bills around here, and maybe we can get something worked out. But if it was up to me, and it pretty much is, I never want you to see her again. Unless, that is, you are able to show me you've changed and are capable of being a good father!"

Seeing her daughter step out of the bus and jump onto the grass yard, Charlotte grabbed David's arm and began pacing toward the back door. She pulled her ex-husband all the way to such door and opened it roughly. "GO!" she shouted. "And don't come back unless you have something good to offer this family!"

"I will," he said. With the door shut before his face, David now wiped the tears out of his eyes and headed around the back of the house. After taking but a few steps, David started weeping, gazing through the window to see his daughter walk in. "Mommy!" she shouted, jumping into Charlotte's arms, who hugged her ever so dearly.

"How was your day, Pumpkin?"

"Amazing! Look, I made it," the girl said, lifting up a boat made out of rubber bands, glue, and popsicle sticks.

"Wow! That looks amazing! We are going to have to put that somewhere!" exclaimed a joyful Charlotte. She bent down to the little girl and said, "Hey, who wants tacos?"

The girl's mouth widened, and she yelled, "Me!"

"Ok. Let me go get the cheese, Pumpkin," said Charlotte. David again wiped off the tears as he took one last look at his daughter. She was such a happy child, with brown hair and brown eyes. He clenched in anger-filled sadness as he ran off. Rain was falling down from the sky and the moon was gleaming onto the world from beyond the clouds that night. The sound of the water droplets hitting the windows was like an army of ants pouncing on them, trying to get inside. David lay in the darkness atop the couch, thinking of a way he could mend his mistakes, fix his life. He thought and thought and thought, but as there was no decent job he would be able to get, he knew it would be months before Charlotte would allow him to see his daughter again. David closed his eyes as hard as he could then, imagining his life if he could, somehow, fix everything. But suddenly, David had a thought, an idea, a solution.

He slowly lifted his eyelids and stood up. He paced to the closet where he rummaged through his jacket until he pulled out the card that Jones had given him. With a sharp grin, David walked into his cousin Jimmy's room, exclaiming, "Jimmy, after tonight, I think I'm gonna go stay with a friend."

"You have friends?" he replied.

"Yes, and he's going to give me a job."

II

Cold and rainy, the dim restaurant was stuffed with fog, making it impossible to see. A young woman with a slender build, blond hair and blue eyes sat at the delightful steakhouse alone, outside in the drizzle. With a nice silver dress, fancy earrings, and a ruby necklace laying atop her chest, the woman's dress sparkled like the flashing lights of heaven. She gazed out into the darkness, where she noticed an approaching man.

The man, with a nice jacket and a good figure, gently stepped up to the lady, looking her in the eyes. "May I sit here?"

"Of course," the woman said, looking up and down at the short man. He took a seat, appearing bewitched by the woman's beauty. "I apologize for walking up here so abruptly, but I was across the restaurant just over there when I saw the most beautiful woman I had ever seen, sitting alone. I thought that was just not right."

"Why thank you. My name is Amanda," the woman said, giggling.

"Amanda. What a pretty name. Mine not so much."

"And yours is…?"

"Sylvester, Sylvester Erellio," he declared as he grabbed the woman's hand and gently plucked it on his smooth lips. "We should order some food now, don't you think?"

"I was actually thinking about ordering some drinks," the woman replied.

With a slight smirk, Sylvester said, "Even better." Hours went by. Sylvester and Amanda talked until the restaurant closed. Filled with alcohol, drenched in their own stink and drunkenness, they continued to talk and talk and talk, but the hour was late, and night fell quickly. Sylvester unusually acted like a gentleman and walked Amanda home. "I should get going," he spoke, looking into Amanda's eyes as they stood in front of her apartment door.

"Of course… or," the woman said, subtly biting the bottom of her juicy, bright red lip. With an amused look, Sylvester leisurely went inside. Taking off their coats, now inside the big, fancy apartment, Amanda gushed, "I'm gonna go pour us some wine."

"More!?" Sylvester exclaimed, chortling. Amanda went to her dresser in her room down the hall, where she took off her jewelry. She then returned back to the kitchen and filled two glasses of wine. Sylvester, noticing her actions, spoke quickly, "I think I drank too much, may I use your restroom?"

"Of course! It is down the hallway to the right. No wait, the left," the woman replied, still blindly drunk. Sylvester nodded and headed down the hall, where at the end he looked to his left, at the bathroom, then to his right. The man then swiftly and sneakily jumped into Amanda's bedroom. Sylvester scavenged through the room until he located the ruby necklace she had just taken off. He quickly grabbed the sparkling ruby-red necklace and tossed it in his back pocket. The crafty man subsequently returned to Amanda, who handed him a glass of wine. "Ah, refreshing," Sylvester chuckled. "This is a lovely home you have here," the man then remarked, gazing around the nice living room with fine couches and furnished rugs.

"Why thank you," she replied.

"What did you say you did again?"

"This!" she hastily replied, smacking Sylvester atop the head with a large, wooden bat. The man's eyes turned red, his face plumpy, and as his nose bled, he fell backward. Slamming onto the ground, Sylvester, with his erupting pupils, did not fail to notice the smirk on Amanda's face, who followed to bend down and search the knocked-out man's pockets. She pulled out of his back pocket the ruby necklace. "I believe this is mine, thank you!" she said.

Sylvester's eyes fluttered for a full minute as he slowly regained consciousness. Still in Amanda's living room, the now tied-up man found his mouth taped over, and he was unable to move from the wooden chair he was stapled to. He found himself completely naked, with all his clothes upon the kitchen counter across from him. The room was cold, he was disrobed, beaten over the head, and wrapped roughly around his sensitive wrists was a large, tough and itchy rope. With not a sign of sense in his eyes, just a flood of confusion and hysteria, Sylvester continued to sit still and did nothing but stare at the beautiful woman in front of him, the same who he vaguely remembered hit him over the head earlier that night.

"Hello Sylvester," she said nefariously. "You've been out for quite a while. Oh my! You really took a hard one with that hit. Ooh-hoo, my bad!"

She rubbed her hand over the blackened bruise on his forehead, causing Sylvester to groan. "You hit me with a bat!" But all Amanda

49

heard was faint mumbling. With a grin on her face, the woman leaned closer and closer to the man, and spoke softly, "Shush. Why don't I do the talking? You know, my father is a very powerful man. He puts all his time and energy into his work. As a little girl, it was upsetting, but after my mother died, he couldn't find a babysitter, so he brought me to work. It was there I understood what he did and why he did it. I became his understudy, and now, I work for him. The other day he was quite embarrassed, and he came to me with another task to do for him. I thought it would be fun, and I must say, you are charming, and this night was most certainly fun, though I haven't been nearly as drunk as I may have let on. Sylvester, I would like you to meet someone, someone very important to me, someone you wronged. My father!"

With shock and fear, Sylvester's eyes widened as Cleo the Cow stepped out from the shadows. "Thought you got away did yuh?" the large mobster asked furiously. The Cow waddled up to Sylvester and smacked him so hard, his eye grew twice as large and twice as red. "No one makes a fool out of me!" he shouted as the back end of his hand hit Sylvester over and over again. Sylvester shouted in pain as Cleo tore the tape off his mouth. The aching man began to laugh uncontrollably from shock and worry. Cleo, angrier now than ever, pulled out his pistol and shoved the barrel into the man's forehead. "Think this is funny do yuh?"

"No!" Sylvester throbbed.

"Yea! Not so funny when you got a guy pointing a gun to your head!"

"Papà," sweet-voiced Amanda whispered to her tempered father.

Cleo calmed himself and withdrew his pistol, then continued speaking, slower this time. "Oh, forgive me my friend. It's just that, well, you have angered me so very much. Here I thought we were good friends, but you embarrassed me. That is just something that I cannot forgive."

Panting ever so heavily, Sylvester groaned, "Cleo, I am sorry! You know guys like us, we wish for the finer things in this life, and we will do whatever it is to get them. I know you and I share many traits, many qualities. I implore you to see reason, to see from my eyes. I know I made a fool of you."

"A big fool," Cleo interrupted.

"Yes, a very big fool! And I am ever so sorry for it. We have made a number of deals in the past, all of which ended happily. Now I know I fouled up on this one, but I beg of you to hear my plead for a chance of redemption, a chance to do right, by you! My friend! Please, if you cannot trust the words of a humble man, trust the words of a bleeding, bruised idiot who is bare, strapped to a wooden chair. I do not wish to die today, and surely you can see that! So understand how much I am willing to do to fix this. Just say the word and I'll do it! Please!"

"My friend, have you ever heard the tale of the Cat and the Mouse?" Cleo asked, pulling up a chair and taking a seat directly in front of a still nude Sylvester.

"The Cat and the Mouse? No, I don't think I have," the shaking man responded.

"When I was a wee boy, and my papà was out at work, I loved to read, and on my seventh birthday, my father gave me a book of German fairytales that I took a great interest in. One of my favorite of these fairytales was 'The Cat and the Mouse'. In the story, a clever cat befriended a little mouse. After the cat convinced the mouse of their great love and kindness, the two decided to live together in a hut. One day, the cat said to the mouse, 'We must make a provision for winter, or else we shall suffer from hunger.' The mouse agreed and so the two went in on a pot of fat. Needing somewhere to hide the pot until winter, the cat suggested a nice spot in the nearby church, right under the altar. The mouse agreed and so they hid it there. But it wasn't long until the cat got a yearning for the fat. So the next day, the cat told the little mouse that her cousin had just given birth to a son and wished for her to be the godmother. The cat asked her roommate if it was alright to leave them in charge of the house for a day while the cat went to the supposed christening. Of course, the polite mouse said yes, only asking her to bring back any wine if there was any at all left. The cat brought no leftovers, however, for there was no christening at all; instead the cat left the house that day to lick clean the top of the pot of fat. The night came, and as the cat remembered the joy of stretching out in the sun, full from the fat, her yearning came back larger than ever. So the cat asked the little mouse to manage the house for one more day, for she had been asked to be godmother again, by another. The polite mouse agreed and the following day while the mouse made busy at home with chores, the cat returned to the church and licked the pot of fat until it was only half full. But like all others, these things come in threes. The cat told the same bullshit story to the little mouse again, who agreed to manage the house all by itself, again. The next day the cat returned home from the church, with the pot of fat licked clean, empty. From that day on, the cat was never asked to be godmother again. But winter came, and when it was time the jolly mouse, with the cat he trusted by their side, walked to the church, and returned to the pot of fat which stood in the same place they had remembered leaving it, yet something was missing, nay, all of it was missing! The mouse realized that he had been duped! He turned to the cat in anger and yelled at him for being an untrustworthy friend. The cat then ate the mouse."

Cleo paused, the truth settling in. "You see, you, Sylvester, have made me feel like that little mouse, being duped by the one he trusted. But I shall not be eaten up! You make a good point, my friend, and that is why I, for the time being, will not pull on your Johnson till it falls off, or shoot you and toss your body in the ocean! I shall be the bigger man. So, here's what's going to happen, dear friend: You are going to pay me back, with interest! Forty percent to be exact. Do you understand, Sylvester?"

Sylvester slowly raised his head and stared into the eyes of the Cow, crying, "Forty percent?! Cleo, where am I going to get that kind of money? Please. I-I will pay you back, ok?"

"Ha! You know what, forty percent does sound a lil' too generous. Let's make it sixty!"

"No. Please, Cleo. Please, I beg of you."

"Oh you beg, you beg?" Cleo mocked as he smacked Sylvester again. "All I know is that if you don't pay me back, then I'll feed you to my wolves! Ha! Got you! I don't have wolves, but if you don't pay me back I will kill you! You have one month. Oh, and just remember, you are not the cat, you are the mouse!"

Cleo tossed his hat on and cloaked himself. One of his men who stood behind him opened the door and everyone left, other than Amanda, who proceeded to untie Sylvester. She handed the man his clothes and walked him out the door, whispering, "See you soon."

The bloodied man walked to the street that night, terrified. Sitting at the curve of the street, all bruised up, he screamed in frustration as loud as he could. He considered running for a minute, then killing Cleo the next minute, and after a while, he concluded that he was going to die. He looked up to the night sky in doubt of his own life.

His head and heart drowned in mixed emotions. He felt angry, sad and afraid all at the same time, and as the rain poured down from above onto Sylvester he accepted. Accept what though? His death, his life, what? He simply accepted. The man slowly reached into his jacket pocket to pull out a blade. As he sadly hasted out his knife, a small index card fell out of his pocket, landing on the pavement and soaking in the puddle's water. Sylvester placed his index finger on the blade and lifted it up. He held out his hands and stretched his arms. The blade of the knife faced the very center of his stomach. The rain flooded Sylvester's ears so much that it was like a bomb went off. He did not want to die, but he must, or else he would find a much more painful reality. As he thrusted his arms inwards, the blade went as fast as a moving train and was about to pierce the very flesh of Sylvester before it suddenly stopped. The man held the knife about an inch away from his stomach as he stared at the ground. Sylvester continued to stare, not at the ground, but at the card that had fallen out of his pocket.

He stared and stared at the card as he read an address. The address on the card, the address that Jones gave him. Sylvester picked up the card and jumped up with excitement. "Haha!" he screamed, tossing his hand up in the air above him. Sylvester then placed the card back in his pocket and walked off into the rainy depths of the night, now with the slight belief he may yet live past Christmas.

III

He knocked, and when the door opened, Jeff said, "Hey Ma."

"So, I heard my son just lost his job. Just when I thought he might not be a failure," the man's mother said, blocking the doorway, arms crossed.

"Good to see you too, mother," Jeff sarcastically replied. "Look, I need to borrow some money. Just to keep me stable for the next couple of weeks until I can find another job."

"Borrow money from me? That's something I've never heard before. Jeff, I am living off the salary of a grocery store attendant. I barely have enough money to feed myself let alone pay for this house. A real man would have just found a job and started working."

"A real mother would take care of her children. No matter what!"

"How dare you! I took care of you and your sister your whole damn lives, and look what it's gotten me! Y'all were supposed to take care of me when I got older, not the other way around. I mean I did everything for you kids, and yet you still come crying back, acting like you've had it so rough! You had every opportunity because of me! Full bellies and a nice roof over your head, because of me! So don't you dare act like I owe you anything else, after all I've done for you!"

"Done for me? Done for us? You really think you took care of us? I cooked every night while you were out at the fancy nightclubs, smooching off other men's fortune. When you dated that architect, you stayed in his fancy hotel for weeks, and you left us at home to fend for ourselves. I went grocery shopping! I took a job at the diner down the street when I was eight! You brought in some rich guys every now and then who would occasionally 'lend you' money, which you would throw away for garbage like your drinks, or your drugs! I come here, standing outside of the house that has five patched-up holes in the ceiling, because of me, asking my mother, who did the absolute bare minimum when I was a child, to lend me a little money to cover one month's rent, just so I can have a roof over my head! But hey, if you're low on cash from your latest bender or sparkly dress that makes you feel luxurious, that's fine! I'm sorry I ever came here!"

With a grizzly face, Jeff's mother slammed the door, and Jeff went back to his apartment to sulk in his own misery. But such wasn't his character, and without a minute to spare, the jobless man ran around the city, grabbing all the newspapers around both old and new, looking for possible jobs. He spent the morning cutting out help wanted ads, and right after he filled his stomach with warm food, he set off for no less than seven applications. The first interview Jeff had was to be a candy man, but the manager deemed him to be too "unhappy". The next job was for a dry cleaner, but since he wasn't very good at the job, and more importantly, he didn't speak Chinese, he again went without employment.

Many more interviews went all sorts of wrong that day. He interviewed for a cook, a waiter, an office manager, a teacher, a construction worker, and a mechanic, all of which, however, he was just not right for. He panicked at spilling oil on himself at the mechanic interview, memorized one thing which was wrong at the waiter interview, burned the food at the cook interview, broke a crane, and destroyed a window. The day was going terrible for him and as soon as he returned home it got worse. He sluggishly stamped up his stairs with oil and ink all over his body with despair in his eyes. When the blue man opened his door and found an envelope in the middle of the floor, he clenched in frustration.

"Dear Mr. Williams in apartment twelve, you have missed the past two rent payments. We know since we have bumped up our prices it has left some people shocked. This is an eviction notice. Due to your missing rent, we will have to evict you if those are not paid back in full. Under the circumstance of our prices going up, we will allow you one week before eviction. Thank you."

One week? he thought, his arms trembling, his face turning the color such of Satan. Jeff still held hope, however, for he had one more interview that day. He was hired unexpectedly. The store was a local bookshop, and the manager was a jolly old fellow who held to his bright spirits as Jeff acted like nothing more than a glum Ogre, grumpy and mad with how the world treated him. Jeff was surprised by his hiring, for he tried very little, but the manager was dimwitted too. The now working man, starting that very hour, was tasked with helping customers, stocking shelves, and cleaning the store. Of course he tried little. With no enthusiasm, Jeff went about the day, without a smile as he slowly worked.

"Hey, do you know where I can find Yellow Kid issue sixty-eight?" a customer asked to Jeff.

"Let me look." The attendant sighed. He walked around the store, searching for the guy's comic. After walking no more than a mere ten feet and taking no extra unnecessary time, Jeff handed over the man's book. "Ok, that will be fifty cents."

"Uh, I'm sorry, this is issue forty-three, I said issue sixty-eight."

"What's the difference?" Jeff frustratedly asked.

"The difference is that I have already read and already bought this issue, and I want the newest issue!"

"Well, I'm sorry sir, but it appears we don't have that one in stock right now."

"That's malarkey! You didn't even look!"

"You didn't look either, you fat leech!"

The manager came out from his office. "Hey, hey!" he shouted. "What's the problem, sir?"

"I asked this gentleman for Yellow Kid number sixty-eight and instead he brought me issue forty-three. Then he refused to even go look for the one I had asked for. See here, all I wanted was to buy this comic for my son's birthday and I would've went to look for it myself, but this store is so damn big I needed an attendant so I could quickly be on my way, yet I am now being held up by a middle-aged brat who doesn't know what it means to work!"

"What's the difference, they're the same thing!" Jeff shouted.

"Sir, I'm sure we have your comic book around here somewhere, I'll go look for it right now," the manager interrupted.

"Forget it, I'll take my business elsewhere. Somewhere where people don't argue with their paying customers." The man stormed out of the shop in fury. The manager looked at Jeff with tilted eyebrows, and just like that, after only three hours, he was fired. Happy yet full of anger, Jeff too, like the customer, stormed out. That night, as he was jobless, broke, and about to be evicted, the depressed man gazed out into the rainy night, eating alone at a local diner. He thought about what he would do with his life. *I'm never going to get a job, and even if I do, it's going to be some degrading bullshit one,* he thought to himself. *How did I end up here! Why has God chosen to punish me! Sure, I'm not the most selfless guy in the room but I just look out for myself, and this is just unfair! I mean, how can a handsome, smart and willing man like me be treated so harshly by the world.*

All of a sudden, a man came up to Jeff and sat down at his table. Jeff slowly tilted his head up to see Bobby. Looking him in the eyes, he asked passive-aggressively, "What are you doing here?"

"I came here for you," Bobby said softly.

"Me? What do you mean?"

Clear in tone, Bobby spoke, "I'm going back tomorrow morning. I'll be honest, I don't have a damn thing left in my life worth fighting for. I have no job, I owe a shit ton of money to a club downtown, I've got no family left, I'm about to be evicted and I am just tired. I am tired of living in depression and fear. I want to be able to leave my home without getting beat on. I want to be in a nice house with a nice woman and some kids. This job might get me tossed in the slammer but it's a fair shot, and one I'm gonna take. I heard you say you love this restaurant and I thought you'd be the least likely to come back besides Sylvester, but I don't know where that guy is, so I decided to come here and see if I could find you and convince you to come back, for Jones said he needs all of us."

With a sarcastic voice, Jeff went, "You want me to come with you?"

"Yes!"

"Look, Bobby, I do agree that it is a great offer," Jeff spoke, "but I have my whole life ahead of me, and stealing from Accardi is not the best thing for me right now."

"Well, if you don't mind me asking, what kind of 'whole life' do you really see for yourself? I for one am going to take a shot at making my life what I dreamed it would be since I was a little boy; I hope you do the same." Bobby, in a manner of mimicking Jones, stood up and silently walked away, leaving Jeff aggravated—not only that he was spoken down upon to a black, but that Bobby just might have been right.

The sun rose with a gleam of aspiration, and Jeff sat on his couch considering what Bobby said, glaring at the card Jones had given to him. He twirled the card in his hands like spinning dice; his mind was ticking, going like a clock from one answer to the other, and he pondered if he should go or not. *I should, I shouldn't, I should, I shouldn't,* Jeff thought in his head over and over again. Finally, he glanced up into the sky and jumped off his weary ass. He grabbed his hat and walked out the door in a hurry, thinking, *I shall.*

The morning sea breeze sang out across the banks, and four cars pulled up at the same time. Simultaneously, four men stepped out of each taxi. The men all looked back and forth at each other in a glaring, sarcastic, embarrassed gaze. They stomped back into the pool house and then into the warehouse. They opened the giant metal door to see Jones sitting on the couch facing directly toward them, smirking. Jones stopped his stopwatch. "Huh, took you longer than I expected."

All the men sat down on the couches as Jones stood up, preparing a speech. "Alright, tell us about the job," the men spoke.

Jones, his smirk unfading, began, "I thought you'd never ask."

Jeff's Recollection

To be honest, I didn't hear all of what Jones said, and why would I? He kept going on and on and on! I'll figure it out as I go. I've never really been one for long-made plans anyway. But holy! This guy had one hell of a plan! Jones went on so long with this heist of his that I really almost saw some Zs! When I changed my mind and decided to go back to hear Jones out, I never imagined I would walk out so sold! He had every little detail for this whole job planned out, and although I don't really like all the work it entails, it is quite a good deal. The kind of money I'm gonna be making is beyond anything I could have ever imagined. So, I went home for the day, as after Jones went through the whole of the plan with all of us, he told us to get some rest and come back tomorrow morning at the same time. But David stayed there, I think. When I got home, I threw my eviction notice out the window and got my stuff packed. I had been fired, and now with no work to do, no job to look for, and nothing to exhaust myself with, I thought I might as well do exactly what my new boss instructed—rest. I only packed up half of my stuff, because I figured when I was done with this job, I'd buy it all again, but better and nicer! When I finished packing the stuff I needed for the following weeks, I decided to go to a nice lunch. There's this little place across town which I've always loved. It had the best soup ever! I drove over to the spot, and per usual, it was a long wait, but I had money to spare now. I handed the guy in the front a bit of a pre-tip, if you will, and sure enough, a table for one at the best soup place in town was mine! I sat down, and without the slightest need of a menu, I ordered the amazing soup that I craved. I was very excited about the shit ton of money I was about to come into, so I got myself a few expensive drinks as well. Wow! It was one good meal, I'll tell you that! It was a peaceful one too, and eating alone with the best food is one of the greatest feelings in the world. But that was cut short, as such always is in my life, when a bunch of my former coworkers came in. With my bad luck, I was sure as shit not surprised when they were seated right next to me too. Now sitting next to me was the chief, my old partner who had fired me just a couple of days ago, the blabbering deputy who no one could ever get to shut up, the boastful inspector named Milo who couldn't talk about anything other than himself, the quiet inspector whom we called Shilton, and the idiot inspector named Carl. They all put on glad faces to see me, and we began conversing thusly, but I knew they were all so full of shit! Just a bunch of dirtbags they were! None of them stood up for me when I left, and when we laughed and spoke at lunch, they tried their absolute best not to mention my exit. They acted so kind and innocent, but really, they were just working to make it the least bit awkward it could've been. I mean all of them except the chief. He was surprisingly quiet. For someone who so confidently fired his friend, he seemed to feel a bit embarrassed, or otherwise afraid. He wouldn't look me in the eye, and every time I tried to address him with a question, he would reply to it with haste, then go right back to staring at the ground. Nothing could have ruined my outing more than those phonies there. Half of the time we all just listened to Milo talk about how he saved the mayor once, and the other half of the time we just listened to idiot Carl's opinions on the latest politics. Anytime I wanted to simply eat in silence, the damn deputy would interrupt, trying to get Shilton to let out a single word. I told them I had to leave when I finished eating; I just couldn't take any more of the bullshit conversations. I finally set off and used my new job as an excuse. They all looked shocked and sort of awkward once I said that. The deputy asked me what job I had, and I told him I was just hired for the lead on a travel agency's new project. They seemed not one bit happy for me, but rather, more shocked of how such a guy could find such a job in such a matter of time. With an abrupt exit, it was then and there I decided to leave them, uncomfortable and holding a clear sign of my opinions toward them. I then decided to go spend my time at the movies. I've always loved Christmas, who doesn't? So I watched the Christmas movie that had just released down on Broadway and spent my next couple of hours there. It was a fine movie, with some good holiday fun, even though it was hardly Christmas time, and the story was quite heartwarming. I love the movies. When I was little, I spent all my time working to provide food for me and my sister while my mother was away doing God knows what. Then, by the time I might've had the time and money to go see films, Black Thursday and Tuesday came, and with it, some of the worst years of my life. Man! I can't wait to finish this job! My life has always been a shitshow! I grew up with nothing but an abusive, drunk mother, then had to live through the greatest economic hardship in modern history. At least I didn't serve though. Ha! My goddamn country puts me through hell for over a decade and then they want me to fight for that same country! What a bunch of bull! Anyways, I went back to my place, took a long nap, then went out to the clubs. It was a bit early, sure, but the way I saw it, I had time to kill, and what better place to kill time? Me and this other fella next to me howled real good that night, though I can't recall his name. We drank and drank together all night, and then I never saw him again. After he left, I decided to get a little exercise in with one of the girls I've known for a stretch, if you know what I mean, All in all it was a fine day, and I was ready to retire home when I stumbled shitfaced out of the bar. For the first few seconds I thought I was imagining his being there, but low and behold, when I walked out, the chief was waiting for me. I'm pretty sure he said he had been waiting for me all night. I asked him why and he told me that the wife didn't like him being in such places. Ha! That loyal pup of a man is a henpecked mama's boy! Does whatever the little women tell him to do. Not me, no, I'll never get bitched around like that! I make my own damn rules! I was too drunk to hardly question his appearance, but it was more than odd, now that I think about it. It was all so hazy, and I remember only fragments. The chief tried his best to pull me to a dark alleyway, or somewhere more discreet. And when he spoke, he whispered. He also constantly looked over his shoulder, God knows why. I do remember not recognizing him at first as well, for he was wrapped in a long coat, with a small but concealing hat on. Why the chief of police, someone who I had known for half my life to be the strongest and bravest man, was hiding, I could not say. It was all weird, especially considering the point of it all. He gave me a business card of a friend of his, someone he said could give me a job. He said he felt bad for firing me and tried to make it better by getting me a new, really good job, but of course I said no. The money that came with The Accardi Job, as we were calling it, as well as the very low chance of it failing, made the gears in my head turn quick. The way Jones had planned it all out with all of these tiny details, it was sure to work. I was definitely skeptical at first, but upon hearing his detailed plan, which I must admit did, at times, seem insane and improbable, I now had a lot of faith in this job. The chief didn't seem to like my answer and kept pressing on me to take the job he was offering. The way he kept speaking was peculiar as well. It seemed, for a moment, that he wanted me not to just accept his job offer, but to specifically leave the job I had just obtained. I can't fathom why he might feel this way, for there was no earthly way that he could've known about Accardi, or Jones, Sylvester, David and that other negro. So why? Why was he so against me doing this? I thought about it all the next day, and all on the plane flight to France, and I think I had come up with an answer. Perhaps he was worried about me, because of all my big busts, particularly the ones I had made just two nights ago. Perhaps he simply wanted me to be under his watch, as after all, up until late, we had been the closest of pals. But I had to deny him, because the gain in The Accardi Job was worth more than the stress and worry the chief would have for me. The next day, I woke up with the biggest hangover! I was also late, so I rushed down to the curb with my stuff and then got a ride back to Jones' warehouse. In Jones' long plan, he gave us the most details on the first part of the plan. It wasn't what we had to do that angered me so, but it was that I was tasked with that other negro! I mean, the guy seemed nice enough the other day when I met him, more than Jones at least, but I did not wish to work with him. My mother raised me and my sister with little effort, but when she was around, she would teach us very certain things, one of them being to hate those mindless jungle bunnies who were taking our power and sneaking their way into our polite, constructed society. There wasn't many colored people in my neighborhood growing up, so I never thought about it much, especially because it came out of my mother's mouth. But as time went on, and I became more familiar with the world, I got what she meant. It was because of those damn people that I had to live on the streets for years, all because they undeservedly took all our jobs! Everything that was supposed to be ours, they were trying to take! But you know, who gives a shit! I was getting paid more than any man I've ever met ever thought of making! I didn't care if I have to work with a couple of these guys. The opportunity this Jones guy had given me was beyond anything! And I would be ready for whatever tried to come between me and that pot of gold that laid at the end of this road!

Chapter 3

The Interview and The Drill

It was noon, and David Cockspy, with two big bags of sandwiches, made his way inside. As he opened the door to the warehouse, everyone's heads turned to cheer. They all rushed to David to grab their lunch, and once they did, they promptly returned to their seats. Whilst the men dug into their meals, Jones stood and began disclosing: "So, in precisely thirty-one days, there will be the annual Mericorn Horse Race. Mericorn is the legit/non-legit company run by the Accardi family, otherwise known as the Accardi mob. Every year they have their famed horse race and make millions off the rich dunces who continue to return on the prospect of winning back a little of what they lost the previous time, and we, my dear friends, are going to rob it! The event gathers high rollers from all around the globe. Business owners, sports champions, actors, and even world leaders come to this high-end event. The point is it has a lot of big players, which is why the race makes so much money.

"When the players make their bets, that money, which they will probably never see again, gets put down a tube. This tube tunnels air all the way down to the vault. It has some of the highest security in history so the tubes will not be accessible. Before the money is sent down, an expert analyzes it to make sure it's authentic. Then, the cash is tossed down another tube where it swiftly flows through a vacuum of air all the way down to a small opening into the steel vault. There, active guards organize the money neatly across the vault. Once the betting hour is over, the guards close the tube, walk out of the fifteen by twenty vault, and seal it shut behind them, making it impossible for anyone to enter until the racing round is over.

"Now, let's discuss the vault. The vault is a large steel box placed in the center of a forty-five-by-sixty-foot lounge, which is located about seventy feet underground. The only way to get to the windowless, underground lounge is via an elevator stationed with two armed guards. If we somehow managed to get onto the elevator, which has only one access point above ground, we would find ourselves in the lounge that has no less than eight armed guards, all tasked with protecting the vault. So, there is no possible way for us to get into the vault without heavy bloodshed, unless the guards weren't there, of course. Therefore, our first step is to make the guards go away. How might we do that, you may ask?

"Ah well, in order for the guards to leave there needs to be a reason for them to leave, and the only thing that these guards would need to leave for is a serious incident. Kingpin of the city, Giovanni Accardi, is at all times the number one concern. So, if we get Accardi to be put at risk, the guards will have no choice but to leave the room to provide extra assistance for the protection of Accardi. Something such as a fake assassination attempt, a fight, or just a hoax of some sort to get Accardi in high risk will be the ample way for us to get the underground lounge cleared of its sentinels. Now, the guards aren't just going to leave without being directed to, which is why we are going to have the head of security tell them to, and that is where dear David comes in."

David halted his chewing mouth and looked up. "Say what?" he exclaimed.

Jones chuckled for a moment, then continued his disclosure: "Recently, Accardi's chief security officer received a very deadly illness, and thus the spot is open for us to send David in."

The shocked man stared at Jones with distress, then cried, "Wait, you want me to physically be next to Accardi? I could get killed if he finds out who I am!"

"Which he won't," Jones stated like fact. "Once you, my friend David, have dismissed a good portion of the lounge's sentinels, the vault will be right for the taking, and that shall be our moment to enter. About three miles away from the stadium, there is an old, abandoned aircraft hangar, now owned by yours truly. This little investment of mine is located practically in the middle of nowhere, which is a vital component of this plan as it ensures we won't be interrupted. Now, this is where we will bring in the drill."

With confused glares and shocked frowns, the four listening men cried, "Drill?!"

"Yes, a drill, and a quite large one at that," Jones continued. "There is a mining hub in northern France, and our dear friends, Jeff and Bobby, shall travel to this region to steal a very specific and quite large drill for us. I have more instructions for the pair of you which I shall address later," Jones went on, pointing to a frown-faced Bobby and Jeff. "Now, once we have retrieved this drill and safely transported it into the hangar, we will secretly drill all the way down to the vault room. It might seem a bit far-fetched, but over the course of four weeks, we shall operate this heavy machinery while it slowly drills at an angle, creating a tunnel capable of driving a truck up and down. This is how we shall enter the underground lounge and thus the vault."

"Drill a three-mile hole at a diagonal trajectory so we may drive a full-sized truck through it? Is that really your plan? That's madness!" cried an unconvinced Jeff, followed by the agreeing faces of the other men.

Jones, never losing confidence, continued, "It will take much work, but many of you have spent fair time in the low-profile manufacturing businesses; Bobby in cars, Jeff a mechanic when he was a boy, and I believe Sylvester spent many years crafting fire extinguishers. Now whether they worked or not doesn't matter; what matters is that you are all fairly familiar with such machinery. The point is that this is very plausible, and given the right amount of effort, all shall go according to plan. Now, shall I continue?"

"Yes, go ahead," the four men replied, now somewhat convinced.

"Very well," Jones resumed. "About two days before the race, the drill's work shall be complete, and we will drive the short miles to the underground lounge. With a couple of sledgehammers, making an entrance will be easy. Of course, however, it is pretty easy to notice a giant-ass hole in the wall. Therefore, we must spend the rest of our preparation time retiling all the walls in the lounge. I have already arranged for this, so when Accardi, his insurer, his staff, or whoever the hell goes down to said lounge, they will see nothing but a well-done renovation job made by the stadium as a thank you to Giovanni Accardi for giving them so much business over the years. What they will not see, however, is the secret door we will have built, covering up the initial hole in the wall we made. So when the time comes, we will enter sneakily into the lounge, take out the few guards that occupy the space, fill up our bags of cold, hard cash, and promptly exit back through which we came, never to be seen again. Of course there are many more details to go over, ones more specific to each of your roles, but this is the general layout of the plan I have put in place to rob Accardi and his annual horse race. Now, hearing all the details, and understanding the full scope of The Accardi Job, I now ask you lifeless mockeries of men, are you in or out?"

With all sincerity in their faces, the men silently nodded. David quickly spoke, however. "I don't understand why I have to be the one working under Accardi." Groaning in grievance over David's not surprising complaining, the men clashed their faces against their hands. "I mean come on! I got food, didn't I? Come on Jones, why don't you let Bobby do it, or Sylvester?"

Jones responded to the foolish question with a grin, saying, "Bobby owes some very dangerous people money which Accardi won't like, and Jeff was in the NYPD for eight years. Sylvester and I have different roles in this. The only option is you."

"Fine," David groaned. "When's the interview?"

"Tomorrow; four o'clock. I'll get you a suit. Any other questions?"

"When do you want me and Bobby to leave, and what are the details on that part?" Jeff asked.

"I have booked two plane tickets for Lens, tomorrow after David's interview," explained Jones. "You will go then. I shall give you the details and specifics of the plan before you leave. Right, now if there is nothing further, everyone go home, pack your things, and get some rest. We reconvene in the morning, and you will be staying here until the job is done." The men finished their meals and left back to their homes. David stayed, however, already being lodged there. Once the other men left, Jones and David spent the day apart, minding their own business, but when night came, and the moon shone over the pool house, the two decided to drink by the outside fireplace.

In the silence of the night, David tried to converse, "So, you know everything about me, but what about you?" he asked. "I mean, what got you here? How did you come up with all of this? Who are you, really?"

"Has anyone ever told you that you talk too much, David? Why don't you just lean back and relax in the warm, windy night?"

To Jones, David solemnly replied, "There's a lot of solitude in prison."

"Very well," said Jones. "If you must know, I lost something important to me. I guess I am here to get, I don't know, closure I suppose. But it is more than that! I have a reputation to uphold! I got to do something better each time, you know? So I thought, what could I do to earn a shit ton of money, and then it hit me. As I turned to a billboard advertising the annual race I had it! So I contacted a few friends, got a few names and a few ideas, and here we are."

"Interesting. Hey, do you really think it is a good idea to send Bobby and Jeff together to Germany?"

"They're going to France, and what do you mean?"

"Well, I've noticed that Jeff is a bit uh, uncharismatic toward your kind of people," David explained.

Jones drank another sip of his beer and said, "We have a long road ahead of us. The sooner they start to understand each other and resolve their conflict the better. Bobby hates the entitled white supremacists, and Jeff, of course, is a Jim Crow lover like his mother. But they are both so guided by their greed that they will not jeopardize anything for such, and perhaps, maybe, you never know. Maybe they can learn from each other. They are more similar than they think, you all are."

Ryder Lim

The next morning, as the sun came up from the east the three men reapproached the warehouse with packed bags. David made breakfast while Jones showed the three other men to their rooms, for there were five total rooms in the back of the warehouse. After everyone settled in and ate, they started a long day. At about one-thirty in the afternoon, Jones drove David to a tailor shop to try on his new suit. The suit was gray, with a black tie, a semi-expensive watch, and nice, buckled shoes. David stood in front of a crystal mirror as he tightened his tie. All the while, Jones was preparing him. "So, one more time," he rehearsed.

"You're going to drop me off on Sixth Avenue, I am going to walk three blocks, take two rights, a left, and another right. I'm going to walk into the big, fancy theater. I will empty my pockets and get checked for weapons. I am going to follow a man into the lounge, where I will wait for my interview. Once I get called in, I will say that I am the best and that I have saved lives and done dirty work and won awards and yotta yotta yotta. Good enough for yuh?"

"Well done, David, you're a natural!"

"Jones, look, there will be at least ten men up for this job, all with actual experience, and I'm just supposed to walk up in there and get the job? How exactly is that gonna work?"

"Well, there's uh, ok, I wasn't going to tell you till tonight, just to uh, not worry you by uh," Jones murmured.

"Jones?!"

"The interview is just to meet you. Wednesday is the real thing."

"The real thing?" David worried. "What is the real thing?"

"On Wednesday, Accardi will put you to a task, a test of who is the best. A sort of game, if you will—he does enjoy games. The winner gets the job. Now what the game is I do not know."

"A game?" David mirrored in angst. "What are you talking about?"

"Look, we will prepare you tomorrow, so that way you will be ready for the game," Jones calmly explained.

"One day is not enough to beat all of these competitors who have been in this type of business since before I was sixteen!"

70

"Let us not worry about this anymore," said Jones. "Today we must focus on the task at hand, the interview. Now remember, all you have to do is talk proudly of yourself and act like you're the strongest, smartest, most dangerous man there! Whatever you do, don't act afraid in any manner. Try to scare the other competitors a bit and make them feel less than you, but you must not, by any means, start a fight!"

"Got it," David replied.

It was time now, and Jones did as he said. He drove his shiny car to the dropoff, about three blocks away from the meet. Jones parked on a clear sidewalk, then turned to David with a glaring look. "You ready?" he asked sincerely. David nodded, and with nothing but deep breaths, dismounted from the vehicle and in turn began walking. Sylvester then jumped into the now vacant front seat as Jeff and Bobby held their bags in their laps. They watched David step away for a few moments as their nerves rattled, but then Jones slowly set the car off and started heading toward the airport.

David followed Jones' directions carefully as he navigated the streets. Suddenly, however, his head began turning and his mind began shrinking. Drops of sweat began pouring down his shiny forehead; he spun around feeling ever so tense, and he saw a homeless man slowly approaching him. "Do you have a quarter?" the man asked David. "Can I borrow a quarter? I need a quarter! Can't you spare a quarter?" the man asked and asked as David continued spinning around, losing sense. Everything became blurry for David, who kept spinning around like a dreidel. His ears were shaking from the loud ringing that had no end, and his chest was tight, ever so tight. This abrupt panic attack caused David to toss up his arm, reaching out for the nearby wall, hoping to find support for his crumbling legs, but his strength did not last, and the man fell to the ground. His ears kept ringing, his sight got more blurred, his chest tighter and his mind weaker. Then, all of a sudden, the sound of his daughter's laugh flooded his ears, and his eyes rolled back as his lids closed shut.

A picture then formed in his mind, one of him playing with his dear daughter. The man kept this picture in his mind, and in the real world he began to let out a smile, his eyes still shut. Those happy memories, however, turned to screams in an instant, and the picture in David's mind faded to a snowy battlefield. He stared at the running, the shooting, and the screaming of men. Suddenly, David saw a man standing in front of him. It was his brother.

Arnom had cold, gray skin, with a hole in his head that caused blood to flow out of every other natural hole in his body.

"Arnom?" David stuttered.

"David?" asked the standing corpse. "You said you would protect me! Why didn't you take the shot, David? Why didn't you take the shot? David?! Why didn't you take the shot!" Coughing and choking on the river of blood that poured from his mouth, the dead man continued to scream, almost to no end. David's face ran with tears and the screams around him grew louder. The icy battlefield then caught on fire, and more concentrated, specific screams spread through the air, ones of a woman and a child.

"Why didn't you take the shot, David!?" the ghost kept howling. David, who was standing in this dream, screamed from all the painful remembrance of his own history and mistakes. He thereafter fell down in this dream, just in the way he had in the real world moments ago. The agonizing screams, the constant shooting, the glaring flames, and the screeches of the bloody corpse grew bigger, louder, brighter, and kept growing, marching on David like Armageddon. In the next second, however, the noises faded and the pictures swelled away. David's true eyes then opened as his chest became looser, with the ringing in his ears becoming faint, and the illusions of his mind dissipating. He blinked a couple of times just to come back to the world, and when he did, he took a deep breath, stood up, pulled out his wallet, handed the homeless man two quarters, and carried on.

Attempting to forget his episode, David kept on his path with all focus, set on not forgetting Jones' instructions and becoming lost, which luckily he did not; in fact, he arrived a touch early. The meeting was held at a well-kept theater, one with colorful lights, furnished walls and a nice carpet. David approached the ticket booth at the entrance to find an old woman reading a book. He paused and waited for a short second, assuming the woman would address him, but after a little time had passed, David asked, somewhat awkwardly, "Excuse me?" The woman kept her pointy nose stuck in her book, intentionally ignoring the man. But, running out of patience, David knocked on the window. Only then did the woman tilt her head up and say, "We're sold out."

"I'm here for the interview," said David with an unusually firm tone. At that very instant, the woman closed her book, then proceeded to pull out a ticket and hand it to David. "Good luck, Mr. Cockspy," the woman said, now with a smile. Quite tense and somewhat horrified, David nodded his head and stepped inside. The theater looked like any other, despite its opulence. David wandered around, trying to figure out where he was supposed to go. Having a hard time telling the staff apart from the theatergoers, for both were lavishly dressed, David entered the concessions line in attempt to ask a worker ahead. Just then, however, a rather large man approached and who rested his hand atop David's shoulder. "Mr. Cockspy, would you care to follow me?" he said calmly.

"Why yes, why yes I would," David quickly replied. And thus, David was led upstairs to a large door, one guarded by another very big man. This man said, also in a calm voice, "May I see your ticket, sir?"

David handed the man his ticket, and after a quick study of it, both large men followed to grab either handle of the large door, then pulled it open for him. "Down that hall." David took his ticket back and moved down the hallway. As he trailed on, he gazed into the artistry of the many paintings on the walls. There was one in particular that caught David's attention. It was a painting of a horse. No background, no title, nothing, just the black frame of a running horse on a brown canvas. David pondered over the painting, admiring its simplicity, and attempted to interpret its meaning, if it even had any. But David quickly continued again, and a few short moments later, he fluttered his eyes as he also took a deep breath in, preparing to step through the door he had come to reach. "You got this! Come on!" David whispered to his anxious self. David's eyes chilled as he saw two guards walking around, and about four other men sitting in nice wooden chairs.

David crossed through the open lobby and strolled past the other applicants till he came upon a woman seated at a large desk. "Can I help you?" the woman asked David.

"Uh yes, I am here for the interview," he said calmly.

"Do you have your ticket?" asked the woman.

"Oh, um yes," he claimed, shuffling through his pockets.

"Mr. Accardi will be with you shortly," the woman said after David handed his found ticket over. "You may take a seat," she said. But David did not move, rather he stood, shocked and more anxious than ever. "You may take a seat," the woman restated as David remained still.

"Mr. Accardi is going to be doing the interview directly?" a shocked David asked. "He-he-he's uh, he's here?" he stuttered anxiously.

"Why yes of course. Mr. Accardi wouldn't let anyone but himself choose his new chief of security."

"Ah, of course!" David replied, nodding intensely. The unsettled man now stepped over to take a seat, moving with the speed of a sloth.

"Here we go," Jones exclaimed, and out of the car stepped the four men. With their bags held high, Jeff and Bobby shook the two men's hands, preparing to depart. Earlier that day, Jones had gone over the entire plan of stealing the drill with the pair. And now with all the need-to-know information in their heads, the travelling accomplices felt confident. "Ready?" Jones asked.

Bobby nodded and Jeff replied, "Yeah." The three men exchanged understanding glances before Sylvester and Jones drove off. As Jones pulled away, though, he chuckled, knowing what Bobby and Jeff were about to learn. The plane flight that the two men were ticketed for had a departure time of eight o'clock, and it was currently one-forty. The travelling companions were angered, of course, and Jeff's particular antipathy being no secret, it was clear what kind of trick Jones had pulled.

Though the two were quite angered by Jones' calculated move, they still followed all of his directions. They waited for the plane, all three hours, and in addition, Jones had declared that the two would not leave each other's side at any cost until they reached Lens. Thus, Jeff and Bobby decided to temporarily exit the airport and find a bench to sit on as they waited for their flight; the airport had different waiting rooms for the alternate races of the two. An hour passed as the two men sat silently in the fresh air. Bobby spoke every now and then, attempting to bring up conversation and break the uncomfortable silence. Jeff, however, was quite stuck on being silent, deliberately ignoring Bobby's chatter.

As time progressed, the awkward silence of the two made Bobby feel tight, like a million seatbelts hauling him to the bench. Jeff, however, did not feel uncomfortable, nor awkward, but restless. In the peacefulness of the fresh air, the sorrowful man looked back upon his life. He remembered his father and mother, along with all the sufferings of his life. Jeff was a man of high ego, and he was always angry. And he did not blame himself for the cause of any grief in his life, even when it was most assuredly his own doing. Jeff, instead, held the world responsible, using bad luck and poor circumstances to blame for, in his eyes, the tragic life he had been cursed with. As Bobby continued to talk on and on, Jeff fell further into deep thoughts, acknowledging every grief in his life. He grew angry, thinking about his demotion, as well as his firing, feeling it was unfair and unjust. He then grew angrier, thinking of how he had been forced to work with Bobby, a man of color. He kept growing angrier and angrier, and whether it was by reliving his mother's abuse, or remembering any other misfortunes, the man had begun to steam like boiling water.

Jeff was livid, and as his jabbering neighbor continued to speak, and speak, and speak, he became more enraged. Bobby, however, hardly noticed Jeff's fury, being too caught up with his chattering. The noisy man was not a fan of silence and found it a good way to clear awkward air. "Yeah, I have a sister up in Jersey. We've never really been close. We actually rarely speak," Bobby rambled on. "I also practically never see my parents, but they live in Philly, so what do they expect me to do?"

Bobby continued on, until Jeff looked over with a grizzly face and shouted, "Shut up! The only reason I am doing this is because of the money. I don't wish to have a heartfelt conversation, nor do I wish to hear about your damn family! Not for the next three days, not for the next three hours, not for the next three seconds! This is a job, and we are here for one reason. So lay back, take a breath of the fresh air, and shut up!" Jeff, enraged by the remembrance of all his other grievances, had found something of use to blow off some steam. As much as he was honest though, Bobby saw this and thought it as nothing more than some built-up anger.

Bobby did not speak for some minutes, but then he promptly continued. "Look, you've had it pretty rough, I get it—you and me both, man," he said in a friendly manner. "I also know you don't like me very much, which I don't blame you for. It's this society that we live in. You were raised to feel certain ways, and that's just how things work. I get it, but hey, I can tell you're mainly just letting off some steam, so I'll forgive yuh, haha. I mean, you won't believe the amount of shit I've got going on in my life! It's unbelievable how much this world can screw one over! This job is gonna change things though, isn't it?" Jeff did nothing but glare at Bobby, who simply passed it off as mocking sarcasm, and continued speaking endlessly.

Around six-twenty, Jeff grew tired of Bobby's conversation, and he too was bored, so he came up with the mighty idea to head to a bar around the corner. It was quite a small bar, but it was calm and had decent drinks. Without invitation, Bobby followed, and when they took places at the counter inside, Jeff said to the bartender, "Give me the strongest bourbon you got."

The young white boy behind the counter rushed to pour the liquor, but as he did, Bobby said, "Wow, that looks spectacular! Let me get one of those!"

The bottle was about a quarter full, enough to make up for three glasses. But the young bartender, as he poured Jeff's glass, flipped the bottle perfectly vertical and filled the glass to the brim. He then said, smirking, "Oh I'm sorry, this man just took the last of it." Bobby turned to Jeff, somewhat hoping he'd say something, but no, Jeff kept a straight face and began sipping on his overfilled glass of bourbon.

"Alright, why don't you get me another type of bourbon," Bobby said, turning back toward the bartender, who sharply and quickly replied, "I'm sorry, but we seem to be out of bourbon."

"What about that bottle there?" Bobby intensely replied, pointing toward another, rather fine bottle on the shelf.

"Oh, I am afraid that bottle is reserved."

"Reserved? Reserved for who? For the captains over at that airport, or just anyone that isn't colored?"

"Yes, the captains," said the bartender.

"Well, what if I were a captain?"

"You're not a captain."

"How do you know? I could be a very good captain, a very proud, wealthy, powerful captain."

"And I could be a very great, strong, skillful Greek warrior," the young bartender sarcastically replied. "I could be the slayer of Achilles just as much as you could be a captain. Achilles is a famed, ancient Trojan warrior, just so you know. I'm aware you people aren't very accustomed to reading."

"Yes, that is a common stereotype, isn't it?" Bobby responded with a strong glare. "One that isn't all that true, especially when it comes to me. I happen to be a Harvard graduate, and I have read Homer's works, as well as Ovid's and Virgil's. I also think you have made a mistake, for Achilles was not a Trojan warrior. No, in fact, I believe he was a great Greek warrior, who died in the tenth year of the Trojan War, shot in the heel by Paris, son of Priam, who sought revenge after Achilles slayed his dear brother Hector."

Embarrassed and humbled, the bartender grabbed the bottle of bourbon and put a glass in front of Bobby. He opened the bottle and began tilting it, but his hand turned fast, and the liquor poured all onto Bobby's lap. The bartender smirked as the colored man jumped up, his pants soaking. Bobby looked like he was about to pounce on the young man, and he might have if Jeff had not leapt in front of him, staring him down like a bull. "Go wash up, remember why we are here!" he hissed. "We cannot afford any issues." Bobby became levelheaded as Jeff spoke, and thus he went to the bathroom to wash up. As the man plodded away, he felt the glaring eyes and the slight chuckles of the many people around, all of whom were white. Jeff returned to his seat and exchanged a look with the bartender as he chuckled.

Bobby walked to the bathrooms in the back of the bar, but he did not enter so promptly. Instead, the hot-headed man stood in front of the two bathrooms. To Bobby's right was a door with a sign on it that read, "Colored." On the door to the left of Bobby, there was a sign that read, "Whites only." His crotch drenching and his fists clenching, the man began to step closer to the door on his left when an older fellow walked out, a white man, of course. This person noticed Bobby's inclination toward the door, and so he walked slowly up to the man of color, saying, "I of course understand the mistake, for I know people of your nature aren't big on words or letters, but that door there says whites only, and that door to your right is for colored folks." Bobby said nothing but clenched his fists even harder. "Is there a problem?" the old fellow asked. Bobby grew red, but then he unclenched his fists suddenly, and remembering what Jeff had said, he withdrew, stating, "No, I was just having trouble reading the sign on the door."

"Ah, very well." He looked down at Bobby's pants. "Oh my, it appears you have some trouble down there, Chap!"

Once cleaned up, Bobby returned to the bench outside as Jeff continued to pour down more drinks. Time went by, and Jeff reappeared at the bench when it was time the plane had arrived. And thereafter, the two returned to the airport to board their flight. Bobby, however, did not speak as frequently as before; in fact he was completely silent.

The two men enjoyed the calmness of their travel. The faint smell of brewing coffee, the occasional clanking of glasses, and the comfortable, leather seats made easy sleep inevitable over the fifteen-hour-long flight. When the pair awoke, they found themselves in France. Located in Nord-Pas-de-Calais, the city of Lens was well known for its industrial economy, led by manufacturing and coalmining. And this city was the place that held the drill of which Bobby and Jeff planned to steal. The accomplices did not so easily find their exit of the French airport, as little English was known in the city. Jeff and Bobby headed toward maps and documents to find a cab.

As they drove to the tiny motel which they were set to lodge at for the remainder of their time here, the two became appalled by the city. There was construction, covering every inch of the city, along with dust in every crevice, dirt in the very air, with the screams of machines and trucks echoing throughout. It felt as if the whole place was a giant factory. In addition, the nice, culturally unique buildings that one might find in visiting a distant city were rarely seen, but those that were either destroyed, abandoned, or had been boarded up with wooden planks were plenty.

Bobby, for the first time since they departed New York, spoke to Jeff, saying, "The war ended years ago. How is there still this much damage left?"

"This place was bombed over and over again, for years on end. It takes a bit more than a few years to rebuild all of it. I mean, look around, some of these buildings have full-sized craters in them."

Bobby and Jeff continued conversing up until they reached the motel they would be staying at, thus ending their long silence. Once they received a room key, the two went away to their door number. Jeff then placed the key in the lock and started to turn. He turned and he turned and he turned, but the door remained closed and the lock locked. "Here, let me try," Bobby exclaimed, reaching his hand out for the key.

"Fine, do exactly what I just did and see if anything different will happen," Jeff said sarcastically, placing the key in the man's hand. Bobby then walked up, put the key in the hole of the lock, and began turning. He turned and he turned and he turned, until he became so furious that he started juggling the knob as hard as he could. He then beat himself up against the door. He continued slamming himself on the door, until finally he put his back into it, and the door busted open. Jeff looked surprised, thinking as if Bobby didn't have it in him. The sheer anger Jeff just saw shocked him. Bobby's huffing and puffing faded away quickly though, and when he began to breathe like a human again, he lifted the key in his hand sarcastically toward Jeff.

The two men, as they entered, cringed at the appalling smell and felt a wave of nausea at the revolting sights of the room. The sheets were unnaturally brown, the floor ran with mold, and the only source of light came from a small dim lamp that stood atop the dusty bedside table. The windows were cracked, the bathroom dirty, the shower smelled of semen, and the paintings were coming out of the frame. With a repulsive tone, Jeff said, "This is where we're staying the next couple of days?"

"Yep," Bobby replied as he dropped his bag and jumped onto the bed, being more used to such spaces than Jeff. Just as he did, however, he felt a big punch in his back, his face quickly turned ill, and his roommate giggled, for the bed was hard as stone. Jeff opened the cabinet in the corner of the room to look for food, yet all his eyes met with were two cans of grinded meat. So he turned without hesitation and said to Bobby, "Restaurant?"

"Yep!" Bobby groaned.

The slight sound of his rapidly tapping foot was heard throughout the whole of the room. His boredom overgrew his anxiety. He went from being as frightened as a kitten in the mouth of a wolf to praying the woman would call his name out next. "Next! David Cockspy!" the woman would shout in his mind. David had now been sitting, waiting for his interview with Accardi for a very long time. So long that his impatience had dispelled his fearful anxiety. The receptionist overcame with dismay when she saw David begin to approach her for the third time. Speaking before the approacher even had the chance, the woman said, "As I told you before, Mr. Cockspy, Mr. Accardi will see you when he is done interviewing the current applicant."

David then clenched his lips a bit, nodded his head softly and paced back to his chair with silence. He once again began tapping his foot as the clock leisurely ticked. Suddenly, time seemed to slow, and David began feeling queasy. With his fearful anxiety returning, he started to ask himself, *What if he knows? What if he knows?* The man continued to worry on, ignoring his confidence and listening to his boredom-spawned, endless what-ifs.

"Next, Mr. Shaw! Next, Mr. Renly!" the man heard in his head as he waited eagerly for the woman to call out his own name. He kept tapping his foot senselessly, not once taking his eyes off the closed door he awaited. David stared and stared at the door without a blink, his hope fading. But just then, the door opened widely, and a big man walked out. "Next! Mr. Cockspy!" the receptionist shouted. David brushed his hair back, fluffed down his suit and breathed deeply as he sped up to the door.

"The next applicant, sir, David Cockspy," the receptionist announced, having led David into the room. A tiny gulp was taken, and David's heart dropped as he looked upon a regular-sized, middle-aged man who donned the nicest of suits, with the most luxurious of watches, and had the silkiest strands of hair. This glorious-faced man, who laid in his leather chair with ease, was certainly Accardi, David thought. With a build that women swooned over and a voice of a god, the most notorious man in the city uttered to David, "Please, be my guest and take a seat!"

"Thank you for having me," David said as he settled himself on the other end of Accardi's desk. "So, you own this place?"

"Yes, well, my company owns it. MX, maybe you've heard of it?"

"Yes, yes, I have. It is a very well-run corporation."

"Why thank you. I assume you know what you're getting yourself into, here?"

"Yes, I do," David said slowly.

"Very good. You see, just recently, my chief of security, a close, personal friend of mine, came about some rather unfortunate circumstances. Circumstances that forced him to depart from me and MX. So, I am now in need of someone new, and someone who can fill his shoes. The men we have are good, but not trustworthy enough. Can I trust you, Mr. Cockspy?"

"Yes! Yes, of course you can trust me."

"Are you sure?"

"Confident," replied David.

"Good! Now, I hear you have recently done time. Arson?"

"Well yes, I did, I did serve some time. And I did do some things, however, that was at a time in my life where I was controlled by my emotions, and that is a state of mind I am no longer in. A state of mind I haven't been in for years, three to be exact."

"Alright," Accardi continued. "So, tell me, Mr. Cockspy, why do you want to get involved in this line of work? The things you will need to do won't be too easy."

"I served three years in prison. I had, *have*, lost everything in my life, and I am ready for a fresh start."

"You think this is a fresh start?"

"A fresh start, to me, is a new beginning. I have nothing, and nowhere to go. With my past, it'll be hard for me to find a job, at least one that pays decently. The truth is, I am tired of living like I have been, but this will change that, this will allow me to be in control of my own life for once! So yes, I think this is a fresh start."

"This job is all about protection, protection of my funds, protection of my very life, as well as those of my acquaintances. As my chief of security, you will be in charge of all personnel. Now, I am not just going to promote someone who already works for me, no, no, I would not do that. I need to have someone who doesn't know how to follow orders, but to give them, as well as someone who hasn't been in this game before, because those that have know how to play it, and I don't like that. Now, while many of my applicants, as I prefer, do not have a history of employment with people in the same line of work as myself, they do, however, all have backgrounds in protection services. You not only have never worked for anyone like myself, but I see here you have never worked in any sort of protection field of any kind. So tell me, Mr. Cockspy, why would I want you as my Chief Security Officer?"

"Because I have something that none of those other candidates out there will ever have, and that is loyalty. I will keep your secrets, keep you safe, and make sure your business is never wronged. You can know this for sure, just look at me, look at my life, both the way I tell it and the way it looks on paper. I have nothing, and I have no way out of this hole, except for you. So as long as I work for you, and as long as you pay me well, I will be in need of you, to continue down this new beginning of mine. The truth is, nobody ever looks after anyone but themselves; it doesn't matter how trustworthy you claim to be, that's just how the world works. So what you must do, is find someone whose needs align with your own. My need is money, and as long as I do my work well, you'll be happy, then I get paid, and I'll be happy. As far as skill, I fought in the war, I know what it means to give commands, to speak only when spoken to, to be stealthy, to be harsh, and to get the job done."

"You make quite an impression, Mr. Cockspy. But, unfortunately, while I must, at least in some part, agree with you, this particular job is one of skill, intuition, leadership, and courage. There are nine other candidates for this job; think of this as only a sort of pre-check to make sure you are all good for the job. But, the contest of who's best will be determined by the real test, the real interview. You see, in order to find out which applicant is the best choice for the job, I must see all of your skills with my own eyes. And being a great fan of games, I have come up with a very good way, a very smart way, and a very fun way of finding out who is best fit. Wednesday, three-thirty, get on South Club Paceway, get off at exit one-thirty-three, take four rights and a left. There you will find me and the other candidates. That is where we will both find out who will be the new Chief Security Officer for MX. And I do hope you like games as much as me."

For many minutes more the two talked, where David continued to answer questions, and even received the chance to ask questions of his own. And when the two were finished conversing, with all sense of formality, David and Accardi shook hands. David thereafter departed from the office, then the waiting room, and once he found fresh air outside, he nearly fell to the ground in disbelief that he was still alive. Bewildered by how well it all went, David found himself frozen in place for more than a few breaths. But then he grew a smile on his face, thinking that perhaps, things were all going to be okay.

While David engaged in his interview with Accardi, and Bobby and Jeff awaited their flight, Jones and Sylvester stood in a booth, eating at a little diner downtown. Jones ate his steak with a fork and knife slowly, while Sylvester, on the other hand, made busy gobbling down his burger and fries. "How much are you going to eat?" Jones asked, disgusted by the man's open-mouthed chewing.

"I'm going to eat until I get my money and move to Ireland," Sylvester replied.

"Ireland? Why Ireland?"

"Well, obviously I have to get the hell out of here when this all ends, and for some reason I thought about Ireland. I mean, what's not to like about it? It's beautiful, nice people, good food, and besides, it would give me a chance to get out of this disgusting city and go out into nature."

Jones nodded his head and said, "That sounds nice, never pegged you as a nature person though."

"Oh yea! Well, it's not that I really love nature, it's more that I hate the city. You know, I've been living here all my life, and to be frank I have made more than a few enemies. In Ireland, no one will ever be able to find me. And when I do get my money, Ireland has beautiful cliffs overlooking the sea where I intend on building a nice home. When I was a young lad, my father, before he died, took me and my cousins camping. We would swim in the water and hike for hours, and when we would finally come back, we would grill out on the fire."

Jones spoke with only his eyes, giving Sylvester an unamused glare.

"Alright, fine!" Sylvester shouted. "I never knew my old man, and I don't got any cousins! To tell the complete truth, I don't even know how to swim. I've never been in nature, I've never been in a small town, and I've never seen great cliffs. But man, do I want to! Living the way I have, growing up with the circumstances I have had, it gives you only one way to live, and I am tired of it! For once I would like to be able to go outside and not have to look over my shoulder, that's what's great

84

about Ireland. It's quiet. And what about you, ever thought about moving somewhere quiet, somewhere small? Maybe find a nice lady, eh? Ever think about kids? You're a fairly old codger, ain't yuh?"

Jones, looking down and not blinking, replied slowly, "I tried that once. Didn't work out."

"Could never hurt to try again. But, anyways, why us?"

"What do you mean?" Jones asked.

"Why the four of us, specifically? I mean, I'm sure that there are better men out there for this job. So why us?"

"Because you have nothing to lose, and everything to gain. Also, because no one else in their right mind, who isn't this desperate, would ever try to rob Accardi. Oh my! Will you look at the time! David will be finished soon. So, let's head out."

Uptown, David paced back and forth impatiently. Keeping the ticking hands of his watch in sight, the eager man looked around for his ride. He waited several minutes before he saw the sight of Jones and Sylvester. "So, how was it?" Jones asked as David hastily jumped in.

"It was uh, it was, uh, uh good, uh re-really good," David stuttered like a baby bird leaving the nest. "Yeah, I think he liked me, and he gave me directions. It's Wednesday, three-thirty, I get on South Club Paceway, then I get off exit one-thirty-three, take four rights and a left."

"Good!" Jones replied, pressing on the gas.

"Why are you so restless?" Sylvester asked.

"Oh I'm sorry, how was your meal?" David shouted sarcastically. "You didn't just have a full conversation with the most dangerous man in the city, who you are planning on robbing, so just keep to yourself, alright!"

"Alright! Chill out why don't yuh! Things around here can get so aggravated. Speaking of, how do we bet the other boys are doing?"

Bobby and Jeff had picked up some food on the way, and now they stood atop a hill overlooking the dig site. The drill the two planned to take was as large as a bus, and as the two men gazed at it from their high view, they could not help but notice the great roar it let out. Digging into the very earth and thundering like a million meteorites crashing into the ground, the jaws of both men fell, and the two grew completely confident. Not confident that they were going to steal the drill, but confident that the task was impossible. How could such a behemoth of a machine, one that is in all seriousness screwed to the land, be moved even a few feet, and how was it that these two were made to move it to another continent, the men thought unceasingly?

"So, what do you think?" asked Bobby.

"The drill we have to steal is in the middle of what looks like a hundred other large machines and is bigger than either of us imagined. So, I think this is going to be very, very, very, hard. Hell, I'd say it's impossible, but I didn't come this far to turn right back, 'cause I got nowhere to go."

"And you think I do? You're right, this is gonna be hard, but we can do it, can't we?"

"I hope so."

"Well then," continued Bobby, "what's our plan of action?"

"When we left, Jones gave us a business card for some guy around here who he said would help us. One of us needs to go speak with that guy and one of us needs to camp out here to watch every move the people here take, so we can have a layout of the operations around here."

"Fair enough."

"I'll go talk to Jones' guy and you stay around here. But make sure you aren't seen; the last thing we want is people poking their noses around us." Jeff left to speak to Jones' contact, and Bobby sat down on the dense grass, breathing in the rusty metal fumes in the air, listening to the deafening work of the machines, and peering at the slow-moving workers along with the guards who patrolled the area.

"This is the place?" Jeff asked when the cab dropped him off. Disgusted by the filth of the warehouse that lay in front of him, which looked similar to Jones', but far less nice, Jeff pointed to the address on the business card, remembering the driver's French tongue. The driver nodded his head at Jeff, then took off.

"Alright," whispered Jeff as he began toward the old and raggedy warehouse. From the outside it appeared as a car mechanic's shop, surrounded by rusted metal Panhards and Simcas. Inside, Jeff found the walls to be falling apart, the roof rusting, and the gutters holding birds' nests. The door was wide open, so the man walked in freely. "Hello!" he shouted repeatedly. For a little bit, no one answered, and as Jeff continued around, he went not seeing nor hearing anything; that was until he heard a few small grunts from afar. He followed these grunts to a lifted red car, seemingly with a man under it.

"Hello?" Jeff asked softly.

"Huh!" The man got up from underneath the car and rubbed his oily hands with a piece of white cloth. He reached out to shake Jeff's hand, who did not move a muscle in return. So the dirty man began to speak, "Uh, ok. Hello, my name is Jeremy. How can I help you today? Ou tu parles Français? Comment puis-je vous aider aujourd'hui?"

"No, I speak English, and listen, I am here to..." Jeff spoke, but he was cut off quickly.

"Ah!" the squirmy man interrupted. "You are here to pick up the roadster aren't ya, because that thing is jogging up space I tell ya, although I could've sworn you said you were coming by tomorrow. So was there a change of plans or am I just imagining things? Ah! Ya know what, it doesn't matter. All that matters is that it gets out of my hands and hey, did you bring the money, 'cause it did cost me a spare buck or two to get the parts ya wanted. Now, I know I told ya it wouldn't be as expensive as it is, but I can assure ya I got it the cheapest, at least cheaper than any of these high-end businessmen could have gotten it. You can trust me on that. Not that I expect you to trust me, I mean I trust you but it's not always a back-to-back thing like I cannot trust someone but they trust me. I mean that's just how it works."

Jeremy, the dirty mechanic, continued to jabber on and on, even as Jeff tried to interrupt. "Hey," he tried. "Hey! Hey! Look! Hey hey hey! I am not here to buy a roadster or any other goddamn car you have! I was sent by Jones. He said you could help me with something."

Jeremy's face went cold, and his voice suddenly changed. The dirty man went from sounding like a rowdy little boy to a stern father. "Follow me," he said slowly. Jeff did so and was guided to a back door. When Jeremy opened this back door, Jeff witnessed a huge garage, one with an enormous truck and a bunch of cables. "So, Jones tells me you need a drill. And a pretty big one at that."

"Yes," Jeff replied.

"Alright, I've done bigger, harder jobs before. Show me the site."

The sun was already setting, and Sylvester and David wanted to go back to the warehouse, but Jones had insisted that they begin training. "Training?" David asked from the back of the car.

"Yes, training. Your interview is in a couple of days, and it has been a while since you have done the type of stuff you will need to do."

"Stuff? Like what stuff?"

"Like run, shoot a gun, knock a guy out, etc."

"Excuse me? First of all, I run all the time. You know they let us outside in prison nearly every day."

"C'mon David, you're a bit of a rounder," Sylvester chimed in. "I mean, I thought when you went to prison you would come out all brawny and ripped."

"I'm pretty fit!"

"Not saying you aren't, just saying that some of the other guys up for this job might be in better shape."

"I don't think that's true, and this is all besides the point!"

"You're right, like really Jones, does David actually have to do all of that, like the knocking guys out and stuff?"

"Yes, as a matter of fact, he does!"

"I do suppose it would be necessary for you, David. Although, I've never heard of any interview be like this gladiator competition type thing, especially with people in these types of businesses."

"I heard a story once," said Jones. "I heard that when Giovanni

Accardi immigrated to America and first began to build his business, he started off by having an underground fight club. I heard that though he and his line moved on to higher things in the world, every Thanksgiving, when the entire family vacationed to Italy, they would reperform this sort of tradition as a way of remembering how they started. They would pay a couple of hopheads on the street to come in and fight bare-handed. Giovanni's grandson, who was named after him, is heard to be one for tradition, and supposedly enjoys such games. After all, we are robbing Accardi's annual horse race."

"I've never heard that before, and even if it were true, bare-handed fighting in a back alley would not be what Accardi has put together for David and these formal men."

"No, but something similar might be."

"Like what?"

"I do not know, but we can only guess what skills it will require. Well, looks like we are here."

"And where exactly is that, Jones?" David asked as he and the other men stepped out of the parked car, surveying the empty darkness of night.

"What's it look like?" Sylvester sarcastically exclaimed. "We are in the middle of nowhere!"

"Precisely my boys!" Jones giggled.

"And why the hell have you brought us out here?"

"This is why," said Jones, turning toward his companions and pulling out from his coat pocket a Luger pistol. David's eyes widened and he took a swift step back as Jones reached for the sky and fired eight shots. The noise blew through David's ears like a train running by. As the other men heard the loud screaming shot of the bullets pierce the sky, they moved not a bit, but David lost his hearing, and then his sight, and then he fell to the ground, as if his muscles just failed him.

"What's happening to him, a stroke, or perhaps a heart attack?" Sylvester asked as Jones simply just grew a vexed look.

Though the sun had fallen, the stars still stood bright, and though the three men were carrying flashlights in the great darkness, David was still unable to see them, nor could he even see the stars. He could, however, see men. Black men, white men, short men, big men, little men, tall men, men all around, rushing together like a school of fish in the ocean. Men running; it's all he could see, all except for the rifles these men carried, and the olive drab they wore.

However, David was a very uneasy man, it was uncommon, quite rare in fact, for him to have two panic attacks in a single day, that being the one he experienced on the way to the interview earlier, and the one Sylvester and Jones fretted about at the moment. Perhaps this job was more stressful than David had anticipated? Perhaps indeed, he later thought, but at the moment, the aching man's sight was gone, and with it his hearing too, but yet, he still saw, and he still heard. That is, he heard the sound of screaming, yelling, and crying, along with the blaring of explosions, shots, and the sound of his own pounding heart. He heard all this, as he stared at the lifeless body that gushed with blood. Though this time, his fallen brother Arnom did not let a word out, nor a cry, nor a scream, nor a gag, nor a choke, nor a groan, nor any sound that would bring David to dread. But this calm silence gave away more dread than any.

Suddenly, the scene of battle left David's senses, and the sorrowful man now found himself in a burning building. With high-pitched screams all around, and blazing light from the very sun, David himself began to scream. He slammed his eyes shut as hard as he could in the midst of the horror, and when he opened them a moment later, he found himself in silence, and from the silence, his name was being called out. "David? David? David? Are you ok?" Before he knew it, David found himself lying in the dirt of the open terrain, Jones and Sylvester's flashlights blinding him from above.

"Uh, yeah, yeah, I'm fine. You mind getting those lights out of my face?"

"Oh yea, sorry," Sylvester said, he and Jones lowering the lights. "What happened to you? You fell down, and your eyes were open for some time, but staring out into nothing."

"Our friend here was merely having a panic attack, I would assume?" said Jones, looking at David who replied with a slow nod.

"Yes, if you don't remember, Sylvester, David here is among us the only one who served, and trauma is quite common with such persons. Now, let's go back to the warehouse. You've done a lot of good work today, David. You could use some rest, and tomorrow morning we will continue training."

It was later that night, when Sylvester had long gone to sleep and David marched to do the same that Jones said, "David, I read your file. I know what happened to your brother. I know your struggles, but this is the role you have to play, and the role you play comes with a gun. So I'm gonna need you to do better tomorrow. If you don't get this right, we could all go home in cuffs or coffins."

"I will," David replied.

The next morning came, and David, Sylvester and Jones went out to the open land once more. Jones had set up three targets, each about ten feet apart from one another. David was handed a gun, and after drawing a quick breath, he held it up. His hand began to shake though, and his arm began to tremble, and sweat began to run down his forehead. He used his other hand to grasp the bottom of the gun to control it more, but he shook, trembled and sweated all the same. He was about twenty-five feet away from the target, and for a good four minutes, he continued to just stare at the center of the target.

With steady eyes and laser focus did David stare at the red circles. But Sylvester and Jones, who had been eagerly awaiting action the entire time, were not surprised one bit when the frozen man lowered the gun and dropped his head with embarrassment. Jones walked over to David then and promptly lifted the sulking man's arm up again. He slowly leaned in and whispered something. As Jones stepped back, Sylvester watched David begin to lift his head, draw his breath, squint his eyes, and aim the gun outward. Growing less and less patient, he took out a box of cigarettes. Sylvester opened the pack and reached for one, but before he could take it out... *BAM!* the gun roared.

BAM! BAM! BAM! the gun fired again and again. Sylvester raised his brows, and in amazement, he saw all the targets holding bullet holes in their centers. David's fear and angst faded; for once he took that first shot, and a weight lifted off his shoulders. "Very good!" Jones shouted proudly. "Now, take five laps," he continued, pointing at a track he had carved out of the dirt earlier with his car tires.

"That was mighty impressive!" Sylvester shouted.

"Why thank you."

"David! Did you not hear me? Take five laps!"

"Easy, Coach Jones. Why do I need to take five laps? I mean, do I really need to do this whole football training thing you've got here? I get getting over my thing with guns, but the rest of this? I mean, one day is not enough."

"One day is better than none."

David did not argue any more but instead dropped his gun and started running through the course. Sylvester lit his cigarette and walked up to Jones, asking, "What did you say to him? Earlier with the gun, I mean?"

"I told him to imagine it was the man that killed his brother he was aiming at."

"Ah, clever!"

"Yes, but don't be fooled, his trauma is quite serious, and one does not simply have an epiphany and find themselves suddenly cured. I'm gonna make him shoot a lot more today, because he needs to learn how to overcome the trauma that returns to him with every shot."

That day, David went through a series of physical and mental workouts. He ran a total of eight miles, shot the targets over a hundred times, and did all sorts of parkour. He also studied Accardi with Jones' help. He learned what Accardi liked, what he hated, his family history, and what he needed from a chief of security. By the end of the day, David's confidence sprung higher than his ego, and he felt far more prepared for the "game" than he did hours earlier. He said to Jones that very night, "I'm going to do this."

"That you are," Jones replied in a confident, formal tone, as always.

The sun rose, and with it came morning. When he awoke, David drove Jones' car to the meet. Under the old bridge where Accardi and his men stood, along with the other candidates, David slid out of the car, anxious yet confident. He walked over proudly and stood with the other men as they waited for the rest of the candidates to arrive. Once they did, Accardi stepped forward and lit a very nice cigar. After taking a large puff out, he spoke:

"You are all here today to compete for the official position of Chief Security Officer for Mericorn Inc., as well as for my personal protection team. With the annual Mericorn Horse Race coming up, I need the toughest, the smartest, and the most loyal man to be in charge of my operations. Now, the time has come to decide which one of you that is. My dear friends here are passing around a briefcase to each and every one of you as we speak. Inside these briefcases, you will find nothing. Down that street over there lies a large, open cornfield. An old farmer friend of mine, who owns the field, has intricately carved a set of paths through the tall, thick crops, creating a kind of maze. You will all go into this maze with your briefcases and a pistol, which is being handed to you as we speak as well. Your objective is to shoot each man's briefcase, and the last man still with their briefcase intact, will be my new head of security."

The men looked at each other in competition before they marched over to the nearby farm and entered the maze. Each man went and hid in a corner of the maze, all awaiting Accardi to start the game. David's briefcase lay on the ground as he prepared his gun. He continued to stare at the firearm, his vision blurring and his hand shaking ever so slightly. But the man grasped it firmly, and with a stubborn face, held his eyes shut until his trembling ceased. Suddenly, David heard Accardi's voice. "Now, gentlemen, the time has come!" he shouted from the top of a tall, wooden platform which overlooked the entirety of the field. "On my mark, you will go through the maze and eliminate each person's briefcase. If anyone here dies today though, the man responsible for killing them will be shot nine times in the head! Now, if there is nothing more to say, let the game begin!"

The men held their guns high and their cases low, now pacing through the maze. David slowly roamed the maze just as well, looking carefully in all directions before turning each corner. It was less than a minute when he heard the first gunshot. "Well, looks like we have our first outed!" Accardi yelled from above. More than a few minutes passed, and while David continued to tread carefully through the narrow lines, he heard shots again and again. They kept ringing through the air, coming from every which direction, and after every batch of shots were heard, he would hear Accardi shout out, just like a game show host would. Whatever he did, he kept moving. After hitting dead ends, and even after seeing people from around corners, he would keep moving, trying his best to avoid anyone and everyone he could. But suddenly, David noticed a man approaching from his right.

The man ran out of the nearest corner and aimed his gun out as he began to shoot. *BAM BAM BAM!* it fired. David scurried around another corner nearer to him as the man shot, and when the same man followed David around the corner, he unexpectedly found David waiting. David suddenly sprung out right then, jumping onto the man with ferocity. He quickly grabbed the man's gun which had fallen onto the ground and tossed it away with the same speed. The two proceeded to fight. Rolling around the ground, punching and kicking each other, David attempted to put the man in a chokehold. But this man was much too large, and much too strong, and it took him little effort to completely stand up, even with David still on his back.

The big man quickly bent over, and used both his hands to grab David's back, shoving him off and sending him flying, face-first to the dirt. Separated, the two stood tall opposite each other and took a moment to catch their breath. But as David took more breaths in, he watched the other man pull out a knife and sprint toward him. He slapped David in the face with his briefcase, which he still managed to hold onto. The man's slap was so powerful that it sent David to the ground. And when the same grounded man looked up the next second, he noticed the large enemy throwing his knife toward the briefcase David held in his left hand, which he too had still managed to hold onto. David swiftly tossed his left arm up though, and his foe, having put so much force into his attempted stab, was sent flying to the caseless ground just as David had been.

David punched his downed opponent in the face and quickly jumped up to the ground. By the time the large man looked back to David, he heard a loud *BAM,*= and just like that, his briefcase was shot. David thereafter dropped his fired gun in relief as his large opponent walked off. *BAM BAM BAM!* he heard. The constant sound of guns screaming reminded David that this was no time to rest. He sprinted off into the maze, and hearing Accardi shout out, "Only four men left!" David held his gun high in preparedness. He ran into a dead end where he decided to catch his breath. He wiped the cold sweat off his forehead and put the knife he had taken from the large man he bested in his pocket. He next began to continue his slow tread through the maze, but suddenly, when he turned the next corner, he was kicked into the dense crops by a skinny, tall man. David threw his briefcase over this man's head to avoid it being shot, and subsequently pulled his own gun out. He aimed at the skinny man's briefcase, which he had tucked under his arm.

Before David could pull the trigger though, the skinny man, seemingly knowing some sort of martial arts, spun around and kicked the gun right out of his hand. The man proceeded with a series of backflips, growing closer to David's briefcase which landed on the ground afar. But David took out his knife and sprung onto the skinny man as fast he could. His enemy turned quickly, and David had suddenly gotten himself into a fist fight. He tried to stab the man's briefcase, which was held tightly, tucked under the man's arm. But the skilled skinny man kept blocking David and continuously hit him in the face as well. Then, with the swiftness of a hare, the man clenched his fist and thrusted his knuckles into David's throat. David took a big step away and nearly blacked out. The skinny man slowly and proudly walked away from his staggering foe. He pulled out his gun to shoot David's case. *BAM!* rung the gun, not the skinny man's gun, but David's gun. With an expressionless face and a shot briefcase, the skinny man walked off.

David, still gasping for breath, relaxed and lowered his gun. He fell to the ground in an ease and closed his eyes in rest. He smiled hard, ever so proud of himself, and began to thrust his fist up into the air with celebration. But then, was it another panic attack? David wondered, hearing a loud blast of a gun. David looked over, and never had he wished to be seeing false things more than he did now, for there was a short man ahead of him, with a pistol in his hand, one which was puffing out smoke. David's briefcase had been shot, and his jaw dropped in sheer unimaginability.

In a spin of worry, David became uneasy. The short man smiled and walked off. But David was so angry, ever so angry he was. It was no panic attack, nor was it out of necessity, but of nothing except his own fury. David leapt up and began to sprint at the man. He held his knife high, God knows why, for he was out of the game, and had never hurt anyone in his entire life; such pacifism was how his brother died, in fact. By the time he was close behind the short man, that same man turned around and aimed his gun at David's head. The two stood still for a moment, staring at each other with intensity, but when David lowered his knife, the short man lowered his gun and walked off yet again.

David fell to his knees. The whole job could not happen now, all because of him. He sat there for a long time in despair, and when he finally began to walk home, he moved with the pace of an old tractor. All he could think about was how everyone would be so mad and disappointed. The sulking man thus found a nearby diner to pout in. He hid there for as long as he could, unable to confront his companions.

It was night. With much conversation and thorough planning, the roadmap to steal the ginormous drill had been made. Jeff and Jeremy lay flat atop the hill that overlooked the mining grounds. The final workers left the area, and as soon as they were out of sight, the two sped down the hill. In the center of the mining complex was a giant lighthouse that was spinning around a beam of blinding light. When they got to the side gates of the digging grounds, Jeff and Jeremy pulled out giant pliers to cut an opening in the tall fencing. But as soon as they began to cut into the iron, the light came upon them. They quickly jumped back into some large bushes. Once the light had passed, they finished their opening and walked through the hole, successfully entering the mining site.

Attempting to be as sneaky and quiet as possible, the two essentially crawled through the place, using the large machines to hide behind whenever the light came across them, and changing directions whenever they came across a patrol officer. The two continued this practice together until they reached the entry points to the tunnels below ground, where they then promptly left each other. Jeremy began to do as the two did, sneaking his way up to the large entrance gate of the whole area. Once he arrived, he sped up the ladder to the top of the gate's watchtower. In this watchtower, which housed the gate's controls, a young man was stationed, peacefully reading a book and sipping on a cup of coffee while Jeremy snuck up. The stationed guard felt a sudden, sharp push right up on his back, as Jeremy slid over to the man's ear and whispered in French, "This is a gun. Make any noise or try to alert anyone and I will shoot."

Pulling out from his backpack a long thing of rope, Jeremy proceeded to tie his hostage up. When he was finished, the man was unable to move or speak and was positioned to face the corner of the wall. Now, Jeremy held up a flashlight out the window, and began to flicker it, rapidly turning it on and off. Suddenly, a large tractor-trailer approached the gate. When it came close enough, Jeremy took the stationed officer's radio, and said in French, "Truck approaching to take item E64 for transport."

"Are you sure?" the officers below asked, confused by the late hour.

"He has official documents. Let him through."

The officers opened the gate, letting the large truck through, and thereafter paid no attention it. One officer, however, found the whole situation suspicious. And while the other guards quickly forgot about the truck, this officer kept an eye on it, so much so that he did not notice Jeremy climb down from the gate tower above him. Jeremy, repeating his earlier method of sneaking through the area, followed the large truck until it parked next to the very large drill. From this truck, out stepped Bobby, who, with Jeremy's help, began to use a tall crane-like machine located in the site. The suspicious officer slowly grew closer and closer as the men jumped to work with questioningly quick speed. He kept his eyes on the two men for the following half-hour while they worked to transport the gigantic drill to the back of the tractor-trailer.

The officer grew bored watching the two men work, and because of how well they handled the equipment, and how knowledgeable they looked doing it, the guard decided to turn back. But something on his way back caught his eye, that being the watchtower. Every day for the past few years, this particular guard had held a job at mining sites such as the one he stood at now. Thus, he knew whenever there was a watchtower to a gate, there was always someone stationed to it. He found it odd that the lights were off. The guard was not so suspicious about this, for he had seen workers go to sleep on the job hundreds of times. As he assumed this was one of those times, he went with no sense of urgency up the ladder.

He opened the door and was quite confused to find no one inside the watchtower. The officer then thought that the guard on duty must have simply gone to the bathroom without calling in someone to cover his position. He began to walk back out to travel to the restrooms and find this foolish officer, but before he made it out the door, the officer heard something. Locating the source of the sound to be right next to him, he closed the door from which he entered, and low and behold, there was the guard on duty, tied up in the corner of the room, blocked from sight with the door opened.

Bobby and Jeremy were close to being finished, but they still needed more time, and as such, when the far away screams and the loud sirens of the alarms began to cry in the air, Jeff decided to initiate the distraction early. He tossed a lighter on the ground and subsequently rushed toward Bobby and Jeremy's direction. All the officers ran to the truck in the center of the site with great speed but fell to the ground when they heard a loud BAM! As every officer turned back, they all dropped their jaws upon seeing the operations center on fire. Home to valuable equipment, vehicles, and other workers, most everyone dashed to the blazing inferno of a building. Two of the officers, however, more angry than concerned, continued to run at the truck.

Jeff caught up and said in a heavy-paced tone to his confederates, "I did it, but we are running out of time. Y'all better be done soon!"

"One more minute," Jeremy replied, strapping the drill down to the truck.

"Arrêtez!" screamed the approaching officers. Bobby and Jeremy froze, quick to hold their hands up. But then, hiding in the dark, Jeff suddenly smacked one officer to the ground with a big metal pole. When the second officer turned to Jeff with his gun raised, Bobby leapt onto him, making the fired bullet barely miss Jeff, gliding just a little over his left shoulder. The first officer, whom Jeff had hit over the head, stood up, only for Jeff to immediately punch him back to the ground. Bobby lay on the ground, holding the second officer he had pounced on in a chokehold. Jeff looked over and was very surprised by Bobby's acts. "Hurry the hell up!" he screamed as Bobby pushed the now unconscious guard off him.

"Ah, done!" Jeremy exclaimed, strapping down the last buckle. The three men then hurriedly got into the truck and drove off. They went at full speed through the machine-filled terrain. With every person and most savable items extracted from the burning building, the officers all screamed at each other to run to the vehicles that were still intact when they saw Jeff, Bobby, and Jeremy drive through the entrance gate. The three men were wise to not yet celebrate, for in an instant, they found four cars chasing after them. Bobby began to panic. "Oh no oh no oh no! They're after us, guys! They're catching up to us!"

"Not for long!" Jeremy yelled to Bobby. Then, being the driver, Jeremy spun the wheel violently and turned right onto a narrow road. The four chasing cars turned as well, nearly swerving off the cliff the road laid next to. As the nearest chasing car closed in, two of the officers in the vehicle, who weren't driving, leaned halfway out the windows and began shooting at the large truck's tires. The tires were reinforced, however, and after successfully hitting two of the back wheels, the officers realized they would never be able to puncture them, at least not with the firearms they held. They all continued down the narrow road until it suddenly widened, and when it finally did, all the chasing cars, generally much faster, quickly sped past the large truck.

"What's going on?" Bobby worriedly asked. "What are they doing? They're going ahead of us."

"They are gonna speed up until they are about a mile ahead of us, and then they are gonna form a blockade in the middle of the road with their cars so we can't get through. But maybe we can turn around?"

"Turn around? How in the hell are we supposed to do that with this mammoth-sized drill?"

"Ah!" yelled Jeremy. "Will you two stop your pissing! Now, get ready!" Bobby and Jeff braced themselves suddenly, preparing for Jeremy to make a quick and witty, unannounced turn. Nothing of the sorts happened, however. Both men faced Jeremy with ghastly expressions and began screaming. "Jeremy, you're going too fast!" cried Bobby.

"Jeremy, the blockade is right in front of us, I can see it!" cried Jeff.

"Oh I see them, lads!" answered Jeremy, still flying straight.

"You're not slowing down!"

"And you're staying straight!"

"You don't think I know that!" Jeremy clapped back at the two.

"Jeremy!" the two men shouted repeatedly. Just as Jeff anticipated, the three men saw the line of parked cars in front of them, and when the officers standing by them saw the approaching truck, still in high motion, they opened fire. Bobby and Jeff ducked down quickly, but Jeremy did not move a muscle. The officers kept shooting, hitting the front of the truck some and the windshield a few times, but they missed Jeremy. And they kept shooting on and on, until the large vehicle was too close. Every officer sped to the sides then, jumping to safety when they all heard a loud, sudden *BAM!*

Sounding like thunder in the clouds, the truck slammed into the cars, driving through them with little trouble. The men started celebrating at their getaway, yelling "Yes!" and "We did it!" But it didn't take them long to notice two of the chasing cars behind them.

"I guess we spoke too soon!" Jeff yelled, staring back at the damaged but fully functional cars that flew by them. The next thing they knew, they had a car on each side of them. The many officers in the cars, aiming at the truck's front seats and leaning out of their own vehicles, continued to fire at the thieves from either side. While Jeff and Bobby once again ducked down to avoid fire, Jeremy pulled out a gun. As he aimed it out to his left, Jeff snatched it from his grasps, yelling, "What are you doing? We don't hurt people!"

"They're gonna kill us, boy!" Jeremy shouted. Distracted by their own quarrel, the two men failed to remember the shooting officers, and so, Bobby quickly grabbed the gun out of both of their hands. He aimed out the truck and thereafter shot. After a few misses, Bobby successfully shot two of the right car's tires, making it go flying behind them. Following this lead, Jeff grabbed the gun from Bobby and shot at the left car's tires. What happened next was hard to later recall, for it was all so fast, but the men's faces went blank as they watched the car swerve out of control. The car sped side to side until it fell off the cliff.

Frozen faced, the men continued to drive on, trying their best to forget the horror of the accident. But it wasn't too steep of a drop, the men thought. They all returned to Jeremy's warehouse with ease, and then they were quick to load the drill onto the cargo plane that landed on the attached runway.

"This is where y'all leave me; good working with you two!" Jeremy exclaimed, shaking Bobby and Jeff's hands. The pilot of the incredibly large cargo plane, of course hired by Jones, flew the drill, Bobby, and Jeff home, sneaking them over with other American imports. Something was different on the way back, though. Bobby and Jeff were silent for a time, as always, but then Jeff began to speak, particularly about the earlier events. The two talked for hours, laughing and reminiscing about their accomplishment.

Ryder Lim

A sleeping David finally opened the door of the car from which he saw and heard Sylvester knock repeatedly. He stepped out, awakening from his night's sleep in the vehicle.

"How long have you been sleeping in my car?" Jones asked.

"I failed, I lost. I'm sorry." Jones and Sylvester looked at each other with a giggle before they looked at David, and said, "Did you now? We went to your cousin's to look for you and he told us that a man dropped by this letter." Jones handed David a letter which he read aloud: "Dear Mr. Cockspy, our first-place winner of today's interview has shot our second-place winner, incapacitating him. Therefore, they were eliminated, and as you came in third, we would like to see you Friday for your first day on the job as our newest Chief Security Officer."

The three men then all began to laugh, and David was filled with hope once more.

102

Stanza's Recollection

"Arrêtez!" I yelled, "Au nom de la loi, arrêtez!" I bolted after the bald man whom I chased. I was lighter and clearly more fit than the man, so it was clear that if I kept up my pace, I would eventually catch up to him. I tried to make the arrest quick and quiet, but my primary partner, wanting to simply embarrass me and laugh at my tremendous failure, tipped the guy off. But, I, of course, was used to such things. After all, I am the only woman in La Gendarmerie Nationale, a male dominated force. Everyone underestimates me. All they see is a beautiful blonde, just waiting to be a housemaid or a wife, but that's not me. I got myself into the force, and I'll be damned if I let these bastards run me out! When my partner tipped off my suspect, and I saw the man I had been tracking down for weeks jump out of the window, I couldn't just sit back and let everyone around me think they were right. Thus, I followed my suspect and proceeded to jump out the window. I ran and ran down the car-flooded streets. My primary partner, along with the other officers with me at the time, of course did nothing but slowly return to their vehicles and very slowly follow after me. And while they drove with no sense of urgency, I, for no less than a mile, continued to run through the open streets after the suspect. I could tell he was worried, for in his back pocket, he clearly carried a firearm, which he would've surely pulled out by now if it weren't for an impending fear of slowing down, and thus allowing me to grow closer. But then, the runaway suspect and I moved our chase indoors, when he sprinted into a cake shop. I came in and was about to run through the back door when the baker and the scared customers pointed upwards. I ran up the steps of the shop and looked far up through the cracks of the zig-zagging staircase to see floors ahead of me, the suspect speeding up to the roof. I followed with a quick step, practically hopping up the stairs. I reached the top and attempted to go to the roof, but the door was locked. I then looked over to see two doors on this top floor. I panicked, not having the slightest idea of which apartment the man had surely broken into. I went to the right door first, pulling out my gun, and thereafter broke down the door. The old lady there seemed quite shook when her door came blazing down, but after a quick inspection of the bathroom and the kitchen, I left. Speeding across the hall and proceeding to break down the other door on the top floor, I then entered. Inside was a young couple. I inspected the kitchen and the bathroom, then ran all around but found nothing. The windows were glued shut as well. I turned and began to run again with all haste when I heard a loud crash. I sped down the hall once more, charging into the old lady's apartment, the very one I had just left. I came in to find the back window broken. My! How could I have been so foolish! The suspect must have been hiding behind the couch, covered up by the old lady he no doubt held at gunpoint. I was, perhaps, too hasty in my inspection. But I have had worse failures. And though he had the upper hand, I jumped through yet another window, refusing to give up. I landed with a heavy impact not on the street this time, but on the roof of the adjoining building. When I looked up, I saw the suspect about three buildings down. Carrying on with my pursuit, I jumped when I came across the ledge at the end of the building I stood on, making a soft landing on the next rooftop. I followed to run, and jump, and run, and jump, and run, and jump after my suspect. However, when the man I chased came across a building simply too far away to jump onto, I witnessed that same man speed down a fire escape. I did the same, and when I reached the ground, I found myself in an alleyway that went in four opposite directions. I spun around in a worry, but then I heard the honking of horns. I ran in the direction of which these loud sounds came. Soon, I stood, yet again, in the middle of the open streets. Seeing my backup a mile down the road, I flung my arms out in an attempt to flag them down. Whether they could see me or not I wasn't sure, but I was running out of time. I continued to run after my suspect who got further and further away. He seemed slower, and as if he was growing short of breath. He went through a nightclub with no top floors, so I figured he was going around to the back. When I looked over to see another entrance to the back alley, I cut through, hoping to surprise him on the other side. As the coughing, sweaty man proved my thoughts true and came rushing out of the back door, he froze quickly, seeing my gun pointed straight at him. With a proud feeling in my veins, I yelled out, "Arrêtez-vous! Mettez vos mains là où je peux les voir!" However, the man did not toss his hands up as I had so instructed but smirked instead. The pride I had briefly felt faded away quickly when I saw from behind the smirking man, the steady approach of two other men. With heavy guns raised at me and cheshire grins across each of their faces, they all shook their heads when I commanded them to surrender themselves. "Lâchez vos armes maintenant!" I shouted. I was overcome with uneasiness, and the grip I held over my own pistol loosened. My coworkers were always, as the Americans say, sleazebags, but they were never devils. The three men, who dropped their guns and fell to the floor quickly, knew they could not run when they saw three officer-filled cars pull down the alleyway from either side. With ease now upon me, and pride returning to my veins, I proceeded to cuff the three men. Armed officers stepped out to help escort my arrests into the vehicles. I said to my primary partner, "Je vous remercie." Though I was pleased and grateful for his help, my fellow officer looked more disappointed in my success than morally satisfied with his own assistance. He turned to me with a stern face and a slight chuckle. "Ces gars auraient pu te buter. C'est pas un endroit pour une petite femme comme toi, tu sais. Peut-être que tu devrais songer à un autre job, un qui te correspondrait mieux. Je sais que les bordels ont été interdits, mais y'en a sûrement des planqués dans le coin où tu pourrais bosser. Et je suis sûr que tu ferais un paquet de fric!" I do not feel the need to translate this, but the general idea is, "You couldn't save your own life, so you don't belong here!" I happily responded to his quite vulgar response, "Quoi, comme un de ces endroits où bosse ta femme?" This, I also do not wish to translate, but I can say that I walked away with more pride than my fellow officer held in that moment. I drove two of the arrested men back to the station myself, for I did not want to have the other officers go back and take all the credit, nor did I wish for them to "accidentally" leave me behind again. These arrests were sure to get me a lot of recognition, and I couldn't wait to shove it in the faces of all of those *trou du culs*! When we arrived at the station, I got our main suspect ready for questioning, which I, of course, wished to do myself. And given my standing on the matter, I assumed I would be able to do so. I became quite enraged, as anyone would, when that was not the case.

I was also sincerely surprised when I understood that it was Commandant Tremblay who took me off the interrogation. Years back, I was recruited as a gendarme, which, though is a starting rank, was quite an accomplishment given my genitalia. It was my sister's husband, a very successful businessman with many connections, who granted me the opportunity. From there it was unlikely for me to get promoted, the other officers thought. While the majority of the force were quite unamused with my presence, there were a few who were more than respectful toward me. With hard work and advancing successes, along with my brother-in-law's constant contributions toward many post-war military forces and other efforts, I quickly ranked up to the title of Adjutant Stanza. One of the officers who always took a respectful liking to me was currently commandant Peter Tremblay. The middle-aged man who always treated me with respect and dignity, unconcerned of my brother-in-law's donations, was one coworker I grew close to. He had sent for me at the same time he took me off the interrogation. So I quickly sped up to his office, wondering what reason he had to take me off the interrogation of the top suspect in my investigation. I knocked on the door and heard my old friend call me in. I shall do my best to translate our conversation to the common English tongue. "You wanted to see me," I politely asked with a hint of passive-aggression. "Oh, Elizabeth!" the commandant shouted. "Good to see you!" he exclaimed. "You too, commandant," I whispered. "Oh come now, call me Peter! Now please, please sit." I nodded and thus sat down as he continued, "I just wanted to congratulate you! You made quite a bust today, and the two men who held you at gunpoint will also prove most useful to the

Ryder Lim

investigation, I am sure. Well done, Elizabeth!" I replied with a straight face, "Thank you, Peter, but I am a bit confused." "About what, my dear?" "Well, you have always been someone I have been able to count on, which is a thing I rarely find around here. And as you yourself say, I have done quite well, yes?" "Yes, you most certainly have!" "Well then, Peter, why did you pull me from the interrogation?" "Oh no, I think you misunderstand. I am taking you off the investigation entirely, Elizabeth." I then cut him off and began to ramble on. "What? Peter! I have been running point on this case all month! This case was a goner when I got it. Actually, that was probably why it was given to me in the first place! And yet, I have turned this case into a possibly extreme bust! We are about to get vast amounts of information on the smuggling rings around here! I found this guy, I chased him when another officer tipped him off, I made the arrest, I made all the discoveries, and now I get no credit! I have gotten used to being treated unfairly, but this?! This is something I would have never thought of!" My. I do wish I had waited a few more seconds to speak my mind. "Ah, Elizabeth, I am terribly sorry for the confusion, but I think you are misunderstanding again. I am taking you off this investigation, because I wish for you to focus on other, more important matters. In fact, I have decided to name you Lieutenant Stanza." My face froze, and I looked like I could hardly believe what the commandant had said. "Wait, are you serious?" I asked. "Yes, the papers are definitely going to be all over this bust, giving us a good look, and the mayor called as well, already praising us." "Oh my god!" I exclaimed. "Oh, Peter! I mean, this is not just a promotion, this is a jump! I am an adjutant right now, and the next rank would be an

108

adjutant-chef, but you… you… you are promoting me to lieutenant? That is two steps below you! I-I, I don't know what to say? And I am incredibly sorry for yelling at you just now." "Oh don't be, Lieutenant Stanza!" He chuckled. "Don't think I don't see the kind of treatment you receive around here. I get the need to let off a little steam. The truth is, you should have been promoted a long time ago, and I blame myself for the wait. But I hope this makes up for it. After all, you have earned it, lieutenant." "I don't know what to say, Peter. You won't regret this! I am going to prove that to everyone!" "I know you are, now get back to work!" he joked. He shook my hand, and I leapt up out of my chair and rushed out. But before I left, I turned to the commandant to thank him. "Peter, I just want to thank you for everything. I know I deserve this, but that doesn't mean I would have gotten it without you. So, thank you!" He said nothing but gave me a smile, so I left, now a lieutenant! How incredible! I couldn't wait to begin working! And I couldn't wait to see what kind of work I'd get into.

Chapter 4

Four Weeks Later

It was night, and celebrations were in order. A few miles south of the stadium in which the horse race would occur lay a large hangar, surrounded by nothing but grass and dirt. Jones, David, and Sylvester sat in chairs, drinking beers and gazing out at the stars. They spent the evening laughing and celebrating like a bunch of bachelors. The conversation had changed many times, and the amount of stories detailed seemed endless. "So there I was, with the diamond necklace in one hand and the rope that held my partner in the other. I had a choice to make," Sylvester narrated. "The police were charging through the museum, and I didn't know what to do, so I grabbed the necklace and ran. About two years later, my partner was released from prison, and the very first thing he did was track me down. He picked the lock on my door and made his way into the place I had lived in at the time. Before I even realized someone had broken in, I was on the floor, beaten half to death. And that's how I got this scar."

As Sylvester pointed to the scar he spoke of that sat on his side, David began to speak. "Very interesting. You know, you and I are quite different, Sylvester. In the army, we were trained to have our comrades' backs at all times. One time, I dragged a man about half a mile through the woods to safety."

"Wow, y'all are just a bunch of buzzkills. Here we are, supposed to be celebrating that we got the drill and that David got the job, but instead, you two are talking about stories where you nearly died. I mean, come on!"

"You're right, I know!" David responded to Jones. "We shall play a game."

"A game?" Sylvester asked.

"Yes, a game. It's called inquiries. We all go around, taking turns, and whosoever turn it is, is asked questions. The answer to the questions may be chosen to be the truth or a lie and we as the inquisitors can call him out whenever we think it's a lie. And if we get it right, that person is out! But if you get it wrong, then it is you that is out."

"Fair enough," the men said.

"Alright, Jones, how 'bout you go first. Ask me anything you want."

"Very well," said Jones. The man then sat there for a minute, utterly silent. As he stared off into space, trying to come up with a question, David drew the last straw. "Alright!" he said. "I'll go first, and Sylvester, I shall ask you. When were you born?"

"August seventeenth, nineteen oh seven."

"What's the most amount of money you ever gambled?"

"I once lost three grand at a casino in Las Vegas."

"Have you ever had a dog?"

"Yes, her name was Daisy."

David stared into Sylvester's eyes for a moment before he yelled, "Liar!" Sylvester sat there for a moment as well, then begun to laugh. "Aha! You got me! Yes, this is fun. Now David does it to Jones."

"Very well," David said, turning to Jones. With a quick breath and a small grin, he began, "What's your favorite food?" he asked.

"Steak," Jones easily responded.

"Have you ever been in love?"

"Once."

"Have you ever killed a man?"

"No."

"Have you ever been arrested?"

"No."

"I say that's a lie!" David exclaimed, quick and confident. Sylvester looked at Jones with open eyes, eagerly awaiting his answer. Jones said, "Yes, it was a lie."

"Hahaha!" David laughed in victory. Sylvester, however, a bit curious, asked Jones, "What for?"

"Sylvester, he doesn't have to tell us specifics, only if it was a lie or not."

"No, no, it's ok," Jones replied. He took a small, dramatic pause before he began his tale. "During that time, I was in an unstable place in my life," he said. "Not everything was going how I wished it to be. I was at a bar one night when a couple of dumb white boys approached me. They didn't seem to like the fact that a colored man was at a decent bar. 'Get out of here,' they told me. I didn't move a muscle. 'Didn't you hear me, nigger!' they yelled. They continued to scream in my ear. They started getting up in my face too. And when they ran out of patience, one of them pushed me completely off the stool.

"I tried to get up, but they kicked me in the chest repeatedly, holding me on the floor. No one stood up for me, why would they? All the stuck-up white men and women didn't want to help a black man. So I laid there, being beaten upon. They tried picking me up and throwing me out, but I was too heavy for the two weak little boys, so their friends who watched over in the corner got up to help. They grabbed my sides and lifted me up. The next thing I knew, I was on the concrete road, outside.

"I was angry. I didn't care they hated me because I was different from them. No. I cared because they messed with the wrong guy on the wrong night. I stood up. I trudged back into the bar, where the laughing, drunk boys enjoyed themselves. They turned when they caught sight of me and stood up quickly, planning to teach me another lesson, I'm sure. The whole pack of 'em walked up to me. Before they said anything, I grabbed my half-filled shot glass that remained on the counter, and I rammed it into the first kid's throat. I threw the second kid over the counter when he grabbed hold of my shoulder. I ducked a heavy punch from the third kid, who I then simply pushed and sent to the ground with his very own force.

"I continued to battle with the young men until I quite easily kicked their asses. But once the other men in the bar saw I was winning, they stepped in. They walked over to me, and before I knew it, I punched one of them so hard they fell to the ground, joining the younger pack of boys. My violent rage did not quit nor slowly fade off. I continued these actions with more men over the next few minutes. Finally, an officer came in and arrested me before I was killed. The cop beat me more on the way to jail, but at least he didn't shoot me. That night was when I knew that if I were going to mess with someone, I was going to do it the smart way."

David and Sylvester's eyes were tapped into Jones' moving lips as they listened to him finish his tale with all intensity. They sat back in their chairs and drank a sip of their drinks. "That's quite the story," David remarked. "Anyway, what's the next step in the plan?" he continued after a minute of silence which the men shared.

"Well, now that you have gotten the job, you will go to work every day and be the loyal, smart, and strong Chief Security Officer for both Mericorn Inc. and Accardi himself. You will continue to learn about the horse race. You will also get closer to Accardi." David nodded his head to Jones' detailing. Suddenly, a little hair on David's arm started moving back and forth. Then all the hairs atop his head began to move, and the three men felt a strong breeze coming in. The men turned to see a plane coming toward them from a great distance. They drank their drinks and watched as the plane landed in the hangar. It was so loud that the men held their hands over their ears, even being quite a far distance from the hangar. As the plane settled to the ground, the men followed its tracks inside. Being three times the size of the enormous cargo plane, out in the middle of nowhere, with enough power to operate a device of the size, the hangar clearly was the perfect place to work the drill. The fact that Jones called it small amazed Bobby and the others.

Jones helped the pilot unload the drill while Jeff and Bobby walked to the rest of the group. They shook hands and made conversation as they recapped their recent adventures. Later on, at Jeff's request, Jones explained how the drill was going to work. "Tomorrow, we will set it up and it will start digging diagonally, eventually coming across the underground lounge where the vault will be kept," he said. "Our job is to operate the drill for the next four weeks while David works for Accardi. We must make sure it goes exactly where it is supposed to or else it will screw everything up and we will not be able to get the truck up and down it. Now, speaking of, while this drill is one of, if not the largest and most unique models in the world, it cannot dig as big as we need it. Thus, we will need some blasting and excavation work to be done, plus many more sets of hands to help out. We can discuss all of that later, but the bottom line is, we've got a shit ton of work to do. But don't forget why we're doing this."

All the questions were summed up. The job began early in the morning, so the men went to bed early, after a small celebration in the pool house. The next day, the men got to work, and the plan was set in motion, the clock for the Mericorn Horse Race ticking down.

Back in Calais, now Lieutenant, Elizabeth Stanza sat in the driver's seat of a moving vehicle, liking to always be the one behind the wheel. It was a show of power for her, and a statement to her coworkers that she was just as capable as them. She gazed out the window, seeing tens of officers documenting the crashes that had ensued the night before. The car pulled up to the site of the stolen drill, and out stepped Stanza. As soon as she did, however, all the officers around her turned and stared at her. While the only female officer on the force was a growing topic of conversation, this was Stanza's first case as lieutenant, and as such, she had a whole new branch of coworkers, types of cases, and abilities. Word had traveled fast through the ranks, but when the many officers saw the insignia upon her kepi and buttons, they were quick to overcome with feelings of jealousy and disbelief.

Though she felt the scowls and sneers around her, the lieutenant was used to ignoring the cold judgmental stares of men. She stepped to the closest officer and spoke in French, "What the hell happened here?" The officer she asked took one look at her and acted as if he didn't hear her. Stanza then stepped closer to the man and asked, "Is my kepi on straight?" She fiddled with it then, acting as if she was attempting to straighten it, when truly she was calling the officer's attention to the lieutenant insignia upon it.

The officer responded with an embarrassed and resentful expression, "Yes, I believe it is. Would you care to hear about what happened last night, lieutenant?"

"I most certainly would," Stanza exclaimed.

"Very well," he replied, again in French. "Last night, three men stole an incredibly large drill via a huge trailer-tractor. There's no telling how big it was, specifically, nor where the drill was made, or anything. The perpetrators torched the operations center along with all the files stowed inside. It's gonna take us a while to figure out the details of everything, but most people around here said the drill could be somewhere between thirty and fifty feet in length. Witnesses say they took control over the gate tower and by the time the officers noticed, they were on the road. As I said, they set fire to that building over there. Evidence seems to suggest no true motivation other than to get the guards' attention. The chase followed about twelve miles down there. All vehicles were destroyed, except the perps', obviously."

"Do we have any leads?"

"Not yet, we've got guys searching all over the place, but we suspect they've already fled the country." Stanza stood there in slight aggravation and amusement, having never seen a stunt like this before. She looked at the officer and asked in a very strange tone, "Who would ever go through this much trouble to steal a drill, and more importantly, why do they want it?" Then Stanza began to walk around, taking a glance at the scene. In the not far distance, one private security officer who had been involved in the chase was detailing events to a gendarme. He looked up and asked the officer he spoke to, "Is that a woman?"

"It sure is," the gendarme replied, distastefully voiced.

"Are those the buttons of a lieutenant?!"

"Right again. That there is Elizabeth Stanza. You got to give it to her, she worked harder than anyone to get to where she is."

"That's probably because La Gendarmerie is no place for a woman!"

"Exactly! She made a big bust a few days ago and then they go and make her lieutenant. It's a fucking joke."

The private security officer promptly walked away from the gendarme, moving toward Stanza. He called out her name. "Elizabeth, right?"

The woman turned with a cold face to the man, speaking, "It's Lieutenant Stanza. May I help you?"

"Yea, look, I had a cousin working here, and he was involved in the event last night," said the man. "Those criminals drove him and a couple more of my coworkers, also good friends of mine, off the goddamn road! They are all in the hospital right now, alive, but in critical condition. I talked with one of the doctors and he told me that he figured there was a high chance of life-long impairments. We're talking paralysis, meaning they can't move! And I, having served in La Gendarmerie myself for nearly ten years, should know. Why don't you let someone else take the reins on this one, sugar? And maybe you could go off and do something else?"

Stanza, with a wry laugh, replied to the man, "You want me to... what? Go off and get pregnant? Or perhaps cook and clean for my husband all day long? Or perhaps I should just work at a brothel since that is all I am good for, right?"

"Look, I am not trying to insult you..."

"No?" Stanza interrupted.

"No. I simply think that this is a case that should be taken seriously and handled by an appropriate officer. One who knows what they're doing."

Stanza slowly walked up closer and closer to the man with an intimidating, confident stance. "Ten years, huh?" she began. "Why are you working here then, for private security instead of La Gendarmerie? You would be a highly decorated officer by now, wouldn't you? Why would someone leave such an esteemed occupation to work at a place like this? I wonder why? It is quite a warm day out today, wouldn't you think? Borderline hot, if you would, and yet, you wear long sleeves. Your uniform is short-sleeved, but you wear an underlayer, one with long sleeves. I wonder why? An officer, who worked ten long years in La Gendarmerie, can now be seen working in a low-level job for a coal-mining company, and he wears, out of choice, long sleeves on this warm summer day? You speak of me being an officer who doesn't know what they're doing, but you are a man who I can determine was dishonorably discharged from the force. One of the only sound reasons I can think of for dismissals like that, in recent years, would be officers who joined the Wehrmacht. I wonder, if I rolled up your sleeves, would I, perhaps, find a swastika?"

The proud man took a slight step back, his face pale and his stance weaker. Lieutenant Stanza then continued, "Many people around here do not take a great liking toward me, a working woman. But I would imagine that they hate, more than a working woman, a Nazi. What do you think, sir?"

The man treaded away as the lieutenant watched with a small grin, but also a closed fist of rage. She thought that making a scene would lower her status far more than it was as of now, so she did not discuss further, but God knew she wanted to. Instead, the woman, feeling the most powerful she had ever felt, returned to her investigation, which she found very interesting.

David was at work, Sylvester and Jeff had gone to pick up the heavy equipment which Jones had ordered, and Bobby went with Jones to Harlem. "Ah, Harlem. Love this place! I had an uncle that lived here; the old man claimed he went on a date with Josephine Baker! Ha! As if! Ah, don't you just love everything! The smells, the scenery, the simple spirit of the people."

"Yes, this place is great, but remind me why we are here?" Bobby interrupted.

"As I told you, Bobby, the tunnel down to Accardi's vault is going to take weeks of work, and we simply do not have the hands to work on it. Sylvester, David, Jeff, you, and I are the only real and necessary players in this job, but this specific part requires a little outside support. Call it a construction crew, if you will."

"Ok, but where are we going to find the people to do this 'construction work'?"

"Look around, my friend."

"In no way, shape, or form did that answer my question."

"Ugh! Just follow me…"

Jones and Bobby walked up in their nicely tailored suits to the long line that stood outside what seemed to be some type of club. "What is this place?" Bobby asked, getting in line.

"What is this place? What is this place? By God's grace, you do not get out a lot, do you? Are you really telling me that you have never been to The Savoy Ballroom? And what are you doing in line? Follow me…" Bobby quickly dashed out of the crowd and ran back up to Jones' side. The line stretched out to the end of the block and was by no means straight, but more like a large concourse of men and women, all pushing past each other to get to the front. The men were all in nice suits, fitted with good shoes, fancy hats, vests, and bowties. The women were in heels, wearing dresses of many sorts, be it cocktail, teacup, or something more elegant, with gloves that went a little low of the elbow, and accessories of many types, be it clutches, scarves, or small purses.

It looked as if every person there put on their best outfit. While all the ladies spent their time complimenting each other on their pearls, earrings, bracelets, and necklaces, the men spoke about sports. Sometimes it was basketball or baseball, but the conversation was most always on boxing. Bobby, a man who lived in different parts of the city his whole life, growing up with little relationships, found the cheerful voices and bright faces of the crowd magnificent. As he and Jones sped past the masses, a sense of joyful hope came over him. Admiring the beautiful women going on about their dresses and the men arguing over if Sugar Ray Robinson could beat Joe Louis in a fight, Bobby said, "When we're done with this job, I'm gonna live somewhere like here, a place where everybody knows and is friends with each other, you know?"

"No better place than Harlem, my friend," Jones said, leading Bobby with him up to the entrance. There was a large man at the door, and at the first sight of Jones, he tossed the door open with his grizzly arms. Bobby was impressed, and a bit curious as to just how many people Jones knew. His curiosity left his mind in an instant, however, when his eyes fell upon the glory of the ballroom, he noticed the men and women all laughing with each other. He discerned people of all sorts—the young, the old, the lonely, the married, the friends, and the businessmen. He caught sight of the electric dancing. He too observed the great tunes of the live band, the flow and rhythm of every twirling person, and the smooth, well-polished wooden floor, specifically designed for the multitude of dancing men and women. He noticed one other thing as well. In fact, it was the thing he took most notice of. Bobby looked all around, finding it hard to believe at first. He asked, "Where are the whites?"

Jones laughed, thinking Bobby like that of a little boy with an insular view of the world.

"My friend, it amazes me that you have yet to see or hear about this glorious neighborhood. Have you never heard of the Harlem Renaissance? I mean, you truly haven't ever gotten out of your own little bubble!"

"I have indeed heard of it, I just never imagined it to be so... so... vibrant."

"Ah yes, vibrant is the perfect word! Now this place is the heart of Harlem. This is the home of the happy feet, and the number one place for social interaction, or in other words, gossip. Now that there is why we are here tonight, my fellow. We're going to go around and talk to all the right people. You see, while no place in the world is completely peaceful and joyously close with each other, this is the closest you're ever going to get to such a thing. Though the men bicker over sports and the looks of ladies, they consider each other brothers. And though the women might talk behind each other's backs, most of the time, they consider each other sisters. No one is gonna say shit, so we know that they aren't gonna go blabbing about anything we say to the police. In fact, most people around here share a common distaste toward the police."

"I wonder why?" Bobby sarcastically replied.

"My friend, we are going to spread word about a discrete, high-paying job, and once we push the first couple of blocks over, these people will fall like dominos, telling the very next person the thing they just heard. We'll give out specific details, such as where to go and when. There's a motel out a couple miles past the hangar. That is where we're going to tell these people to meet, at exactly four-forty-five, tomorrow. Now, while there are more than a few gangsters and crooks around here, there are also more than a few on the straight and narrow. So we gotta let it be known that this job must be kept under wraps, but that it is just a simple construction project, as to not scare off any of the men who play strictly by the book."

"You're telling me that you just want me to go around, partying, dancing, and socializing with these people to simply bring up the job every now and then with a few minor details."

"Exactly!" Jones exclaimed with a jolly face, leaving Bobby to his own, who just so went about the ballroom, dancing with the women and drinking with the men. He made new friends, he heard gossip, he met new people and new ways of enjoying life. He had never seen such a community full of wonder. Jones had busied himself at the bar while Bobby conversed with people on the dance floor. Sure enough, after both men told more than a fair share of people, those people went home to tell their neighbors and families, who told their coworkers in the morning, who told their spouses at lunch, and by the meeting time of the following day, thirty men arrived at the motel for the job. Jones was right; for every person they told, that person would tell two more who would tell three more, and so on and so on.

David returned to the warehouse from his new job that day. Finding no one there, he went to the hangar in search of his friends. Sure enough, although it was quite late, he pulled into the hangar and found Bobby working on the drill, Jeff and Sylvester giving out orders, and about thirty men working large vehicles, machines, and other excavation equipment. This digging and excavation job was really something, and for the next month, things ran like clockwork. The thirty men had told their wives and families that they had been employed at an overseas construction job that would last for a month. They were, however, just some miles outside the city, sleeping in the hangar, tucked into bunk beds similar to those soldiers in the military or voyaging crews would have.

The five men, Bobby, Sylvester, David, Jeff, and Jones would wake up at six, and they would have breakfast before David left for his job. The men would then drive over to the hangar that hid in the desolate valley. Jones owned a large, vertically positioned, golden circle called a gong. He claimed it was gifted to him by a Chinese business friend of his. At seven o'clock every day, Jones would bang the gong with a mallet which would let out a loud toll and consequently wake up the crew of thirty men. The thirty workers could always expect to have food lying on the long table next to all the machinery when they awoke. Their meals would always be from various restaurants which Jones and the others would pick up on their way in the morning. Most of the time though, the crew's food would come from a curry place of which Jones had heavy ties with. In fact, Jones and the other four men knew well of this restaurant and held hypothetical plans for it.

After the men would eat, around seven-thirty, Jones would split them all up into three groups. To keep things new and engaging, Jones liked to have new groups every day, allowing the men to remain interested in the work and thus work harder, he thought. One group would be in charge of organizing supplies and resources. The second group was in charge of planning and designing the tunnel, along with building beams, poles, and other metal or wooden structures to hold the tunnel firm and prevent it from collapsing. The third and largest group was in command of excavation. Jeff or Sylvester typically operated the drill itself, and the excavation crew would be in charge of excavating the dirt and rock with heavy machines as well as blasting with explosives.

For four weeks this ran like clockwork. From sunup till sundown, through the weekends and until the job was done, did everyone work. There was hardly any complaining, however, due to the incredibly substantial wages. The thirty men had also seemed to be accustomed to the rigid schedules and long hours of work, as was typical for blue-collar jobs into which society had placed them. Aside from all being colored, the thirty men all resembled each other. Each man held towering statures, with bulking shoulders and general herculean builds. Sylvester along with Bobby and Jones usually ate with the many workers, while Jeff begrudgingly would eat outside. Jeff, in the beginning, had no intentions of having relations with the many colored men.

Each day and at every meal, Sylvester would get the many men to play cards with him. Whether it was, the skin game or three-card monte, he tried to hustle the workers at every given moment. When he discovered that many of the men were already taken with the sinister implications of the games, he went on to poker and other such things. As the weeks progressed, they all bonded and grew to know each other more. Sylvester stopped scamming the men then, feeling he had grown a relationship with them. He truly realized they didn't have much money. Jeff, too, after about the first week and a half, began to sit with the workers. He said nothing to begin with, but by the later half of the tunneling project, he grew to have decent conversations with them all.

As said, it all ran like clockwork, and while there were a few hiccups along the way, be it a fifth of the tunnel caving in, the drill not working, or the tractors getting turned over, Jones had intricately planned for such accidents to occur. As such, everything would be completed precisely on time. Some would think the long hours might make things slower, but in fact, the many working men felt the time fly by due to Jones' strict schedule. The first week went by, then the second, then the third, and then the fourth and final week sped away, with the progress being most visible.

Everyone woke up on the final Wednesday of work and did what they had grown to be so good at doing. Meanwhile, back in the city, it was dark, rainy, and the clouds covered up the sun like a wrapped present. David ran across the flooded street to the tall building of which he entered with pride. As soon as he arrived at the highest floor, he began, "Mr. Accardi wishes to confirm these numbers for next week's race."

He tossed a sealed folder onto the man's desk in front of him and the man then replied. "Yes, of course, Mr. Accardi and all of Mericorn surely know how much we value their clientele," he said.

"Indeed, and Mr. Accardi wishes to confirm that if anything were to occur during this race, his worth would not be compromised, and this company would support him in rebuilding his lost fortunes. Confirming this with Mr. Accardi would surely show your gratitude."

The man stood up and said with a grin, "Yes, of course. I will have Mrs. Miranda go over my schedule with you, now thank you for your time."

"Oh no, thank you," David replied, walking out of his very brief meeting.

"Uh, Mr. Cockspy?"

"Yes?" David responded, his body rotated.

"Remind Mr. Accardi that it is our company's policy to go through security details thoroughly."

"Yes, of course." Some minutes later, David walked to the highest floor of the Mericorn building across town, of which he too entered with pride. "Ah, Mr. Cockspy, how was the meeting?" Accardi asked as he saw his Chief Security Officer enter his office.

"Excellent. I got an appointment for you on Friday at four. Everything seems to be fine, there's just a few things they have to go over."

"Excellent indeed!" Accardi replied. "You know what David? You've had a long day, and you have an early meeting tomorrow. So why don't you take the rest of the evening off."

"Why thank you, sir," said David. About forty-five minutes later, David pulled Jones' car into the hangar. You could hear nothing from the main road, but up close, it was like a nuke going off in your ear. David stepped down to the tunnel. He took about twenty paces before he found himself in the underground highway, surrounded by swarms of large machines, dust, dirt, and helmeted men. He walked up to Jones, Sylvester, Bobby and Jeff, who were in the middle of moving the drill back to the hangar above them.

"Hey! What are you doing here so early?" Bobby asked.

"Boss let me off early. How's everything going down here?"

"Good, very good," Jeff replied. "We're nearly to the vault room. And right now, we're just cleaning up the tunnel and getting rid of the majority of the equipment."

"Good!" David replied.

"So, how's the job?" Jeff asked David, now outside the hangar with a cigarette between his coarse fingers.

"Actually not bad. To be honest, the man's quite nice."

"Don't go enjoying him too much. In one week, you will never see him again, nor him you."

"Yeah, I suppose so. But still, of all the jobs I've had, this is surprisingly not the worst. He's kind, he's generous, yes, I have to do some bad things every now and then, but you know, he treats me well."

"Yeah, that was what it was like for me at the station before I got axed."

"I'm sorry; it sucks that you were; you have no real relation to your father other than blood. It was just wrong what they did to you."

"Yeah well, life sucks. You should be glad the man hasn't made you kill anyone yet."

"Yeah, I did have to beat on that one guy a couple of weeks ago though. To be honest, if there wasn't as much violence involved, I would seriously consider, I suppose I already have, holding down this job for real."

The two kept smoking outside in the fresh air. Four weeks had gone by and everything was going smoothly. David had gotten close to Accardi and was very involved with the security details of the race. And the rest of the gang was about to reach the underground lounge, where the vault was.

Back in Calais, Lieutenant Stanza, after a month of investigating, had found the culprits of the drill heist to be in New York City. She walked fast into the commandant's office. "Commandant, I've got it!" she exclaimed in French.

"Got what?" the commandant asked, putting down the file he was reading.

"The drill thieves, they're in New York!"

"America? We don't have jurisdiction there."

"Which is why I got this," Stanza said as she tossed a short stack of papers on the man's desk. The commandant looked through the papers to find diplomatic clearance forms from the Ministry of Foreign Affairs, Interpol notices, letters from the Federal Bureau of Investigation, travel authorization forms facilitated by the French Embassy, and other international papers. Knowing Stanza wished to go to America and further investigate the case, the commandant threw his head in his hands. With a hint of reluctance in his voice, he spoke. "Elizabeth, when I promoted you to lieutenant, I thought you would be a value to all of our investigations and not just this one goddamn case. I mean here we go, after four weeks of pursuing this dreaded thing, you finally have one small lead? How much more wasted time and energy will you use?"

"Peter, I can get these guys if you would just sign these documents. The Americans have already agreed to assist us in our efforts."

"Don't you mean they have already agreed to assist *you* in *your* efforts?"

"Look, all you have to do is write your name down on a piece of paper."

"Why should I? What will it do for me, other than cause me to lose a valuable officer for the next week? If you ever find these guys, you will just realize that you could have caught twenty of them by now. They stole a goddamn drill! They didn't bomb the city! Drop it!"

The two exchanged glares, both moderately inflamed. Stanza drew a quick breath and said, "Commandant, I became an officer to show people that a woman could put the bad guys away. I don't care about how many guys I get; I care about showing people that the law isn't just some wall they can climb over or smash through any time they want to. Now I know I can catch these guys. They broke the law, they hurt people, and I can get them after some small signatures. It doesn't seem like a hard choice to me, sir."

The commandant looked at her, and as he huffed and puffed, he contemplated. He kept his eyes firm on Stanza's, and with a solid tone he said, "I was once like you. I thought that anyone who broke the law should be a priority, but then I learned that there are hundreds and thousands of people breaking the law every day, hurting people in horrific ways, and plotting to commit heinous acts. You are more needed here. I promise you will soon realize this, but until you do, I will respect your beliefs and choices. So fine, I'll sign it."

"Thank you, sir," Stanza replied with a grateful grin. The commandant lifted his pen and signed all the forms, one by one. He finished and handed everything over to the lieutenant. "You get these guys!"

"Will do, sir," Stanza exclaimed. The next thing the lieutenant noticed was the stiff, compact seat of the plane that carried her to America.

The hairy man spoke with an accent which was so foreign, David had a hard time comprehending his words. "Right here we got an MP40, sum' M1 Grands, an' a bunch o' StG 44's. Take yer' pick o' the lot."

"I'll take them all," David said as he handed a fat stack of cold cash over to the short gentleman. He leaned over to grab the guns, but right as he did the man exclaimed, "T-t-t-t-t-t-t, no, it's too light my friend, y'm gonna need 'nother hundred."

"Excuse me?" David responded, quite invoked.

"Well, these things, they worth a lot, an' if yer' takin' the whole lot, well, y'm gonna to need a bit more to make it good."

David came closer and closer upon the stubbed man, speaking with a growing voice, "May I remind you that I am here on Mr. Accardi's request?"

"No, ah don't. Ah know Mr. Accardi."

"Well then you must be familiar with his certain... profound ways of handling situations, or should I say problems. Now I would like to avoid having a problem here, but that's just me."

"Ya think ya can scar' me? Nah-nah-nah, ah got balls the size o' yer' mama's ass, an' ah ain't gonna be pushed 'round by no lil' boy like ya!"

"You got quite a strong accent there. Let me guess, Irish?"

"Ya think ah'm Irish? Nah my boy, ah ain't Irish. ah'm Cajun, straight down from Louisiana!"

"Oh, my sincere apologies! You see, I only ask because you sound like you belong to another corner of the world."

"My ancestors come down from Canada, 'nd they come from French heritage, y'know."

"Ah yes, of course! You got family back there, in Louisiana I mean?"

"Shoor, ah' got two sisters that live back there."

"Well, you must care for them a lot."

"Shoor."

"And what are their names?"

"They names is Annette an' Marie."

"Oh, what beautiful names. I would bet that you try to see your sisters as much as possible."

"Shoor."

"When you go to visit them, do you travel by plane or car? Because it is a rather long trip if you go by road, as I'm sure going all the way to Crowley would take you at least a few days. But someone with your occupation might not do well by air travel and other such public transportation methods."

"Ah' never said my sisters live in Crowley."

"No, you did not. But they do live in Crowley, do they not?"

"This deal is ova'! Tell yer' boss that he can buy his guns elsewhe'!"

"Woah! Why? I thought you wanted our business, but I suppose not? I wonder, is it because you've got to pack for that flight that leaves at four today? Or is it because you're worried that some of Mr. Accardi's close personal friends would admire his new guns, and they would wish to purchase some for themselves, only to come and find out that those guns are their own, stolen by a short, fat, hairy, little Cajun man who thinks he can call the shots with anyone and everyone he does business with? Let's get one thing straight, pal, I work for the most powerful man in the city, and I served in the war. I am no stranger to violence. And if I end up doing anything rash, I'm sure Mr. Accardi will help me in my efforts to clean up any such mess I may or may not have made in his name."

David, already towering over the man, grew closer now, grasping the grip of his gun which laid on his waist. The stubbed man changed his face, and after a short moment of frowning, smiled. The man said nothing, but simply stepped back, gesturing David to take all the guns. David placed the purchased items in his car trunk, then grinned at the short man before he got in the driver's seat. As he drove off, his face released a smile. For the first time in his life, David was calling the shots. The last few weeks gave him a sense of power he had never felt before, and a sort of dominion over anyone who had ever heard the name Accardi.

David drove back to Accardi's home where he parked in an open ring of gravel after passing through the large gate. He handed off the car to his coworker, Doc. "Mr. Accardi wants to see ya," the man said.

"Does he?" David replied, stepping inside. The house was no regular-sized house, but a mansion of three stories. The first floor was made up of the living room, dining room, conservatory, kitchen, and wine cellar. The living room had a large chimney opposite the many ornately patterned sofas. The dining room held a long mahogany table, with golden silverware at every seat, and a glistening chandelier made of French crystal. The conservatory was on the edge of the house. It had walls of glass and rows of dirt with vegetables of all sorts growing from within them. The back of the first floor held the kitchen, which took up half the entire floor. It was fitted with the most expensive and accommodating equipment of the time, with a pantry the size of a grocery store, and it all sat directly next to the wine cellar, which held the finest and most exotic wines around.

The second floor held the cocktail room, billiard room, and the library. As soon as you walked up the first flight of stairs, you would find yourself in the dimly lit, wide-open room that took up most of the second floor. Though they weren't separate spaces, the left-most side was considered the cocktail room, for it contained a giant bar, stuffed with drinks of all sorts, and multiple sets of stools and high tables. The right side, on the other hand was considered the billiard room, which held a pool table for games of eight ball and a classic billiard table for carom, along with more seating and the tallest cigar humidor any man ever saw. If you went around the corner of the billiard room, you would find the brightly lit library. This room had shelves upon shelves inside, all stuffed with books of new and old, along with chairs hiding in every corner and two large tables in the center of the selections. The first and second floors were for clients, friends, and other acquaintances of the sorts. The third floor, however, was the family floor.

On this top floor, Accardi's room, Accardi's office, and multiple other bedrooms for Accardi's extensive family were held. Behind the mansion were a few small cottages which housed the servant's quarters as well as the laundry room. There was a bathroom on every floor, with an extra one on the third. Italian rugs made up every inch of all three stories' floors. The mansion had a stye of framing that was a glorious testament to Italian Renaissance Revival trends. And on the third floor, the current head of the Accardi crime family, whom everyone referred to as "Mr. Accardi," was sitting in his office and working at his walnut desk when he heard a knock on the door.

"Mr. Accardi," David said.

"Ah David, come in," Accardi replied, instantly recognizing the man's voice. David did just so, and Accardi continued, "My dear friend, you have outdone yourself today! Joey tells me you got all the product and only paid three-fourths of the price. I hope you didn't run into any trouble?"

"No, of course not, sir."

"Well good! Now, meet me out front in five minutes, because you and I are having lunch at Café di Luigi. You will join me, won't you?"

"Of course," David responded with delight.

Fifteen minutes later, David found himself seated at a round table with a red-and-white checkered cloth draping over the edges, a tiny vase of basil standing tall in the center, and across from him was Accardi. "I think I will have the Veal Piccata," Accardi said to the waiter who took his order.

"Molto bene, and for you?" the waiter said, now turning toward David.

"I will have the Fettuccine Alfredo," said David. The waiter gave a nod, grabbed the menus and walked off into the kitchen.

"So David, tell me a bit about yourself."

"Excuse me?" David asked, shocked.

"Well to be honest, I didn't expect you to be as good at this job as you have been, and so I had refrained myself from getting to know you, thinking there was a good chance you wouldn't last more than a week. But now, seeing how you've since proved my cynicism wrong, I wish to know more about you."

"Well, I-I, uh, I have a daughter."

"Oh really, children! You gotta love them!"

"Yeah, yeah, well she-uh, she doesn't know me quite well. I'm still trying to patch things up with the ex."

"I hear that! You know, when my ancestors came to this country, they had nothing but the clothes on their backs and what strength was left in their bones. For years they were driven into harsh labor in agricultural fields, small shops and restaurants in the poor parts of towns, but my great-grandfather, the man who's name I carry, grew tired of his families' treatment and overall lifestyle. He already had one son, my father, who was just two when my great-grandmother and the child she was bearing were killed by marauders. Like much of the family did, my great-grandfather could've spent his life chasing vengeance, or drowned himself in wine, or simply drowned himself. But no, my great-grandfather chose to lead his family into the big city. From there they started an assortment of shops, restaurants, and other businesses of the like. And after the marauders rampaged through their former settlement, they learned to be more prepared. They took to violence when other people tried to take what was theirs, and they made a business out of that. My great-grandfather would continue to lead my family in growing a large business that would last for nearly a century. I'm telling you this, David, to help you understand two things. One, that no matter what life throws at you, you must stand strong and never back down from a fight! And two, loyalty is everything, and we are all stronger together."

Their meal went on for quite some time. David enjoyed the outing more than he would have thought. If he had not known what Accardi did for a living, he would've felt bad for robbing the man. There were times when he considered taking up a real position for Accardi, to have an actual living, but he was constantly reminded by the tense nature of the job and the violence that came with it. All he cared about was getting the money so he could provide for his daughter and be with her again. His motives never changed, he wasn't doing this for fun, for the money, or for the delight, but for the chance to begin a new relationship with his child.

Stanza landed in New York around nine o'clock. Visibly eager to continue her investigation, she went straight to the local police station. She knocked on the door of Lieutenant Dan Rivers.

"Come in," he said, his face stuffed in paperwork.

"Lieutenant Daniel Rivers?"

"That's the name on the door, isn't it?" he replied, his eyes still stuck on his papers.

"Good to meet you, lieutenant."

"What do you want, lady? I'm very busy. If you're here for the sergeant, tell him I was very clear about the Willie Sutton search."

"No, I am actually here about the Nord Horizon Drilling Co. case."

Finally taking his head out of his paperwork enough to notice the French woman's very apparent accent, the American lieutenant threw his head up. With tinted eyebrows and slightly parted lips, the lieutenant responded, "I was told a French officer that goes by the title of Lieutenant Stanza was coming by later today regarding a case on a few high-level thieves they believed were hiding here in the city."

"Yes sir, that is me. The name is Elizabeth, Elizabeth Stanza."

With an even more shocked expression, Lieutenant Rivers whispered, "This is a joke, right?"

"No sir, this is not a joke, but rather a very serious case. One of which I have traveled across continents to further investigate. Now, shall we discuss plans of cooperation, or should I inform your captain, an old and dear friend of my own captain, that you are not helping La Gendarmerie's pressing matters?"

"Of course, Madam Standa, why don't we go get some coffee?"

"Coffee sounds nice, and once more, it is Stanza, Lieutenant Stanza."

"Of course, sorry."

Lieutenant Rivers gave Lieutenant Stanza specific directions to the nearby café where they planned to go. He told Stanza, "Why don't you go on ahead? I need to drop off this paperwork." Stanza nodded and set off. As soon as she walked off, Lieutenant Rivers went not to drop off paperwork, but to speak with his captain. He stormed into the office with an ego larger than himself. "What the hell is going on with this French case?" he asked with a heavy tone.

"What's all this about?" asked the American captain.

"I was told that the station was working with some foreign force to investigate some things here in the city. I was expecting the head officer on the case this afternoon, but I was not expecting a woman to come to me. A woman who says she is not only an officer of the law, but a goddamn lieutenant!"

"First of all, Dan, watch your mouth with me!"

"Right, sorry sir."

"You ought to be. Now listen carefully. La Gendarmerie, which is like a militaristic version of us based in France, has been in contact with us for multiple weeks on an investigation they believe to have spread over here. We agreed to cooperate, and we will. This is about a relationship between nations, not a couple of lieutenants. I did not know that she was a woman. And frankly, it does not matter. Just adhere to her interests and get her out of here as fast as you can. She is not your captain, but you will do your best to help her. Is that clear, lieutenant?"

"Fine," huffed Rivers begrudgingly. With an irritated face, he walked out of the captain's office. He went down to the café where he found Lieutenant Stanza sitting and waiting. His eyebrows tinted, and his jaw clenched with slight rage as he whispered to the French woman, "So, how can the NYPD help you, ma'am?"

"Well, sir, have you read through the case file we sent over yet?"

"No, I've been real busy lately, why don't you fill me in?"

"Fine. About a month ago, a coal mining company was robbed by three unidentified men. There was a chase involved, and shots were fired between them and the private security team employed there. The culprits shot out a few of the officers' tires, causing them to skid off the road and off the cliffside of the mountain. Most of those men are still in intense medical care as we speak. We scoured the streets and heard from local witnesses that no one had seen any men of the sort. When we considered the culprits had already fled the country, we found the only plane big enough to hold the stolen tool in the time frame to be a direct flight to Havana. It was said to be carrying a full load of automobile parts, but when I looked through its inventory documents, I found that the aircraft had only held a third of the normal amount of parts."

"So? He could've just had a small load that day. And how exactly does this relate to my city?"

"That's not all. The plane landed here."

"I thought you said it was a direct flight?"

"That's what its flight plan said. But when I looked carefully through it, its flight time was much longer than an average estimated time from Lens to Havana. I checked with the ATC, and they confirmed my suspicion that the plane made an unscheduled stop in the United States, particularly here in New York City. But here's the twist: there were no customs and immigration records."

"Well, that isn't too weird. Those types of records are falsified all the time."

"I didn't say they were falsified, I said there were no documents whatsoever on the plane. According to those records, as well as the flight plan for the plane, the aircraft never went through, in, or near the United States."

Lieutenant Rivers, beginning to be genuinely intrigued, leaned up and said, "Have you checked airport logs?"

"Every single one where the plane could possibly have landed, and I found nothing. LaGuardia, Newark Liberty, and Teterboro all had zero records of any such plane."

"Could they have falsified airport logs?"

"No. I also spoke with ten workers over the phone who were on rollcall the day it would've landed."

"I think we need to talk to the pilot."

"Good, because he'll be here in two hours."

"Excuse me?"

"I pulled some strings and got info on the cargo plane, along with the pilot who was running the show that day, bringing in select imports for a company here in the city. He'll be landing soon, and after they unload the cargo, he'll be staying at a nearby hotel until his departure the following morning. We'll wait for him at the hotel about the time he'll be done with the day's work."

"Sounds like a plan, a very specific plan."

"It's a very specific crime."

"Right, a... a... What was it again? A stolen tractor?"

"A drill."

"Right, a drill. Now who the hell would go through all of this for a drill? And what in God's name would they be using it for in this God-forsaken city?"

"That's what we're going to figure out. Now, are you going to help me with my investigations?"

"What do you mean? I'm here, aren't I?"

"Sure, but you see, back home, I am often taken for a joke, an insult, an embarrassment to the force, simply because I am a woman. I'm aware that Americans are stubborn; my brother-in-law was raised here. I'm also aware that they share similar opinions of which many of my coworkers carry. You think I am just a dumb, little girl, wanting to be seen, don't you?"

"No, I don't. In fact, I think there should be more women on the force."

"Really?"

"Yea."

"So when you said you were going to go turn in some documents, you weren't going to complain to your boss about me?"

"W–w–w–wait, were you spying on me?"

"No, I've just been doing this long enough to know what men think of me. French, German, American, it doesn't matter. First you complain to your hire-ups and when they don't do what you want them to, you think that you can belittle me. You think you can pretend to be on my side so you can get into my pants just to turn around and take all the credit for any work I've done around here."

"Fine, I'll admit it, I was and am highly uncomfortable with your being here. I think that this world has dark corners and this is a job that deals solely in that part of the world. I don't think, just like most others don't think, that this is a place for women. And perhaps if everyone thinks the same, maybe they're not the ones who are wrong."

"Maybe… but frankly, oh what is the American phrase? Ah yes, as you people say, I don't give a fuck what they think."

"Hmmm. You know, while I may not like you much, I have to help you, so says my captain. And while if I had the choice to, I would rather not work with you, however, I must say that this case you have brought here is quite interesting. So, let's say we make a deal?"

"A deal?"

"Yes, a deal."

"I'm listening…"

"Here's the thing, my captain has been on the force for decades, and he's getting a little old. About a month ago, he made a bad call on a case, and we ended up losing a couple of our men on a stakeout gone wrong. I know the department would force him into a semi-early retirement, which believe me, is best for him, if they thought that someone truly great would be taking over. This thing you've got here, it sounds like it goes deep. I wouldn't be surprised if it was connected to the Italian crime families or the Tong rivalry. If I help you take down these guys and whoever they're connected to, I need all the credit here in America, and I'll tell your higher-ups back in Paris whatever you want."

"So we work together on this case equally, and we both take all the credit in front of our own superiors?"

"Sounds good, doesn't it?"

"It does."

"Well then, shall we shake on it? That's a thing we do in America, by the way."

Stanza chuckled and lifted her hand for a firm shake with the stubborn man she had begun to befriend. That afternoon, when the pilot had finished his long day's work, he walked into the luxurious hotel with a full suitcase and a satchel around his shoulder. He went up to the front desk and told his name to the receptionist, expecting to receive a room number. But instead, Lieutenant Rivers and Lieutenant Stanza walked out. "What is this?" he asked.

"Mr. Manier, you mind if we have a quick word with you?"

"We?"

"Yes, I am Lieutenant Rivers and this here is Lieutenant Stanza."

"Lieutenant…?"

"Yes, lieutenant," said Stanza.

"Nice accent, buttercup. French?"

"You know your stuff."

"Je parle très bien Français, belle dame."

"Je m'y attendais, étant donné combien vous voyagez dans ces régions."

"Alors, permettez-nous de vous poser quelques questions, s'il vous plaît."

"Je pense que je voudrais un avocat."

"Vous ne voulez pas ça, croyez-moi. Vous voyez, nous ne voulons pas vous causer de problèmes, nous voulons simplement vous poser quelques questions, et ensuite vous pourrez repartir."

"…Bien."

"English please," Rivers whispered.

"Sorry, I was just discussing with our pilot here about potentially asking him a few questions, which he has agreed to."

"Very good, shall we then?" said Rivers. In the nearby diner located inside the beautiful hotel, the three sat, Stanza and Rivers asking questions, and the pilot answering with the utmost vagueness.

"Have you ever been in contact with any Italian criminal families?"

"No."

"Hmmm, well, have you got any family that has?"

"No."

"Hmmm, well then, what about Russian?"

"No."

"Any crime families or organizations of the sorts?"

"No."

"Well then tell me how a pilot can afford to stay in such a luxurious hotel, for I'm sure you don't have the highest of salaries?"

"The company pays for it."

"Oh the company, the same company which holds your aircraft's travel plans?" Stanza chimed in.

"Yes."

"Well do you mind clearing something up for me then? You see, a few weeks ago, you flew a cargo plane to Havana, carrying, according to your company's official logs, a bunch of automobile parts, however, not nearly as much as your usual load."

"I remember that, actually," replied the pilot. "It was a long week, as I'm sure you, madame, know quite well that—"

"You can call me Lieutenant Stanza."

"Eheh, ok, well anyway, as I'm sure you can understand, Lieutenant Stanza, things in that part of the world can't always stick to itineraries and strict schedules right now."

"Listen," Rivers interrupted, "we know you stopped here on your way to Havana, and while we are sure of that, we aren't sure where you landed, or why you would be anywhere near this city during a direct flight to somewhere outside of this country."

"I don't know why I would be here, do you?"

"Perhaps you were paid to travel here."

"I work only for my company, who has authentic documentation about every shipment I hold, where it goes, where it came from, and how I had it delivered."

"Yea, but maybe they didn't know. Maybe the person who paid *you* got you false documentation to enter the country and sneakily depart it. And perhaps they had friends inside the Customs and Immigrations Office as well as your very own company."

"What would I be carrying in this hypothetical of yours?"

"A rather large stolen drill in addition to some of the culprits behind such a scandal," Stanza interrupted.

"A drill? That is insane!"

"Is it?" Rivers exclaimed. "Be careful about what you say next, because I'm beginning to lose my patience."

"Mr. Manier," Stanza jumped back in, "please understand that lying to an officer of the law, both of the New York Police Department and La Gendarmerie, is a serious crime."

"What makes you think I was ever in this city?"

"Not only did it take you much longer to travel to Havana than it normally would," Rivers took the reins once more, "but we checked with the ATC, and they assured us that a cargo plane with proper clearance passed through the United States. And yet we can't seem to find any documents pertaining to an aircraft like that, including its clearance. We also found that the only plane of the sorts to have possibly been the very one the ATC confirmed was either your aircraft, or Santa's sleigh."

"That sounds like a conspiracy."

"It sounds like evidence," Stanza replied.

"Fine, it's evidence, but it's not proof. And besides, evidence of what?"

"Evidence that you brought a stolen drill and perhaps the very people who stole it with you," Rivers exclaimed.

"Or maybe you are one of the people we are looking for," Stanza said.

"Am I under arrest?"

"No, not as of now."

"Then I think I'm going to leave, *as of now*."

"Fine, but don't attempt to leave this state, we have already spoken to your boss and relayed the message that you will not be able to fly his aircraft to Cuba tomorrow."

"Fine by me, lieutenant. This is not such a horrible place to be stuck in."

The pilot got up and walked off, leaving Stanza and Rivers to continue conversing without him. "Well, what now? What about the other pilot?"

"That's a no-go. He was let go a week ago, and according to his papers, he doesn't have an address. Tracking him down would take too long, besides, I think I might have our lead."

"And that is…?"

"Look at him," Stanza said, turning her head to the man who had just left them. He walked with a proud strut past the men wearing crimson, double-breasted tunics and bold pillbox caps, over the uniquely patterned Persian rugs, directly under the golden-warm chandelier to the receptionist's desk. He stood in line to get his room key, which he was unable to receive earlier. But the line was long, and around his shoulder was his satchel.

"We might be able to find something in that satchel," Stanza whispered.

"And how do you intend to get his satchel?"

"This is New York City, I'm sure we can find some help around somewhere."

It was later that night when the pilot took to a club, at which he was approached by a slender and beautiful blonde woman in a stunning, sparkling dress. Manier, with no avail to have the woman leave, spoke and flirted with her. They had drinks for some time, and when the hour grew late, the woman, intense by nature, tossed her hand on the man's right knee. "Why don't we have some fun?" she said, her palm slowly creeping up and around the man's leg. With a small gulp and drunken eyes, the pilot grabbed the woman's other hand with a lustful force. He took her around the block to the hotel. They went up to his room, and it was no more than an hour later that the man fell into a deep slumber after a satisfying time with the blonde. The woman, however, did not fall asleep, but rather scoured the fancy room when Manier begun to snore. She looked in his satchel and found cash, a watch, a knife, some glasses, and a small business card with nothing on it but an address.

The woman paced downstairs and across the street to a bar. She tossed the small card with the address on the counter where Stanza and Rivers sat drinking. "Thank you Cindy," Lieutenant Rivers exclaimed.

"Uh huh…" she uttered, holding her arm out, her thumb and index finger rubbing slowly against each other. Rivers handed over an envelope of cash to the woman, and once she fluttered through the bills that hid inside, she spun around, stepping out the door.

"She seems like a charmer," Stanza said.

"Ha, you can say that again. I met her when she and a couple of the girls she was with broke into a barber shop that messed up their hair."

"Wow!"

"Yep, we got gangsters, murderers, rapists, arsonists, kidnappers, junkies, and most of all, drunk idiots. What about you? I know everybody over by you are still rebuilding."

"Oh yea, everywhere has dust in the air, it always smells like literal shit, and the ground's always got something crawling through it."

"Sounds awful, sorry."

"I've lived in worse places, trust me. I know when I should be thankful for what I've got."

"We all have. You ever lived here?"

"I've mainly only ever lived in Arras."

"How is your English so good then?"

"My sister moved here about a decade ago, right when the war was starting to get bad."

"Wait, you said Arras?"

"Yea."

"Like you've been there for a while?"

"Since I was a child."

"So then, you…"

"Like I said, I've lived in worse places."

"Right. Um, well anyway, hopefully this address is our smoking gun."

"Hope so."

"Look, um…"

"Elizabeth."

"Elizabeth, I've got to say, this is a pretty hard case, and after even one week the guys around here would have probably just quit. You've been working on this for what, three weeks?"

"Four."

"Four, well that is mighty impressive. Look, I'm sorry if I was overly rude to you this morning."

"Overly rude?"

"Well, a guy can still have an opinion, can't he."

"I guess. And look, it's alright, I'm used to it. It's not just cops. I can't walk down the street without getting a disgusted look. And it's not just men either. When I leave for work every morning, I see all the wives on my street walking out to say goodbye to their husbands, and all together, they stare at me. They shake their heads in a condescending way. They don't invite me to any of the social functions, and they spread rumors about me. Some say I slept with every man in the office to get where I am. Some say I'm a German spy. You know, a lot of times I think to myself, I should just quit, I should just become a housewife. But no matter how hard I try, at the end of the day, I'm the same person, driven to this line of work."

"And why's that?"

"That's a story for another time."

The truck pulled up to the small, suspicious building. From it, outstepped Jones and Bobby. "I don't like this place," said Bobby.

"Where else would you suppose we get what we need?" Jones replied. The two men continued conversing as they walked into the old building. It was a small drugstore, in which a few customers sat patiently waiting in chairs. Jones walked up to the receptionist and said lightly, "Hello, I'm here to pick up a package that I believe y'all are storing."

"Of course, sir, right this way," the woman said, standing up and leading the two men to the back. When they found themselves in a new setting, Jones went up to hug a large man with various tattoos who was present in the room. This large man began speaking in a deep voice, and Jones slowly walked away with him, leaving Bobby to do nothing but eavesdrop. He couldn't understand what they were talking about, however, for they spoke in another language, a very foreign language, Russian, Bobby guessed. After a minute or two, Jones turned to Bobby and waved him over. Bobby walked up, and as Jones and the large man finished sharing a few chuckles, the man led them to a large mound covered by a brown tarp. The Russian man grasped it firmly and tugged it down, revealing a mound of dynamite.

A little later, inside the truck of which was now carrying the explosives, Bobby, in the front, stuttered, "Jones, uh, uh–"

"What is it?"

"Do you... do you think this is dangerous?"

"Incredibly."

"Aren't you worried?"

"Not at all, my dear fellow. I have spent an enormous amount of time on this plan, and I wouldn't be going through with it if I was not one hundred percent confident. Besides, what have you got to lose?"

"Nothing I suppose. Say, if we do succeed…"

"When," Jones interrupted.

"When we succeed," Bobby continued, "what will you do with your share?"

"I suppose I will get everything I want, and you?"

"Wow, not an incredibly vague answer at all! You really are sticking to this mysterious man persona, aren't you? Anyhow, I would buy a house somewhere nice. Not anywhere that has too many white people around. I don't want to grow old and still get beat on twice a week. I thought about Harlem, you know, the place you and I went a couple of weeks ago. But Sylvester is saying that we've all got to get out of the country. So that takes away a lot of my options. I also want to meet a nice girl, have some kids, and maybe start a business. You know, I actually did start a business a couple of years back. In fact, I've started a lot of businesses. None of them ever really worked out though. When I started a café, it got robbed at least two times a week, and shit like that has just kept on knocking me down. My last business went up in flames, literally. Even still, I've always seen myself as an entrepreneur. I guess that's mainly because I've always liked to be my own boss, and that type of thing isn't in the cards for guys like you and me. That is, unless we act as the dealers."

Jones sat listening to Bobby speak on and on and on. He began to muffle the banter out after a little while, however. Then he let his mind run endlessly in its own thoughts and questions. They were halfway back to the hangar when he heard his name being called out. "Jones?" he heard.

"What?" he responded.

"Did you not hear me?"

"To be honest, I stopped listening ten minutes ago."

"I do love that brutal honesty of yours. What I asked was if you had ever thought of settling down? Get a woman and some kids? Maybe live in a small town?"

"No."

"No, you've never thought about it?"

"No, I don't think it's for me."

"Why?"

"I tried it once with a young French woman, but it didn't work out. I don't think I'm cut out to be a husband or a father."

"Oh come on, you'd be a great father, Jones."

"Well, I haven't exactly put women first in the past; imagine how I would be with a child. I'm sure I'd fail them."

"I'm imagining you with a little Jones right now, and it's a nice view."

Jones did not respond. And Bobby stopped speaking, sensing some sort of sensitivity around the subject. When the men returned to the hangar, they made their way down the tunnel to greet Sylvester and Jeff. Jones and Bobby's faces were covered with grins when they approached. "Took y'all long enough," Sylvester said. He and Jeff had made the final blasts nearly an hour ago, and now they sat on the ground with beers in their hands, waiting on the other two men to arrive. Jones and Bobby grew closer and closer to the concrete wall that lay ahead of them. When they came close enough, they stepped through the giant hole in the middle, which Jeff and Sylvester had hammered. With its clean and colorful rugs, wine-filled bar, three velvet couches with nailheaded trimmings and an oddly open space in the middle of the large room, it was certain that this was a lounge. And it being seventy feet underground with an elevator at the head of the room, it was certain that this was the lounge the men had been working to get to.

The next stage of the plan was now in motion. Jones had paid the thirty workers from Harlem and sent them on their way with the surety that they would never speak a word of them or the job. Now, everyone was hard at work. Their plan was simple: to enter the lounge when the vault was present and full of cash. They had dug down to the lounge and created an entrance for themselves. However, they could never just walk through a clear hole in the wall. No. They had to be more discrete, and so they planned on crafting a secret door over the hole. The door would be coated in travertine tile. Obviously, it would not be such a secret if it was an outlier, so the entire room needed to be covered with the same tile and fronted as a remodeling job.

Bobby was cleaning and dusting the walls before proceeding to cover them with a scratch coat of mortar. Jones was cutting the tile and then used abrasive stones to smoothen it all out. Jeff and Sylvester were mixing the mortar, placing it and then the tile on the walls. Bobby then checked the alignment of the tile. They worked quietly and rarely spoke to each other in conversation, all worn-out by the week's work. Hours upon hours went by, and the four men, having limited time, in addition to a strict schedule, worked with declining spirits.

The men were nearly done with placing the tile on the wall. They only had to cover a little more of the walls, and the small, wooden trapdoor, which the men had also crafted out of a few pieces of wood and some screws. While they all worked hard, eagerly awaiting their near finish and time for rest, David stood inside a local restaurant in town, owned by a dear friend of Accardi's. He walked around the room with endless boredom, along with three other men on the boss' security team. Accardi sat in a small booth at the far side of the empty restaurant, cleared of people for the powerful man's security and preference. He and his guest sat and spoke in the large, uninhabited space. He was meeting with Mr. Crutcher, the insurance man. David truly couldn't care less about the men's conversation. It was all business talk, numbers, systems, bills, and other boring things that made David yawn. So he continued his slow pace about the room, counting the minutes until the meeting would come to an end.

As much as he tried not to waste his energy on listening to the dull conversation, the two men's voices were the only sound in the entire restaurant, making them hard to ignore completely. Just so, David spun

around when he heard Accardi say, "Why yes, actually, I do not have any more meetings today, would you like to see the stadium right now?"

"That sounds quite excellent," said the insurance man. "I am most curious about the vault room. Would you mind showing it to me?"

"Of course, I actually heard they are doing some remodeling."

"How interesting. Well, shall we?"

"After you."

David froze in fear, knowing well that his friends had not finished by now, and it would not take long for Accardi to get there. He must do something. But what? There was no way to get in touch with the rest of the group, so he would just have to stall and pray. David was to drive one of the cars there. He purposely got into the one containing Accardi. Sweat began to fall from his face, and he clasped the rims of the steering wheel as hard as he could when he began to drive. After a few minutes, David slowed the car and asked, sounding confused, "Oh dear, did I make a wrong turn back there? Sorry Mr. Accardi, it seems I have."

"No worries, I've got all day," said the insurance man. David apologized once more, then continued his roundabout way to the stadium. Twice more he pulled a stunt like that, but it wouldn't work forever, so for the next half-hour, he brainstormed ideas to get out of the situation.

Back at the stadium, down in the lounge, the men had completed tiling the entirety of the walls and had begun working on the trapdoor. Bobby walked across the room to grab a tool, and when he began his journey back, he paused. He stepped to the side and realized they had made a grave error. "Oh dear," he exclaimed.

"What is it?" Sylvester asked.

"We've done it wrong! The two on the very left, they are turned the wrong way." The men all stepped back to see that what Bobby spoke of was true. "Ah damn!" all three men exclaimed simultaneously. They looked back and forth at each other in frustration, then sluggishly walked over to fix their mistakes. While the men unhurriedly worked on the walls in the lounge, David began driving the correct way, to counteract any suspicion. And as he traveled down the road, he brainstormed ways to further suspend their arrival to the stadium. He pondered for minutes, but the time kept flying by and his mind remained empty. He didn't know what to do. He grew worrisome. His veins began to glow and sweat began to crawl out of his skin. He looked to his right to see a fast-moving car and without thinking, he spun the wheel, ramming into the vehicle.

A loud crash fluttered through the air. All the women around let out sudden screams, cars began honking and the men all stepped out of Accardi's car. Though nothing around was damaged, nor was anyone hurt, the car was wrecked. The entire left side of the car was dented, with torn-off patches of paint revealing the bare metal beneath, the bumper was bent inwards as well, and shattered glass from the windows spread across the road. The other car, of which David crashed into, looked about the same.

"Oh! I am so, so sorry, Mr. Accardi. I-uh, I don't know what happened. I-uh, must've just blacked out."

"It's perfectly fine, Mr. Cockspy," Accardi whispered back, quite infuriated.

"Hey!" the other driver roared, jumping out of his car. "I got somewhere to be, pal! I don't have time to deal with this crap!"

"Sir," David began, holding his open palms out at the man. "I am very sorry. I see a policeman trying to make his way past the traffic a few blocks down. I'm sure we'll both get on our way in no time. Truly, I am so sor—"

"That's bullshit, pal! Look at my Buik! The side's a different color, the door is busted, and the engine's sticking out of the hood!" While the angry man continued, another on Accardi's security personnel walked up to David, whispering, "Hey, we all are going to take Mr. Accardi and Mr. Crutcher up to the stadium while you deal with this."

"Oh um, um, ok," replied David, "but make sure you drive slow! These roads are all bent out of shape."

There David stood, watching Accardi drive off with sharp eyes. And as the honking of cars and the screaming of the other driver kept going, he could do nothing more than pray that his friends would get the job done in time. But at that same moment, the men down in the lounge across town worked without a worry in the world.

"Ah! There we go!" Sylvester exclaimed. "Team, we have finished tiling the walls!"

Jones, Jeff, and Bobby, who busied themselves with tiling the secret door, looked up. "Well done!" said Jones. "Now all we have to do is finish this door, attach it to the wall, clean up, and go home! And hey, you know what? You and Bobby did most of the work, so why don't y'all go up for a quick smoke while me and Jeff keep on with this."

"Thanks Jones," replied the two men. A second later, they jumped in the truck, beginning to drive back up to the surface. The accomplished work was remarkable. If one were to travel through the large tunnel, they would find as they went carefully placed poles that supported the tunnel's integrity, lights that made day a constant, and compact dirt that sat flat on the ground. It took about eight minutes for the men to return to the surface. They then proceeded to walk out of the hangar and into the huge, clear valley, covered with short green grass and slightly clouded skies. It was quite a place to be, so they thought.

Bobby and Sylvester stood and smoked in silence as they enjoyed their break in the fresh air. "Remind me where the road is," asked Sylvester, still taken away by the long miles that held nothing.

"It's right over that short hill right there," Bobby answered, pointing.

"I don't see it."

"Here!" Bobby replied as he left for the hangar. Sylvester kept still, continuing to squint his eyes in search of the road.

Bobby returned and handed over a pair of binoculars. "Now look where I point," he said. Sylvester put his cigarette in his mouth and his eyes in the binoculars. He looked left, then right, then left, then right until he saw the tiny sliver of gray that bled across the view. "Oh, how nice." The two sat in peaceful silence for a minute before Sylvester continued, his face still stuffed in the binoculars, "Hey, which way is the stadium?"

"It's just down that road to the left."

"Is there anything else down that road?"

"No? Why do you ask?"

"Because there is a car driving left!"

"What!?" Bobby exclaimed, hastily snatching the binoculars from Sylvester and shoving his own face in them. "Well... looks like you're right. Seems like it's a nice car. And looks like a stretch!" Bobby and Sylvester tossed their eyes onto each others', simultaneously saying, "Accardi."

"C'mon, we gotta hurry," Sylvester exclaimed. The two dropped their cigarettes and rushed back toward the truck. They sped down the wide tunnel, nearly running over Jeff when they returned. "What the hell!?" he yelled.

"Sorry," Bobby exclaimed. "Jones! It's Accardi! He's coming this way." Jeff and Jones' eyes widened, their faces full of shock and worry. Without delay, Jones replied, "Jeff, go up top and try to delay them as much as possible. Do whatever you can. But do not get yourself into any trouble!"

"Got it!" Jeff answered, speeding up the lounge's elevator.

"Bobby, Sylvester... we must place the rest of the tile and mount the door to the wall as quickly as we can!" The men nodded and immediately rushed toward the assortment of tools which laid on the ground. Bobby spread the mortar across the flat surface, Sylvester began placing the tiles, and Jones continued to cut the tiles they would soon use. Meanwhile, Jeff ran like a lion after its prey across the huge, empty stadium. Having an idea, he rushed to the staff's locker room. He quickly picked the lock and followed to search every inch of the place until he found a fitting janitor's outfit inside a random locker. He then sped to the storage room to grab whatever he could find that would help him pull off his quick scheme.

Before he knew it, Accardi and his men were out of the car, already beginning to make their way inside. As he was preparing for their approach, Jeff continuously looked up and over the edge of the railing. His apprehensions kept him doing this every other second. But on what felt like his fiftieth check, Accardi, Mr. Crutcher, and about six other men on Accardi's security walked across the dirt track which sat in the middle of the stadium, surrounded by concrete walls and bleachers. Jeff, standing on the highest level of these concrete floors, remained still with shock at Accardi's appearance. However, when he saw one of the guards pull out their pistol, moving it to another pocket, he was reminded of what was at stake. Jeff jumped back to work.

Down below, Accardi and Mr. Crutcher, now entering the stables within the stadium, spoke. "For a place that carries nothing but bugs and animal shit, your stables here are quite elegant, a little too much, perhaps," Mr. Crutcher began.

"Well, here at Mericorn, we provide the best things for our best people. And as it so happens, these horses here are by far, some of our best people!"

"You sure do make a pretty penny at these events."

"We both do, my friend."

"Indeed. Now, who is this glorious pony?"

Accardi turned toward the large, golden-brown horse with a glowing mane and said, "Ah! Now that there is Goldilox, my horse. Yep, my grandfather started the whole horse-racing thing, and he gave this one to me on my thirtieth birthday, sweet ol' Goldilox. Raised her myself, trained her myself, and now she is the only horse I bet on. She is the fastest runner there is. Would you care to take a ride, Mr. Crutcher?"

"Oh no, I couldn't, I am here on business."

"There's no reason you can't test the strength of the horses."

"I'm afraid I must take a rain check."

"Very well, shall we see the box then?"

"I think that is an excellent idea."

Accardi showed Mr. Crutcher the box where all the richest and most successful people would sit, then the cash office where people would make their bets, then the kitchens of the two restaurants located in the stadium, then finally, they made their way toward the underground lounge. They walked down the open floor to the lounge's elevator until they heard, from a distance in front of them, a janitor call out, "Oh, hey-hey-hey!" exclaimed Jeff, disguised as a janitor. "Don't step on that!" he said.

"On what?" Accardi asked.

"I just put a new coat on the ground!"

Accardi looked carefully down at the floor to see an overly shiny reflection. Jeff shouted again, "I am sealing the floors for the upcoming race and any interruption it has with the concrete can ruin the whole process!"

"We would just like to cross," said one of Accardi's guards.

"Well unless you want hundreds of dollars to be put to waste and hours of work to mean nothing, then I suggest you go around the other way to wherever it is you're headed." Accardi and all the men exchanged glances before nodding, turning around, and going the other way. Jeff watched them all with spiked eyes until they were out of sight. As soon as they were, he toook off his hat and janitor coveralls. He sped back to the lounge's close by elevator. He came down it, and when he got to the bottom, he saw his three friends cleaning up the area, having finished the door's tiling.

"I stalled them as long as I could, but y'all better hurry!" Jeff exclaimed.

"Well, why don't you help us rather than yell about it!" Sylvester clapped back. Jeff ran over to help the men clean up their tools and supplies. This took only a couple of minutes, and when the cleanup was done, the men began on the final task: mounting the door to the wall. Accardi, Mr. Crutcher, and the many armed guards that followed were about fifty feet from the elevator. Bobby was screwing the door's hinges as Jones and Sylvester held the door high in place. They finished, and a quick breath of ease was puffed out from each of their mouths. They all prepared to leave, but then Sylvester noticed the door was wide, too wide, causing it to stick out of the wall in the most unsubtle way.

After a march of uneasy sighs, the men quickly unscrewed the door, placed it on the ground, and began sawing off the appropriate amount. While they were fixing this problem, Jones ran over to the elevator where he placed a piece of wood in between a couple of cogs hiding behind the old thing. He had bought some time, how much though was uncertain. In a few long-felt moments, the men finished the cutting, then jumped back to mounting the door.

"What's taking so long!" Jones yelled, still standing on the other side of the lounge. With heavy breaths and sweat-soaked faces, the men choked up, "We can't get it to fit! It looks like when we took the door off the first time, one of the screws broke in half and is stuck in there now, blocking the hinges."

Upstairs, Accardi, Mr. Crutcher and the armed guards that followed pressed the button to the elevator. "I wonder what's taking so long?" asked Accardi, minutes later. Seventy feet below, Jones, who had run over to help his coworkers, used a pair of pliers to pick and pull the stuck screw out of the wall. He kept at it for many fleeting seconds, picking and picking continuously at the screw, but not even touching it most times. After much aggravated attempts, however, Jones managed to grab a good hold on the screw, and he used all of his might to send it flying out. The men had no celebrations, though. Instead, they ran right back to work, picking up the door they had just sat down. As they began for the third time to mount the door, focus was at its most. That was until all the men spun their heads around like owls with jaws dropped, hearing the slight thud of a piece of wood. The same piece blocking the elevator from going up. The men, seeing the fallen wood, carried on working with twitching fingers, thundering hearts, and clenched jaws. Meanwhile, the elevator rose.

The elevator arrived at the surface. "Finally!" Accardi exclaimed. He and all the men around him then entered the large elevator. They went down, and the whole compartment shook upon landing at the bottom. When one of the guards pulled open the door for Accardi a moment later, everyone stepped out into the lounge, seeing nothing but beautiful, newly placed tile on the walls. No one noticed, nor suspected, that there was a secret passageway hidden in plain sight. And through it, a big, long tunnel, in which Jones, Sylvester, Bobby and Jeff now sped up victoriously.

Hours later, David stormed into the warehouse winded. He paused to take a huge grasp for air when he saw the men eating sandwiches and making conversation. Once David finished catching his breath enough to speak, he paced over to his friends and said, "What happened!?"

"What do you mean?" Bobby asked.

"I mean I just spent two hours dealing with the wreck I purposefully got into to make sure Accardi didn't get to the stadium, even when he did! So what happened!?"

The men took one last bite before all setting down their meals, interrupting in between each other to tell the story. "Well, Jeff here had to dress up as a janitor to distract them while we finished the job."

David stood in slight disbelief for a few long-felt moments. He nodded his head with fury and exclaimed, "So you're telling me that I spent the whole day worrying I was going to prison again or getting killed when really only a sentence of shit happened?"

"Pretty much."

"No," Jones interrupted as the other men giggled. "Truth be told it was quite stressful. I had to block the elevator from going up and we got out only by the skin of our teeth. To be honest, Jeff and Sylvester saw them because of good timing and sheer dumb luck. They were having a smoke when the car was going down the long road. If you hadn't gotten into that wreck, we probably would all be dead right about now."

"Thank you, Jones," said David. "This is why he is my favorite."

The rest of the night was mostly quiet. It was now two nights away from the race and the men were sitting around the fire that crackled in the pool house. They drank and laughed the whole night. They repeated told stories and laughed at them nonetheless. They had had so much adventure on this one job they couldn't believe it. And it was all coming into play now.

The men started to realize that the real event of which the job was about were only some hours away, and it made their skin crawl. If Jones were not there to reassure them that they would not be caught, the men would have drowned in their own worries. It was late, David had gone to bed because he had an early morning, Sylvester was making a midnight snack and Bobby, Jones and Jeff went out for a walk. The three men smoked out on the midnight seashore, staring up at the bright moon. They began conversing. "So much I feel has changed. We all have bonded, some of us have changed as people, like Jeff, and we have all done so many incredible things, it's hard to believe it was mostly luck."

Jeff took his cigarette out of his mouth and turned to Bobby. "What do you mean I've changed?" he asked.

"Well, a month ago you were quite, um, filled with disdain for me and Jones. But now, you are more comfortable with us."

"What's that supposed to mean?"

"Oh c'mon! It's no secret you don't fully enjoy the presence of colored folk, but I feel you and I have begun to be friends, different from when we first met."

Jeff stopped, looked at Bobby, and said in a sincere tone, "You're right. I grew up in such a place where even the sight of you people would invoke some outrage in us. I not only apologize, but I never gave you a true thank you."

"Thank you?"

"When we stole the drill, you saved my life with that officer. I am saying a long overdue thank you, and I apologize for putting the color of your skin over your heart, and you too Jones. I don't know what I would do if you had never given me this opportunity, so thank you, to both of you. I can't deny my opinion of your people still stands strong, but I do think of you as my equals, and as good, kind-hearted people. I'm sorry for treating you otherwise."

The men nodded in thanks, and the smoking men's conversation continued on. Meanwhile, David turned off his light and fell asleep in one of the rooms of the warehouse. His bedroom was located right behind the kitchen; it was more of an added square than a true bedroom. It was still a bed to sleep on though, and a bed David had grown to enjoy over the past weeks, for it was comfier than those in prison. Sylvester sat down on the couch as he lifted up the spoon full of milk-flooded cereal. Up and down the spoon went. The bowl was half empty when Lieutenant

Stanza and the many cops with her stampeded into the warehouse, all with guns raised.

"Get down! Get down on the ground! Now! Now! Do it!"

Sylvester's eyes froze, and he dropped his cereal on the ground without a thought. He attempted to put his hands up in fearful surrender. But before he could, he was pulled down to the hard floor by Lieutenant Rivers. David slowly stepped out of bed, trying as hard as he could not to believe he heard what he had just heard. However, before he could find a reason why it was just in his head, he heard the large voice of a commanding woman say, "Go get a look around! Rivers, put that squirmy guy in the car!"

David, hearing the cries of the lieutenant, grabbed his watch and one of his duffel bags, making a run for the back door. The officers turned the corner with their guns raised when the door behind David had slammed shut.

The three smoking men outside kept laughing and speaking. But then Jeff said, "Oh shit!" The men all turned around, gasping at the sight. They put out their smokes and walked closer, not believing their eyes, but sure enough, they witnessed an army of cops going into the warehouse.

The men began running for the warehouse before Jones called out, "No! Sylvester and David are gone! We will get them later but right now we need to leave!" The men's hearts pounded like thunder, their sweat stinking the cool air, their brains rumbling, all because they didn't know what to do, what to say, or what to think. They were terrified, even when they ran away, leaving Sylvester and David. The three men fled the scene quickly, grabbing a taxi after walking a mile away. Then they left for the backup meeting spot, filled with worry and fear.

David's Recollection

It was a few weeks ago when I first started working for Accardi. We had already met twice, first at the theater where he wished to meet the applicants for the job in person, and then at the interview the following Wednesday. Accardi is, as Jones said, "A man who enjoys the little things," and a man who will play games as long as it makes him smile. For our interview, he made us play a game, and the winner would receive the job. After a bit of training and preparation, I went to the meet, and that's where I lost the game, along with the job. I spent the next bunch of hours feeling sorry for myself until Jones and Sylvester came to me saying that I actually had gotten the job because the top applicants were disqualified. So there I was, standing in front of Accardi's God-like palace on my first day. Jones and the others were off making the tunnel's excavations. And I was doing my best to give a good first impression with Accardi, along with all his other men. Out of some accident or illness, I can't really remember, Accardi's Chief Officer of Security had left the position, and weeks before the race, Accardi was in need of someone to fill those shoes. When we spoke for the first time, he claimed that the only reason he didn't just promote one of his pre-existing workers was because he did not trust them. That also meant he wouldn't trust me either out of his ingenious suspicion of everyone. Anyway, since I, who had never worked in security before, especially in this type of scenery, came in at the highest possible position, there was surely going to be some backlash. I remember I entered the golden mansion with a big smile and a well-tailored suit. I knocked on the door and someone opened it immediately. I walked through the large open halls until Mr. Accardi himself came to me. He called me to his office, and we spent the next four to five hours going over what my job would involve. He kindly walked me through how his personal, corporations, and race security should be managed. When we finished going over the many details, Accardi went off to a meeting. A meeting that I would be driving him to. Many days I act as Accardi's personal chauffeur, even though he quite literally has one of those. I've lived in this city long enough to know how to get to places, but when Accardi told me to go to some farm out of the city, I was at a loss. I had to pull out a map to guide me all the way to the place. When we got there, I got out and followed behind Accardi into the open barn. We had only taken one car out that time, with only Accardi in the back seat, me in the drivers', and another man on Accardi's security team next to me. This guy who was with us was called Pasta, a nickname given to him because he always made the best pasta. Pasta never really spoke much. If you asked him a question, he would nod for yes and shake his head for no, even when it wasn't a yes or no question. Pasta always held a poker face. The only way to really get to know and understand him was through his cooking. Anytime he cooked for all of the staff, you could taste how he felt in each bite. There was no doubt about Pasta's perfection. If you got super tough pasta with watery sauce and no spices, it meant that he didn't like you, but on the other hand, if you got a perfect blend of seasoning, sauce and pasta, it meant that you were one of his favorites. As much as he didn't talk, he did sit with the group and always looked sad or depressed whenever there was a conversation going on without him. But again, he never spoke a word.

157

Over the weeks, Pasta got to be my best pal. He was always by Accardi's side. I think Accardi wanted him there just because he never talked. Pasta and I would always eat together at meals, take the same car to places, and work the same spots. We had one of those friendships that meant a little more than being a friend, and it was really nice. But like I said, I was new to this line of work, and I started at the very top, so naturally I got a lot of looks, bad mouthing and glares. We have a meeting every week to go over the security protocols and schedules for the next seven days. My first meeting was the second morning of the job. At the barn Accardi had me drive him to the day before, I asked Pasta about it while Accardi talked with a guy who trained the horses for the race. All he did was shrug his shoulders, though. I came in at seven o'clock sharp to the Mericorn headquarters building downtown, and on the third floor of which I then walked in, was a huge floor with confusing halls and doors on every corner. It took me about ten minutes just to find the conference room, and by the time I did, Accardi was there with a sharp grin, saying, "Ah, Mr. Cockspy, nice of you to stop by." I didn't care much for his joke, but I was glad it wasn't made a big deal. Accardi had already debriefed me on how these things were supposed to work, and the night before, Jones further prepared me. There were no less than fifty men who all sat with arms crossed, staring at me in the front of the room. I went up and began the debriefing. I tasked all the men with different jobs at alternate places for the next week. I've never been in charge before; in fact it's always been the opposite for me. I took orders in the army and at all the other jobs I've worked my entire life. I wasn't all that confident on my standing with my coworkers, and the others saw that in me. I remember after the first meeting, three men came up to me. There names were Johnny, Frank, and Frank, but everyone called the second Frank "Monopoly" because of how he used to earn a living by forcing people on the streets to pay rent for not being robbed by him and his crew. Frank (not Monopoly) was the talker, and Johnny was the one with the ego. Truth be told he was waiting for that promotion to Chief Officer of Security. There's even a rumor that he's the one who got the former chief out, getting him sick or injured. He made it clear to me that he wanted my position, and that he would do close to anything to get it. The first time he came up to me he said, "So youse' the new Chief Security Officer?" I replied, "That's me." "Ah' thought so. Yea-yea, so how lawn' youse' known the boss?" "Oh, I just met him a few days ago." "So youse' new to this family? And yet youse' startin' out at such uh' high position? How did that happen, exactly?" "I just applied and won the game." "Game?" "Yea, Mr. Accardi made us play a game to see who would get the job." "Ah see. Y'know that does seem like the boss, he's always been uh' guy to enjoy the lil' thins'. Anyhow, if youse' ever need anythin', youse' come to me. Yuh'see, ah' been in this business for uh' lawn' time, and ah' know how everythin' 'round here works. Why don't ah do youse' uh' favor and run them security drills for the next couple uh' weeks. And maybe ah' help youse' out with positionin' the crew as well. Y'know, just to be nice." I replied with a growing grin, perhaps out of shaking nerves. "Oh yea, well as much as I appreciate that, I think I'm gonna have to say no." "No? Ah offerin' youse' uh' bit of help, uh' service born out of the kindness of my heart. And youse' saying no?" "Yea well you see here, Johnny, everything you're offering to do is pretty much my entire job. If I let you 'Help me out' then I would have no work to do." "Woah-woah-woah. What's that sposta' mean?" "Sorry?" "Youse' just said 'Help me out' in uh' weird way, uh' way that makes it sound like there's another reason for me wantin' to help youse' out?" "Look, Johnny I understand that a few people who have been here a while are a bit angry with me fulfilling the role of Chief Officer of Security, but that's what Accardi wants, and so I'm not going anywhere. Ok?" "Ah see, youse' think that just cuz' youse' technically our boss youse' get to call all the shots. Well listen carefully, pal, this ain't yuh' place to be. 'Round here, we got uh' system. The crew and ah' all understand how to do our own work, and so if youse' think youse' can make all them decisions yuh' be flat wrong! Yuh' job is to oversee our work, not to be our goddamn general, and since youse' ain't really my superior, youse' probably would want to show me uh' bit of respect 'round here. Is that...ok?" "Yea, I get it," I replied. I walked away feeling a slight fever of anxiety. It wasn't just Johnny though. It seemed like everyone was out to get me. Everyone but Pasta. I kept at it for another six days. Every morning, I would come into the office and adhere to Accardi's schedule, driving him around and overseeing all the guys' work. I would check places before he entered, I would tell the other guys on the crew where to go, what to do and when to do it. Every time I gave out a task or assignment, however, they would always laugh at me, only ever following my demands when Accardi was with me. It was on the sixth day when Accardi went up to me that he said, "Tell me how the race's security systems are going, Mr. Cockspy." "Well, we're working on escape routes for the entirety of the race, including the gambling booths.

160

I'm trying to figure out who wants to be on watch during the event and who wants to be on guard for all the exits, then we have the vault which is—" "I thought you were supposed to finish all those markups two days ago?" Accardi interrupted. "Well um, yes sir I was, but um, I haven't received an answer from the rest of the crew for where they wish to be stationed." "Their voices don't matter, only yours, Mr. Cockspy." "But sir they are very selective about where and when—" "Listen here, Mr. Cockspy, those *piccoli cani* are all simply pissed because they have to answer to a greenhorn who's barely Italian. They're gonna resent you, in fact, I wouldn't be surprised if they were already digging your grave. But it's your job to show them who's the boss." "And how exactly do I do that?" "Finish marking up the stations of the race for tomorrow's meeting. If, or rather when, anyone gets real angry, clock them right in the face and beat them to the ground." I began to laugh, considering Accardi's advice to be a joke. But when he turned to me with a cold face, I knew he not only was being serious, but he expected me to take his advice. I nodded and went home that night where Jones gave me the same advice. I was a bit frightened, for I had never really been a man of violence. I returned from the war having only shot a few enemy troops in the leg, and as a kid I would always run away from a fight. But that day I decided to wake up and be the boss. I walked in and gave out the schedule. I told Viggo, Emilio, and Joey to go see who's been messing up the filing for Mericorn trading documents as well as to teach them a lesson. I told Sal, Nico, Leo, and Dario to be on house duty for the week. I put Raffa, Johnny, Lenny, Stubs, Rico, and Luca on station at Mericorn. You see, the idea of this big security team is just the nice face in the front of the company. In truth, we're just a bunch of guys who help Accardi with all of his endeavors. I assigned Frank, Bart, Pasquale and Angelo to transport truck shipment arrivals and departures. Fabrizio, Cesare, Monopoly, and Bruno were all the guys I put on Warehouse Number One guard duty. Then me, Pasta, Doc, and Tino with Accardi. I kept listing out positions, jobs, tasks, and work for the week, but before I could even finish that, let alone get to the race or company reports, I heard an overlaying crowd of laughter. At the front of the room was a podium where one would put the many documents they would read out on, and at the sides of it, little pads to place your drinks or rest your hands. I wondered what the crowd was laughing at, and a second later, when I attempted to lift my hand from the pad I had placed it, I found that I couldn't. Whether it was glue, sap, molasses, or whatever, I didn't know. But it was nearly impossible to see, being either transparent or a well-blending color. And it was not too liquidy, but I found myself standing there like a fool, with two hands practically stapled to the podium. I kept pulling and pulling and pulling as hard as I could until I pulled so hard that my right hand came flying out, and with its force, my entire body came crashing down as well with the podium still stuck to my left hand. The crowd burst into laughter and Accardi, from the other side of the room sat with a shaking head and an encouraging nod. I stood up after about two minutes of pulling and fidgeting with the podium. I had finally gotten my hand unstuck, but with bits of my skin torn off, and my palm was a different shade from the agitating force. I looked out into the crowd, tossing my eyes side to side to see if I could spot out who did it. Low and behold, at the very front of the pack of chairs which the men of fifty sat, Johnny with his glistening teeth, his slick back hair, and his nice jacket looked like a fish on the sidewalk, gasping for air. I knew it was him when I saw Cesare and Viggo patting him on the back from the row behind, with Frank and Monopoly constantly looking over to him with smirks. I looked back at Accardi where he gave a stern, slow nod. Just then, I clenched my fist and began to walk towards Johnny. I was so full of rage that I had taken no account of how there was a half-foot drop from the front stage to the floor. And with my heavy steps, I fell to the ground, landing right in front of Johnny, who continued on laughing even more now with the crowd. I looked up, and seeing his huge cheshire smile, I leaped to my feet and uppercut him. I slammed my roaring fist into his chin and then a half-second later, his nose. I jumped a big step back with my fists clenched and up high. Johnny let out no words, but with a bloody nose he got to his feet and quickly pulled out a slick piece of clean wood. And from that clean wood, shot he out a flat spike of steel. The bloody man spun his Stiletto around like a pair of nun chucks. Seeing the fear in my eyes, I'm sure, he ran at me. I can't lie; I was a complete pansy. I flung both my hands up in the shape of an X over my face. And when Johnny successfully stabbed me in the arm, he did so with such force that I fell to the ground for the third time in five minutes. Ever since Arnim, my brother died, I get these sort of daydreams. I never talk about them, afraid that I'll get confused for a looney, or worse, I find that I am a looney. My dad fought in The Great War, as they called it. He saw heavy combat but thankfully returned after a long year. When he came back, he was different though. He would hardly sleep, and when he did, he would have a gun under his pillow. That would always scare my ma. He would often wake up from a horrible nightmare, screaming and crying. It got worse over time. He would often mumble to himself and visibly tremor when we were in public or large crowds. I remember waking up in the middle of the night one time to get some milk and to use the bathroom, but when I went to do the latter, I found my father's head stuffed in the toilet, throwing up a monsoon. I overheard the doctor talk to my mom about something called shellshock, which was something soldiers might get after seeing battle. I remember him always being paranoid as well. After about a month of him being home, he got into drinking. He would come home late and sometimes not at all. I didn't understand much of it at the time, but when my ma took us to stay with her parents, and I heard her crying in the middle of the night, I knew that my father had a real sickness. I was never afraid of him, but I couldn't deny that he was going mad. It got bad, and then it got worse, and one night we got the knock at the door. My mother told us with tears in her eyes that he was gone. He had gotten drunk and thought someone was following him, so he used the gun he always carried to threaten the guy. The police came, and when my father took the first missed shot, the officers reciprocated, but they did not miss. When Arnim and I shipped out a little over twenty years later, I prayed every night that I would never end up like my father, and that my daughter would never have to see what I saw growing up. I saw disaster. And though I rarely had the nerve to pull the trigger, I saw more than any man could. It wasn't all that gave me nightmares, though; it was seeing my brother slowly turn cold, seeing the life pour out of his soul, and the shock in his eyes. In many ways I turned out to be just like my father, and I paid the price for it. It's

gotten much better over the years, ever since my epiphany. But nearly
every night, I still see the horror of that day, the day I failed to protect my
own brother. At least twice a week, I get these nightmares during the day.
My heart always tightens, my head always aches, and I most always fall
to the floor in sheer uncontrollability. I see my brother in the daylight of
the bloody battlefield, and a lot of the time, it's random when they occur.
But sometimes when I get very stressed or scared, I return to that
moment. This is what happened when Johnny pinned his foot against my
neck. I traveled back to that day I can't seem to forget, only this time it
was different. This time, I wasn't myself in the dream, but instead I was
Arnim, on the ground, bleeding out, and I looked at myself failing to
protect Arnim, who was me in the moment. I saw from Arnim's point of
view, and it opened my eyes. Watching myself fail made me understand.
I realized that the only person holding me back was me. Somehow, my
fear turned to sadness, and my sadness turned to anger, and that anger
turned to action. Back in reality, I rolled over and out from Johnny's
boot. I jumped up, and without thinking, but by a pure rush of adrenaline,
I reached behind, pulling out my Colt M1911. I stared into Johnny's
frightful eyes as I, without hesitation, pulled the trigger. The room fell to
silence, and laying where I had just gotten up from was Johnny, with a
burst of red pouring from the middle of his torso. Sense came to me, and
normally I would have screamed with fright or cried in regret, if it
weren't for the pat on the shoulder Accardi gave me then. I looked out
into the crowd, seeing eyes of respect. I understood then what Jones had
been saying all along. These people did not hate me for what I did and
barely feared me for it. Instead, they respected me. I grew a stern face,

filled with pride from that moment, and three more times in the center of the chest did I shoot Johnny. "Now," I said, "Who's gonna clean this shit up?" Frank and Monopoly ran up instantly, grabbing the body by the sides and carrying it out of the room. Viggo and Cesare then went to the back to get a mop and a bucket. I walked slowly back up to the podium, and after I ripped the pranked pads off, tossing them away, I continued on with the announcements. Ever since that morning, I felt something unusual, a feeling of sheer power that I thought I would never feel. The crew began to include me in jokes, get me food as well as coffee without me having to ask. They offered to do things for me, and whenever we were out, they'd introduce me to any known associates we'd run into. They'd talk me up to be some great gangster. It was clear my name had gotten around, along with the story of how I shot Johnny. Sylvester and Jeff liked to tease me for how I began to dress, but I didn't care. I began to wear the nicest suits, with great watches, ties, and hats too. Accardi paid quite well, more than well, in fact. It was my third week when Accardi sent me, Pasta and Doc to deal with somebody who owed him money. Before I left, Accardi gave me a few hundred bucks, saying, "Why don't you and the boys go to that nice place around the corner and get yourself something nice when you're done." "Thanks boss," I replied with a jolly smile. I remember that morning like it was yesterday, because that was the day I had a change of heart. Over the few weeks, I had become a man of high esteem. Everywhere I went I felt respect and admiration around me, more than I had ever felt before. I had power, money, and quite frankly, the job was fun. I'd just boss people around, run errands where I threatened people, and calculated the many possibilities of how something could go wrong in the business. I hadn't told the guys yet, because I hadn't decided for sure yet, but I thought that I would keep the job, even after the heist. I thought that there was no way Accardi could find out that I was working with the thieves, and if he had any suspicion, I would just frame somebody else. The job gave me purpose and a level of authority I truly loved. But my pride got to me in these thoughts, and as I walked into the parlor with Doc and Pasta, I saw an old man, no younger than eighty, sweeping the floor. Doc, who got the nickname from how he got kicked out of medical school for beating some guy, and was well known for having a rage problem, walked up to the old man. "Hey, long time no see, Liam." The old man turned with a big frown, and coughed up the words, "Hey Doc, look I-I-I got most of the money, but things have been a bit slow around here." "Oh ya, oh ya, I'm sure o' dat'," Doc mocked. "You know I'm good for the money. I just need another week, and then I'll give you more… with… uh… um… in-in-interest." Doc nodded and stepped closer. "Look, I know ya good for it, Liam, but it ain't my doe, is it? Na-na, it's da' boss', and da' boss gave ya a strict deadline for payback." The old man began to shake, and he dropped the broom, turning to step to the cash register on the nearby counter. He said, "I understand, I do, I do, but hey, look here, I've got more than half of it right here, you see?" The old man took out two hundred bucks, holding them out with shaking hands. Doc practically slapped the old man's hand getting the money. He counted it and quickly exclaimed, "Liam, t-t-t-t-t, ya low, pal." The old man stuttered, "Like I said, Doc, that's all I got." Doc pushed past the old man to the back-room door. He rummaged through the many coats in the closet until he found a small safe, a safe which he opened in an instant. Inside the safe was another two hundred. "T-t-t-t-t, Mr. Hart, why do ya lie to me? I'm da' one who gotchya' dis' safe. Y'know, I should probably take dis' extra hundred ya got right here as a lesson for ya not to lie no more." The old man slapped his hands together pleading, crying out, "Doc please, please I beg of you! That money is for my wife, she's very ill. She needs some very expensive treatment. I-I-I wasn't lying before. The money I gave you is all the money I can give you right now." "Ah, ma che fai? Do ya tink' I care about ya lady, or better yet, do ya think da boss cares about ya lady?" The old man began to sob, and I walked up to Doc then. I whispered in his ear, "Hey, Doc, I think this guy is telling the truth. Why don't we let him slide on this and give him another week." Doc quickly replied, "Oh I know he telling da' truth. Why ya tink' he borrowed da money from da boss in da first place? But da boss sent us to collect his debts." "Ok, then why don't we just tell Mr. Accardi that the man here needs an extra week?" "Da boss is expecting us to bring him tree' hundred. Ya gonna take ya own wallet out to cover dat' missing hundred for dis' old mook?" I knew there was no way around it. What was the point of me paying a hundred bucks for the guy? I mean, I didn't know him. So I stepped back and watched as Doc lost his shit. The old man got on his knees. He begged, "Doc, please! I beg of you! I just need another week! I need that money for my wife." Doc spoke with a deep voice, "Fine. I was gonna take dis' extra hundred as punishment for ya lying to me. But if ya need it so damn bad, ten' I'll use ya body to make da' point." Right then, Doc grabbed the old man's shoulders and rammed him into the nearby mirror, which shattered into a hundred pieces, cutting the old man's wrinkly skin. Doc then kicked the old man to the ground, who sobbed all while Doc hit him, and hit him, and hit him, and hit him. I thought he was gonna kill the poor guy, but another reason everyone calls him Doc is because of how precise he is. The man beats people like surgery. He hits them in places where they have the most nerves and sensitivity, like the face, neck, or crotch. And he cuts them in the places most visible, be it the hands, arms, or face. When Doc finished his assault on the elderly man, he dropped the extra hundred in the pool of blood on the ground, laughing devilishly. "Say hey to ya wife for me, Liam!" I may not be the best guy, not by a long shot, but I don't think I'm a monster. I'd done a bunch of these kinds of errands for Accardi, but each time the guys paid up, and even when they didn't, all it would take was a deadly stare on my part to get them to. However, anytime someone didn't have the money, something like what Doc did to that old man would happen. I heard about that man later the same day, actually. His name was Liam Hart, a stand-up guy who served for most of his life, and now worked day and night for peanuts. That day, the day I saw one of the nicest guys I had met on the job unleash hell on a man double his age, I knew I wasn't cut out for this work. The job got worse from then on as well. It was a week before the race, and I had to do inspections of each and every employee. I also had to drive Accardi around, be in charge of all his other guys, and work with Jones to complete an entire run-through of the day-long race's security. It was a shit ton of work. But what kept me going all the way, what has kept me going for all these years, is my daughter. In just a little over a week, we would be done with The Accardi Job, and I'd get to sit on a faraway beach with my ex, who would hopefully remarry me once I get all this money, and we'd watch our daughter play in the sand. It's like that old British dude once said, "It's always darkest before the sun comes up." And my sun was about to come up!

Chapter 5

The Night Before

It was morning. The sun rose, and the roosters crowed. David jumped out from the taxi and into the tiny curry restaurant. As he stepped inside the colorful, dirty, cramped establishment, he was greeted by a young waitress. "Just you, or you have more people?" she asked.

"Uh, I'm looking for a party of three. They probably arrived here some time ago."

The warm-skinned waitress glanced at David with slightly widened eyes. "Of course," she replied, "right this way, sir." The waitress walked across the restaurant, through the kitchen in the back, and up to a big not-so-shiny freezer door. David clenched his jaw in the unexpected mess that was this restaurant. He thought in his head, *This is where Jones has been getting our lunches for the past month?* As he continued to turn his head around, noticing every stain and crumb in the kitchen, he heard the young woman cough, "Ahem." The disgusted man turned to see the woman give an upward nod toward the door. David gave a slight nod and opened the metal door in front of him. Inside, he found a great table topped with three empty plates of curry, two nice couches, soothing music playing, fine books on the tall shelves, and most prominently, Jones, Bobby and Jeff. David, with a somber face groaned, "What do we do now?"

"Good to see you too, David," Jones answered. "What took you so long?"

"I lost the address for the backup place, which I expected a bit more from, by the way."

"Beauty is bought by the judgment of the eye."

"You read too much Whitman, Jones."

"It's Shakespeare, actually, David."

"I don't care. Sylvester's been arrested, you know?"

As the men all sat with ease, listening to the humming box in the corner, Jones responded, "Look who you're talking to, of course I know!"

"Then why are y'all tuned into the radio without a worry in the world?"

"You stress too much, David. It's all fine. We prepared for such a thing as this. Now look, the police have no real evidence to incriminate him, meaning he'll be free as a bird when the cops finish asking him all of their questions."

"Questions? You sure he's not gonna roll over?"

"Please, Sylvester wants this money more than anybody, and out of everyone here, he's got the most experience with talking off cops. I will go to the station this afternoon to pick him up. As for everything else, the plan will continue as it shall. You, David, will go to work as usual."

"I already spoke with Accardi this morning. I said I needed the day off, and he said it was fine, but I have a lot of work to do tomorrow."

"Good! You and Jeff can go pick up the supplies I ordered."

"What about me?" asked Bobby.

"You may come with me to pick up Sylvester."

Down at the police station in the middle of the city, Sylvester sat still with a deadly glare. Locked in a small, dark room, surrounded by thick bricks, he sat silent, not saying a word or making a noise. Though his breath was easy, and from afar he looked calm, he indeed was not. His heart was bouncing like it was on a trampoline, the quick twitches of his nose made a small whisper, and he clenched his fists with the strength of an ox to stop them from shaking. He was uneasy, but he knew that the chances of the cops having any dirt on him were shy. So to not give them any reason to suspect him, he tried to make as little movement as possible. He was particularly successful in that part, but then he broke a sweat.

He wanted to act patient and calm, but he just couldn't bear the silence. His sweat made him feel he'd had enough, so he jumped out of his chair and walked over to the locked door. He banged on it, shouting, "Hey! Don't you arrest a man for no reason and then lock him in a warm room for over an hour! Where's your common decency!? Now I want to know why I'm here, and I want to know why you people think you can just take a man out of his home like that, make him spend the night in a rat-infested cell, and then stuff him in a room with not a word! Now I know you can hear me, you little blue damns! Let me speak with someone, or you bet your ass, you'll regret it!"

Lieutenant Stanza entered the room, slapping Sylvester in the face with the door she thrusted open. "Mr. Erellio," she calmly said, holding a folder in her hand and a grin on her face.

Sylvester squinted his eyes and dropped his mouth ever so slightly. "You're a—"

"A woman?" Stanza interrupted.

Before Sylvester could let out a sarcastic reply, or a clever insult, he froze in worry. He noticed the lieutenant wore a different uniform when she first walked in, but only when he looked and listened closer did Sylvester understand her to be a French officer. With recollection of Jeff and Bobby's tales from France, the open-eyed man soon found chills in his skin. "Would you care to have a seat?" the lieutenant asked to the man she clearly had frightened. Sylvester drew a quick breath in and sat down with a slight nod. Once he was well seated, the lieutenant put her case file on the table and took a seat herself. With her confidence more apparent than her strong accent in her voice, she spoke, saying, "I take it from your temper tantrum that you are a bit confused about why you are here right now?"

"Yes, I have no earthly idea why I'm here, and from the looks of things, that's fine with y'all."

"Oh, it most certainly is, Mr. Erellio. A quite large robbery occurred about a month ago, and I'm here to find the perpetrators. I tracked the plane that transported the stolen tool and interrogated the pilot. He gave me clear directions on where your so-called 'Base of

Operations' was located. Naturally, we went there and found you. Mr. Erellio, we've brought you in here today to ask you a few questions. Is that ok with you?"

"You have no charges, do you?"

"No."

"Then technically, I'm free to leave."

"Yes, but mind you, if you leave here without answering my questions… you bet your ass you'll regret it."

With a mix of hilarity at the female officer and a fearful tremble from his bones, Sylvester said quickly, with a smile, "Of course, I was just asking out of curiosity. I would definitely like to help you in any way I can."

"Very good," Stanza said. "Now, the first question I have for you is, why were you at this warehouse? I have been informed it's not your home address, and it's under a different man's name."

"Well yea, this man is a dear friend of mine, and uh-uh, well, he is currently out of town, and there have been a lot of break-ins around the area, so he asked me to house-sit for a couple of weeks. That simple." The lieutenant nodded slowly. She stared at Sylvester for some time before continuing.

"Ok then," she went on, "well, if I can, might I ask you about the stolen tool?"

"Of course."

"Have you seen or heard of anything relating to a stolen drill?"

"A drill? Like for construction?"

"No, I am looking for a much larger, much more unique type of drill. One that's often used at dig sites."

"How big would you say this drill is?"

"As tall as this building and as wide as a car." Sylvester's shocked expression furthered his act.

"Why, wait, what, how, how-how could someone even steal such a thing?"

"Well, it must have involved a lot of thinking. The people who did this are smart, hasty, and not afraid to take action. They had the right tools and the right plan at the right time and somehow… they pulled it off."

"Beg your pardon, madam, but why would someone go all the way to France, I presume?" The lieutenant nodded. "Well, madam, why would someone go to France to steal... a drill?"

The lieutenant took a slight pause before she leaned forward. She said softly with her eyes locked on Sylvester's, "I believe the men who stole this needed it for something. Something big, something that would take a lot of hands, effort, and would be very noticeable to the world."

"And you think I am involved? Ha! I don't know how much you know about me, but I am not a team player. I'm a loner, a wolf in the late night."

"Is that so?"

"It is, and I do not have the brain capacity for something like you're alluding to. How would I even go about doing this?"

"Now that I believe."

"Now you believe what?"

"I believe you are not the mastermind here, but I do believe you are involved, and I do believe you can lead me to the man behind all of this."

The room fell to silence. Sylvester and the lieutenant sat with their eyes fixed upon each other. Sylvester said without a blink of an eye, "Believe whatever you want, madam, but since you have no real evidence to incriminate me in any way, I ask you now, as a free man under no criminal proceedings in place, may I go?"

The lieutenant, with a sharp smirk, said, "Yes, Mr. Erellio, you may." Sylvester got up from his chair and walked over to the door. He placed his palm on the knob, and the lieutenant then exclaimed, "Now, since you say you are innocent, I find that it will cause you no distress to hear that we are keeping your friend's warehouse for forty-eight hours so we may properly investigate it."

"Good. I get to go home for a couple of days." Sylvester stepped into the lobby where he was greeted by his two friends, Jones and Bobby. Sylvester stopped for an instant before he walked right past them, stepping outside. Jones and Bobby followed him back to the car, where they all drove off, not saying a word in public. Watching from a few stories up, the lieutenant stared out of a small window with eagle eyes. The American lieutenant walked in and saw her with a fixed gaze and arms crossed. "Lieutenant Stanza, what are you doing?"

"I'm going to follow him," she said.

"What? Who?"

"The man that just walked out, the one I interrogated but moments ago."

"Woah-woah-woah. Look, I was assigned to look after you and this case. And I don't think that following someone who we just released around all day will get us any closer to finding that drill. He knows he is on our map now, so there is no way he will go anywhere near that drill."

"Oh, mon dieu! It's not about the goddamn drill. Don't you see? These people flew thousands upon thousands of miles to steal that drill. Why would they go through that unless they needed it for something?"

"What do you mean?"

"I mean, I think that whoever stole this drill stole it for something big, maybe some sort of high-paying job."

"Like what?"

"I don't know, but I do know that they stole the largest drill in the world, and I don't think they would go through all of that trouble just to toss it on the market."

The American lieutenant, Rivers, looked at Stanza with a modestly staggered expression. He bit back his compliment to Stanza, not daring to give the female officer too much praise. "Very well, do what you feel you should do," he said, deciding to trust her unpredictable method.

"Thank you," Stanza replied, walking off.

In the car, and now about a mile down the road, the three men finally began to converse. "So, how was jail?" Bobby joked. Sylvester kept his unjolly frown as the other two chuckled. But Jones quickly stopped, asking, "So what did happen in there?"

"A French detective is here. She followed us from Europe! The lady knows I'm involved. I denied everything, of course, but I know she knows. So I might need to lay low for a bit. But besides that, nothing much."

"Did you say lady?"

"She's French; who knows what they're like over there."

Jones, thinking through it all, said, "That could work."

"Oh," Sylvester added, "and they're holding the warehouse for a couple of days to properly inspect it or something, so we've got to sleep at the curry place for the next couple of nights."

Jones quickly swerved over to the side of the road, slamming on the brakes, and with great importance, he yelled out, "What!?"

"Shit, man!" the two passengers shouted. "What the hell was that?"

"How could you leave something like that out!?"

"What's the big deal? We'll stay at the restaurant for the next few nights; if not, we can go to a motel or something."

"It's not about where we sleep, you buffoon! It's about the pounds of illegal dynamite we have hidden in the warehouse!"

"Oh..." Sylvester groaned.

"Yea! 'Oh...' is right! We need those explosives, and we don't have time to get more. You're going to have to go and get them."

"I can't. They'll be on the lookout for me. If I get caught, I will get arrested again, and then I don't think they'll be as keen on letting me out." Jones turned his head slightly, giving Bobby a hinting look. Bobby looked at Sylvester and then at Jones. He rolled his eyes and without another word, Jones drove back onto the road, now headed for the warehouse.

At the same time, but across town in one of the trucks, Jeff and David rode together to pick up one more thing they needed for the heist. They were about ten minutes out from the seller, and they both had a smoke on their way down the long road. David drew a deep breath in, then an elongated huff out. He tilted his head over to Jeff, who was driving. He said in a low voice, "So, over four weeks in the making, and it's almost here now."

"Yeah, I'll be glad when it's all over."

"What will you do?" David asked. Jeff nodded his head up and down, his eyes watering ever so slightly. In a somewhat tragic tone, he explained, "When I'm done with all this, I'm going to go somewhere far, far, far away. And I'm going to bring my sister and her son too. Go to Europe or somewhere that has beaches, then I'll put my father, my mother, and all that other shit out of my mind. I will wake up every morning to the gentle breeze of the ocean waves, with a new broad wrapped around my arms."

"Sounds nice. And if you don't mind me asking another question, what was it like for you? Y'know, growing up the way you did?"

"What's there to say? My father was never around. He would always come home late with the stench of liquor, same as yours. And every night, I would hear the cries of my mother being groped, and the sounds of the dogs barking. As time went on, pops just showed up less and less. It got to the point where we might only be seeing him once or twice a month. He eventually left, for good that is. I was eight at the time. We assumed he was dead, but he wasn't, no-no-no, he was quite alive. But everything changed the day it happened. When my mother picked up the news on that Thursday morning, it took her all but ten seconds to drop her coffee.

"My father was treacherous to me, my sister, and my mother. And when he left, we were relieved. But it didn't matter. It didn't matter how much I hated him or how close he was to my family. All that mattered was that my father shot up a bank for cash and then when chased, ran to a nearby hospital, where he killed over ten people, including himself, with a stick of dynamite he had strapped on to get into that bank's vault. And shit, look at me, at us... I guess that's the definition of irony.

"My friends stopped talking to me; my teachers would beat me; and my neighbors would let their dogs on me whenever they had the chance. Like they were any better? My mother had the worst of it, though. She could never find a job, and she could never find any friends. We had to move a thousand miles away, and even then, she had hard times with it all. I was twelve when the hypocrite began drinking. She became just like my father. She would leave with a man three times a week and not return till the following morning. She fed us now and then, let us stay in her home, but other than that she was an awful mother. I don't care what happens to her. It's not like she gives a damn about me. All I know is when I get my money, I'm going to go live the life I've always deserved, and my sister and her son are coming with me."

Jeff grew a smile as he envisioned what could become of him after the job.

"Just so you know, none of us have had the perfect life."

"Yeah maybe, but what about you?"

"What about me?"

"What will you do with your share of the money?"

"When I get my money, I will first brush myself up with the ex. I'm going to be in my daughter's life. I'm going to be a father. That's all I want. Just to be a father to my daughter and a son to my dying mother. I'm going to be there when she goes, and I'm going to be there, holding my daughter's hand as we both cry and mourn together. I've made many mistakes, but I will do everything that I possibly can to correct the one that took me away from all that I had."

"I hope it works out. I've made mistakes too, just so you know."

"Thanks."

"Aha! We're here."

The two men had arrived at a dock. The water surrounding it was murky, and the building next to it looked like a hundred-year-old tower, with the paint falling off and the walls holding critters. Jeff and David headed straight for the building where they were scheduled to meet. Inside, they found an empty lobby with two hallways springing out from it. Jeff said, "This way," as he stepped down the left, David following. They continued until they reached an open door with loud screeches coming from it. They entered and saw a huge open room, one that looked like a science lab.

"Hello, may I help you?" a man in a white overcoat asked.

"Yes, I am Jeff, and this is David. We are here to pick up the suit."

"Yes, of course," he said, "Jones said you would be here, and I have the best model for my dear old friend."

It was twelve-thirty in the afternoon. Jones sat in the driver's seat, eating a hot dog, the other men doing the same. They were atop a hill overlooking the warehouse about a quarter of a mile out. Jones tossed the final chunk of bread and meat down his throat, then picked up the binoculars. He lifted them up to his squinting eyes. He turned his head from left to right and found no sign of any cops. "Alright, Bobby, you're up," he exclaimed. Bobby gave the two men a dark look as he shoved the last piece of hot dog down his throat and jumped out of the car.

"You think he'll get it?" Sylvester asked, watching the man scurry down the long hill.

"No cops are around, as long as it stays that way, we are good as gold," Jones answered. Bobby tumbled down the hill and ran across the big open road toward the empty warehouse. When he reached the building, he found the door locked. He tried the key, but it wouldn't budge. He went around to the back door, which was also closed, and so was every window. He remembered the backup plan Jones had told him, though. He headed down to the seashore where he climbed the staircase of rocks down to the water. Once close enough to touch his foot in the salty ocean, he lifted his head up, looking around in search. Though not without a heavy sigh and a deep, aggravated breath, as soon as Bobby spotted the sewage pipe, he headed in.

He covered his nose and treaded with heavy steps through the huge, human-sized pipe. The water was thick and mushy. The smell ran into his ears and mouth. Even though his nose was shut airtight, he could still smell the horrid stench of shit and piss the pipe was painted with.

The tunnel was gradually shrinking, and when his back wouldn't bend anymore, Bobby clenched every muscle in his body and allowed his knees to fall over, sinking into the shit. He shook his head as he almost burst with disgust. His teeth slammed against each other when he lowered his hands under the sewage. Looking like a toddler, Bobby crawled on both hands and knees through the harsh river of feces.

The pipe started like a sewer, big enough for Bobby to walk through, but it slowly got smaller and somehow deeper. And there Bobby was, half his body practically swimming through a liquid he could neither see through nor truly call a liquid. There were several rats running along the edges, and with the vacancy of light, Bobby could never be sure there wasn't one running up his back. Now with his clothes drenched, sticking to his thighs and arms, he had finally reached the end of the tunnel, where a ladder lay, spiking up to a metal plate. Bobby sprung up the ladder as fast as a cheetah chasing after its prey. He tossed the plate over as he reached the inside of the warehouse.

Jones and Sylvester sat in the car, conversing every few minutes. Sylvester, being slightly bored, looked through the binoculars. "Jones!" he screamed.

"What?"

"Look!"

Sylvester tossed the binoculars over to Jones. When he looked through them, he saw two cop cars pull in front of the warehouse. Jones looked at Sylvester with a face of great distress, saying, "You need to go down there!"

"What?"

"You need to stall them while Bobby gets the explosives."

"I can't! What if they recognize me from the station?"

"Very well," Jones exclaimed, hopping out of the car and down the hill. He rolled along the ground and tossed dirt in his hair before continuing to run. The two officers stepped out of their own vehicles and began speaking. "What exactly are we supposed to be doing here?" one of them asked.

"The lieutenant said he wanted us to patrol the area and ensure there's nothing out of line."

"Alright, let's head in then."

"Excuse me, officers!" Jones shouted. Covered in dirt, his posture lowered, his eyes half shut and with his ruffled voice, he continued, "Officers, thank God I found someone!"

"Hey, hey!" shouted the first officer. "You're ok right there!" Both cops put up their right palms toward Jones, laying their left against their pistols.

Jones lifted both his hands up, and after taking a couple of steps back, he slowly explained, "Officers, forgive me, I did not wish to startle you."

"What's a man like you doing out here?"

"Ha! Well, my great-grandfather moved to this beautiful country in search of a new home—"

"Not this country! This area!"

"Oh right! Forgive me. You see, I was in my car, going to visit my Great Aunt Lisa about nine miles north, and it's her birthday, so naturally I gotta get her a present. She's a pretty old gal but she can still glare like a rotting corpse."

"Get to the point."

"Right-right-right, sorry. Anyway, I was planning on getting her a present and some gas on the way, but I woke up late from my afternoon nap, and already being extremely late, I ran out of the house as fast as a fetching dog. So fast that I forgot my wallet. I didn't even realize until I was about halfway there. I could not miss my Great Aunt Lisa's birthday; she would never forgive me. So I just hoped for the best and kept driving, but of course, my car gave out. You can understand that a black man on the road is not something people would normally stop for."

"Yes, I can," the officer spoke.

"Listen, good sirs, I know you have a lot of duties on your hand, but I haven't had a drink in hours."

"And?"

"And I'm parched."

"What do you want from us, do we look like milkmen to you?"

"No, of course not, good sirs. But you see, my Great Aunt Lisa is probably worried sick about her little Gio, and as she is a very wealthy woman, I think she would be quite rewarding to some fellow guardians of the law who helped out her favorite nephew. So if I could just enter this here warehouse and fill myself a glass of water to satisfy my thirst, I'm sure Great Aunt Lisa would be very grateful."

The officers exchanged looks as they withdrew their hands from their pistols. "A wealthy negro, I find that hard to believe," said one officer.

"Well, you would be interested to know that she isn't the same color as I am. You see, one of her nephews, my father, some years ago, had an affair with a young maid of color. A bit later, I popped out of the oven, and I'm not the best at biology, but as you can see, I got my father's eyes and my mother's skin. Now gentlemen, I know you both have important work to do, but I'd very much appreciate it if you would let me into this building that looks like it's got several home commodities to fetch myself a tall glass of water." As Jones finished his persuasive story, the officers exchanged another look. Right then, they both turned to Jones with broad smiles and said, "Of course, sir. Please, be our guest. We'll go unlock the door for you to refresh yourself, and then afterward we'll drive you those miles to your Great Aunt Lisa's."

"Oh, you gentlemen are too kind! I'll never forget this, and I'm sure Great Aunt Lisa won't either."

"Haha." The men laughed. "We'll get the key," the first officer said, walking to the car. The second officer stood still with a wide smile and bright eyes, while Jones kept his sights on the warehouse door, hoping Bobby was almost done.

On the other side of that door, Bobby heaved for breath with every step. He was covered in all sorts of filth that made insects crawl up his anus and muck solidify in his shoes. He stepped heavily, aching with every move.

Bobby went into Jones' room where he quickly waddled past the bed and the nightstand to the closet. He opened the door and grabbed all of Jones' clothes. He threw them all out onto the floor until the closet was empty. Then he pulled out a blade, raised his hand, and slammed the sharp point into the ground. The oak floorboards of the closet were incredibly hollow, and the blade punctured it like a bullet running through glass. Bobby tilted the blade side to side, carving out a hole in the floor. Once it was a big enough opening, he wasted no time to reach in and pull out a small duffel bag. He placed it on the floor for him to open, and sure enough, all of the dynamite was there. He closed up the bag, covered the hole he had made back up with tape and a pile of clothes, then darted for the sewer.

Bobby went back through the warehouse to the underground pipe, but on his way, he suddenly stopped. He looked along the ground and saw a series of muddy footprints. He took a deep breath in and went into the nearby bathroom. He grabbed a towel and cleaned up all of his tracks. When he finished, he got back over to the sewer. He tossed the duffel bag down before he jumped in himself. Like in a comic, he lifted his hand up from the ground, grabbing the sewer plate and sliding it back over the open sewer entry. Once the lid was back in its place and Bobby had all the explosives, he ran out of the sewer, back up the hill and into the car.

Sylvester held disgusted eyes when he saw the brown monster. "What the hell happened to you?" he asked an approaching Bobby.

"I don't want to talk about it," he replied, grabbing the prepacked bag of clean, dry clothes. "Where's Jones?"

"He went down to distract those policemen," Sylvester answered, looking away as Bobby stripped and rinsed himself off with a bottle of water. He dressed to the best of his ability, but he still stunk like a dead gorilla and walked over to the edge of the hill. "So what's the plan now?" he asked. "Do we wait for Jones?" As soon as Bobby finished asking his question, Sylvester, who was standing right behind him, and facing toward him, looked a little to his left. When he saw Jones and the two cops walking toward them, he shouted, "Oh shit!" He plopped down onto the ground. Bobby, turning and seeing the same thing, jumped down as well a second later. Fortunately, the cops didn't notice them. Instead, they returned to their vehicles and drove off with Jones.

"Where is Jones going?"

"I don't know, but he's not in handcuffs. It's fine, he knows how to get out of a fix if he's ever in one, let's just go." Sylvester got up and walked back to the car. Bobby remained still for a minute before he followed. The two then left Jones off to fend for himself, traveling back to the restaurant. When they returned, they made their way to the back room, meeting up with David and Jeff. The first thing the two noticed when they walked in was the giant suit standing in the center of the room. "Where's Jones?" David asked.

"He left, he's fine, but more importantly, what on God's green earth is that?" Sylvester asked, pointing to the black rubber body with clear goggles and giant duck-like feet.

"Oh, this is the swimsuit. It's top of the line and has this bag of air that recycles your oxygen, allowing you to hold your breath underwater for up to an hour!" The four continued conversing, talking about the suit, who would wear it, and where Jones went, but about halfway through the ensemble of topics, Bobby left to take a shower, for the other men wouldn't stop giving him shit about his stench. That night, Jones returned looking exhausted. He spoke of his day's journey, in which the policeman drove him to his "Great Aunt Lisa's house" and "Yotta yotta yotta," as he said it. He went over the plan for tomorrow before he and the other men fell asleep like a whisper in the night.

The next morning was an exciting one, for it was the day before the heist. Weeks of preparation all went to something that was only a dear day away. There was much work to be done, and the men started early in the morning. David was the first to leave. He headed straight for the stadium, where he spent his day reviewing security details, getting everything cleaned, and making sure the horses and the vault were properly dealt with. The other men spent the day simply getting everything prepared. All their supplies and resources were in the exact place they needed to be by the end of the day.

All five men spent thirteen hours hard at work on various tasks, planning, prepping, and laboring. It was a little past seven that night when Jones, Bobby, Sylvester and Jeff, who were all dripping in sweat, covered in dirt, and held aching bones from the labor they had done all day, labor too bland to describe, rejoiced to realize they had started on their final task. The men, ready to call it a night, rushed to put up the dynamite. Though David would get most of the guards out of the underground lounge, there was no way to get everyone out. So when the guys would come out from the hidden trapdoor into the lounge, they would be found out. Since no one wanted to kill the couple of guards who would still be down there, they would need to collapse the tunnel to avoid being followed. So now, a few mere hours from the race, the men carefully stuck the dynamite onto the walls around their side of the trapdoor into the lounge. When they were done sticking the putty to the wooden surface, they wired it all together, connecting it to a medium-sized box with a tall handle to push down on from the top to ignite the explosion.

When the men finished this and their day's work was done, they headed over to a bar for a night of relaxation. Meanwhile, once everything was finished at the stadium, David went to Accardi's office, having been told to come over for a debriefing when his day's work was done. At the golden palace, full of the nicest and most unnecessary things, David and Accardi sat alone in the dining room. David ate an extravagant chicken dish topped with a hundred spices at one end of the long, mahogany table. At the other end, Accardi ate his crispy steak, leaving a dozen empty seats in between them. Accardi barely had to ask David anything; David simply knew what to say. He spoke of each and every horse's medical examination results, as well as their riders'. He told of the security layout and the personnel on every side and level of the stadium. Then he explained every possible detail of the underground vault, the money transportation tubes, the employee background checks, the gambling booths, and the meals of all the kitchens.

"Great! Very great indeed. All of it. I must tell you, Mr. Cockspy, you've done an outstanding job. You've impressed me."

"Why thank you, sir."

"To be honest, I expected less, much less. But over these few weeks, you have proved me wrong, which is, by no means, an easy thing to do."

"Why thank you, sir. I do enjoy the work."

"You know, Mr. Cockspy, you have shown a great amount of work and effort on behalf of this estate. However, I'm just not sure where your loyalties lie."

"Whatever do you mean, sir?"

"Well, though you seem like an honorable man, my father always told me that you should never trust anyone, especially one that seems too good to be true. Based on what you've brought to the table since you were hired only four weeks ago, I find you ever so suspicious. So, if you don't mind my asking, why are you here, Mr. Cockspy?"

"It's quite simple, sir, I need money to see my daughter, and I was looking for a job when I heard of a high-paying one. I know I mostly do work on the business side of things, but that doesn't shy away from the fact that you are not an honest man, Mr. Accardi. And whether you are or not, I simply don't care. As long as I am paid enough to give me an offset chance of having a second shot at life, I will do whatever goddamn job you will provide. So maybe you can't trust me, but I do a great job, there is no denying that. And I feel the one who does it the best should be the one who keeps doing it. I want to keep doing this."

"Well said, Mr. Cockspy. But you've told me all of that before. Money, your daughter, a second chance at life. Sure, good enough, but not great enough. I want to know what drives you beneath all of that. I know why you got sent to prison. I know what you did, and I understand why you did it. What I don't understand is why you are trying so hard not to do it now. So... why are you here, Mr. Cockspy."

"I..." David paused. "I..." he tried again. Accardi sat patiently staring into David's eyes and into his soul. David looked down, trying to figure out the answer to Accardi's question, a question he had never bothered to ask himself, and thus he didn't know the answer to. After a full minute of silence, David looked up, finally figuring out what brought him his life-changing epiphany all those years ago. He said, "I wanted to get out of the hole I was in. I wanted to get rid of all the regret, the hate, the sadness, the anger. But then I realized that those are the things worth living for. If you never had regret, you would never take any chances. If you never had hate, you would never know kindness. If you never had sadness and anger, happiness and joy would never be as precious. I had an epiphany before I went to prison, and that realization, though I only now am able to put it into words, is what has been driving me."

"There we go. That is why you are here. Don't ever forget what you just said here. Allow that knowledge to continue to drive you. Now, tomorrow is a big day, so why don't you go get some rest."

"Thank you, sir," David said, standing up.

"Ah-ah-ah-ah," exclaimed Accardi with a shaking head. "It took five hours for Marshall to get that chicken just right. Don't insult him by not wiping that plate clean."

"Of course, sir."

As David sat back down, continuing to eat, he asked a question that slightly shocked Accardi. "Hey, um, what was the story for Johnny?" he asked.

"Excuse me?"

"Well, you know Johnny, the guy I... I... I..."

"The man you shot and killed."

"Yea, right, him. Um, I know his funeral was a couple of weeks ago, and I was just wondering what his family was told. How he died, I mean?"

"Why do you ask?"

"I don't know. I've never killed anyone before. It just feels like... I don't know."

"I thought you served?"

"Yea, I did. I saw heavy combat too. But I only ever shot a few people, every time in the leg. I never had the best aim. I've done some hand-to-hand combat as well. I've stabbed people, torn off limbs with grenades, but I had never ended a life until that day. Until Johnny."

The Accardi Job

"Let me explain something to you, Mr. Cockspy. You were insulted by the man, and you warned him. You tried to give him a second chance, which most people in this world never get. But he tried to kill you, and in return, you ended his life. He had all the blame, and frankly, if he didn't, so what? It's not like the man had any prospects. Sure, he might've had some friends, a couple of hobbies, and a few dames on the side, but all in all, he was a walking trash can. His life was meaningless. It's a cold, cruel world, and people die all the time. Feeling guilty ain't something you get to feel in this line of work. So man up and accept what you did. Learn to spit on a grave, not bring it flowers!"

"Right. Thank you, sir." David finished his meal, got up, and went home for the night, deciding to let go of any guilt he had for killing Johnny, if he had any to begin with, that is. David soon joined his fellow comrades at a nice bar a few blocks down from the curry restaurant. He walked into a heavy conversation on politics. He didn't want to enter that arena, so he simply ordered a beer and waited for the next conversation. The rest of the night was full of fun, silly jokes, laughable tales and pure excitement for the great wealth they believed they would soon acquire. But little did they know that across the bar, paying close attention, was Lieutenat Stanza.

An hour passed, and while the men kept drunkenly conversing, Stanza listened in, waiting for something that could allow her to make an arrest. The table once topped with nothing but four beer-filled glasses, now held four times that with empty glasses. The five men squabbled, laughed, and shared, stepping over their own words sentence after sentence. They sat in a corner booth to draw as little attention as possible, but that didn't stop the rest of the bar from hearing their loud conversations. Bobby, his head full of liquor, stood up. "Going to get s'more drinks." He laughed.

Somehow, in this acclaimed bar made for white men, no one in the entire hour challenged Jones or Bobby's appearance. This, of course, did not last. Right when Bobby got up to fetch more drinks, a pair of drunken white boys came bursting through the door, stinking of hard tequila and yelling damned words. The bar throughout the night was

189

filled with the glares of proud white men. Their patience was almost up, and with every minute, their eyes lingered longer on the two colored men. The pair of drunken skunks they would call men walked up to the counter, speaking loudly about their recent debacle at another bar.

The men ordered a few drinks right about the time Bobby received his. The first man tapped the other and pointed with a daring glare. Bobby stumbled back to his seat with his drinks, but close behind followed these two men. They looked at each other, and then back at Bobby, too drunk to process their own words. "Ay!" they shouted, urging the attention of the bar on Bobby and them. "What the 'ell do yuh think yuh doin', bud?"

Bobby turned, his friends returning the glares of the two men. Bobby said with a scared, helpless look, "I'm-uh, I'm-uh, just-uh, giving me here companions some drinks, if that doesn't disagree with you?"

"It does disagree with us, though. I'm fairly new to this land, but as far as I can tell, people around here have similar opinions toward niggers. That is what yuh' are, isn't it? A nigger?" The crowd surrounding the blazing tension between the two groups slowly leaned further in. The sitting turned, the standing drew closer, and the lieutenant grasped the grip of her gun in preparation for a brawl.

"Why yes, yes I am a-uh, a-uh…"

"A nigger!" the second drunk man interrupted. Jeff gained an angry frown and stood up with a proud posture. He'd had enough of Bobby's torment. "You may think of my friend here as you like, but you will not insult him as such," he exclaimed, stepping in front of Bobby.

"Who ze 'ell is vis? Yuh really standin' up for zis nigger?"

"Yeah, I am, and if you call him that one more time…"

"What? What yuh gonna do?"

"Look, you don't wanna fight me."

"Us!" David exclaimed as he, Sylvester, and Jones stood up. Bobby looked at his friends, and then back at the pair of men who could barely speak, remembering all of the times he had been beaten, discarded, insulted, and mistreated by guys like the two that stood in front of him now. He'd too had enough, and with friends by his side, he found the courage to fight back with the greatest strength. He leaned against the table, slowly reaching his hand behind his back to the handle of an empty glass.

The other men of the bar who were done holding their tongues gathered around the two drunks, forming a wall around Bobby and his friends. Fists began clenching, faces began turning, and eyes stood still. For a second, everything stopped, frozen, unclear, with every man in the bar eagerly awaiting something to happen. The lieutenant, watching this western standoff carefully, grasped her gun as she slowly stood up as well. The men did not speak, nor move, nor blink. They simply stood, waiting for what would happ—CRASH! Bobby grabbed the empty glass and chucked it across the room, sending it flying into the forehead of the first drunken man so hard it shattered.

A trail of blood dripped down the man's face before his body made a loud thud, falling on the floor. Angry screams were let out, and just like that, the men were off, jumping on each other like grasshoppers, running into each other like bison, kicking each other like kangaroo, and slamming each other into tables like birds flying into windows. The street, in a matter of seconds, howled with crashes and bangs and thuds and bams of the epic bar fight. Bobby rushed at the second man, picking up another empty glass. He tossed his arm up and slammed it down on the man's head, who, already having trouble standing, came down on the ground like a brick.

Bobby drew a quick breath in before another man grabbed him by the shoulder, turned him and smacked his fist so hard in the colored man's nose, it turned sideways. David saw this and immediately tackled the man to the ground. With everyone leaping into the all-out brawl, Stanza held her gun high, beginning to shout "Stop!" But before she could even yell a second time, a stool, thrown by a three-hundred-pound man, smacked into her face, causing her to fall down to the ground with her pistol flying to the other end of the room.

While Stanza was stuck to the ground, feeling like she was shot above the eye, Jeff jumped onto a man. He took his right arm and wrapped it around the neck, holding the guy in a chokehold, his left fist hitting him in the face until it was red. Sylvester, like the coward he is, ran behind a booth, his head sticking out slightly, watching the action from afar. Jones, shocking all around him, beat everyone like a master of martial arts. He kicked one man into a table, and he grabbed another by the neck, who he sent like a running bull into another guy. He grabbed another drunken man by the shirt and pulled him closer, hitting him like a punching bag. Jones grabbed the leg of the now-broken stool that hit Stanza earlier and flung it out like a baseball bat, striking two men in the face and sending them both crashing down like a plane with a bad engine.

Bobby, having been blinded by the heavy hit he took earlier, now sat up from the floor he had been stapled to. As he gagged for breath, his eyes fluttered and his head slowly rose; he saw a revolver two feet away, pointed right at him.

"Night night, nigger!" the bloody-faced man who Bobby first hit said as he reached for the trigger. WACK! Jeff used a full bottle of whiskey to hit the back of the drunken man's skull. The bottle shattered, and Bobby caught the revolver as it fell from the now unconscious man's grasp. Meanwhile, on the other side of the bar, Lieutenant Stanza crawled to grab her own gun, which had been knocked out of her hand and across the room. She reached it, and still with a throbbing headache, stood up. She then ran into the crowd, dodging every clash of heads and duel of barstools, trying to get to David, Jones, Bobby and Jeff. Sylvester still hid behind the booth in the corner, watching the chaotic battle. He spotted the lieutenant moving through the masses of drunken fools with a gun in her hand. He gasped.

Looking back and forth at his friends and the lieutenant, Sylvester knew he needed to do something quick, or he could kiss his fortune goodbye. He jumped out and before Stanza could come close enough, he screamed, "Hey! Cop!" The whole room stopped moving and turned toward the woman. "Everybody freeze!" the lieutenant shouted, her badge raised. The crowd stood still, except for Jones, who slowly reached over the counter for a glass. He grabbed it, lifted it up, and quickly smashed it into the man in front of him.

As the big, bald drunk stumbled over, knocking into three other men, the lieutenant's eyes fell, and as the room would not listen to a woman, the fighting continued. Stanza twisted around with her gun high, looking for Sylvester and the unidentified men he was with, but it was too late.

Around the block, the men fell to their knees in search of breath. "That was a close one," Sylvester exclaimed, the men looking at the weakling with enraged faces. Those faces turned quickly, however, for behind Sylvester ran up one of the first drunken men to insult Bobby. The man pulled out a knife, and close enough to stab Sylvester through the heart, he threw his arm out. But a bang went off first, and when Sylvester spun around, he didn't find himself stabbed, but the drunk man shot in the shoulder, dropping his knife and screaming in agony. He ran off, and before Sylvester could react, David, with the gun he'd been carrying since his employment with Accardi, grabbed Sylvester by the shoulders. With smoke still rising from the pistol in his right hand, David spun his startled friend back around, shouting, "That French lady must've heard that! We need to go, now!"

And so all the men ran off, Sylvester still in shock. David had saved his life after he'd hid behind a booth while the others fought in the bar. This shock did not dissipate anytime soon for Sylvester, but the others soon forgot about it. When they all returned to the curry restaurant where they now slept, they used no time recapping the many near-death experiences they'd had in the last hour. Rather, they went straight to bed, with Jones saying, "Tomorrow is the big day, and we need as much sleep as possible." Nearly all of the men turned in right then. And so the countdown began. It was time for the heist.

Sylvester's Recollection

If there's one thing life has taught me, it's to be self-reliant. I never knew my pops, or my ma. All I had was my Uncle Barley. He reared me to be the handsome, clever, amazing man I am today. He didn't have much to give me, but what he did have was the knowledge of how to get it myself. By the time I was twelve, I was scamming banks. By fifteen, I was robbing moving trains. Sure, things didn't always go so great. Whether I stabbed the wrong people in the back, or stole the wrong thing, there was always someone after me. But in the end, I always did fine for myself. Uncle Barley had just gotten back from a job in Cairo. He wrote me a letter saying how he had scored big, and that he was coming back to the city to celebrate. He said he was flying in for a week before heading to Vegas. It was near the end of the job, and I met my dear uncle at one hell of a nice restaurant on the ground floor of The Plaza. I walked in, wondering how in the Sam Hill my slow, dimwitted uncle managed this. I saw him at a table in the back, and I went up. Instead of hugging or shaking hands, we bowed to each other. It was our thing. We always admired the wealthy, though at the same time thought they took advantage of what they had. We began mocking them by bowing to each other like those rich kings and queens who never took one glance at us small folk. So my uncle stood up, bowed, and then we both took a seat. "Aha! It's so good to see you, my boy!" he cried. It took me a minute to respond, for I was so taken back by the plush seating and crystal chandeliers of the room. "You too, uncle," said I. "So, you must tell me about the job that got you all this!" "Ah, of course, and it is a good tale,

194

but perhaps we should order first, I'm starving!" I agreed and so, to my uncle's request, I ordered the fanciest steak on the menu, Steak au Poivre. Uncle Barley ordered the Filet Mignon, topped with a bottle of Château Mouton Rothschild, and then a bottle of Vino Nobile di Montepulciano. To no surprise, I barely got two cups. My uncle's tale was quite something. He began, "So you remember how me and the boys torched up that nightclub down by the docs for Albert Anastasia?" "Of course," I replied, "it's what got you run out of the city by the Barones. It's actually what gave me that idea to sell false fire extinguishers." "Ha! Genius! Right, well, I thought it best to go out to Nantucket. Not too costly, and it'd be a long time before the Barones found me. Got the idea from that shark book, *Moby Dickens*. I thought doing some shark hunting overseas would be nice, but when I got to the little island, I found that all that was a dead tradition. And what was growing up on the place was real estate. The place was bringing in some new people what seemed like every week. I began to do some investing, y'know, in myself. I won some land off a game of Bridge with this old lot, and then I began selling that land to these little business ventures. People who wanted to start little shops or restaurants, y'know? So, what I did was go down by the docs, and all around town. After looking intensely, I found about twenty strong guys who agreed to labor for me. First, they put pipes and poles and all this shit in the ground, then I would sell that land. And when the new owners realized they wouldn't have a well, electricity, septic tank, and all this other crap, they'd call me and I'd recommend them twenty laborers, who secretly work for me, and they'd go to simply dig up what they'd put in the ground, all for much more than their work was worth. I carried on with this scheme for a couple of years. Now I got to make some good money, sure, but I lost a fair bit of it at cards, and one night I got a little too tipsy. Long story short, I bet more than I had. I reached into the laborers' pockets to square off my debts, but when those guys found out I'd spent all their dough, they were ready to kill me. They trashed my place looking for me. They knew I'd try to skip town, so they guarded the airports, the docs, everywhere! Them guys wouldn't let me off the hook any time soon, so I hid in the basement of an old church for a straight week. I didn't know what to do until I woke up one morning to hear above me a couple of men talking. I listened in, and turned out, there was a little woodworker in town who made high-quality coffins. A funeral director from Jersey came by to purchase some for his fancy business. I paid that guy with all I had left to sneak me into one of those coffins, and next thing I knew, I was shipped out to Jersey. I got there and quickly found a gig as a bouncer for this one club. That's where I met this guy who told me about a job in Cairo. I was very intrigued, so I went. Me and about seven other guys then took a ship out to the place. There was this big building. I can't remember what it was, exactly. Maybe a bank, or hotel, or something like that. Anyway, when it was the dead of night, we broke in and took a bunch of these dusty old pots. Next thing I know, I'm handed thirty large ones." "No shit!" "Oh yes, my boy. Like I said, tonight is on me!" "Well alright, but the next one is all mine. As it happens, I've got a job right now. Been working on it for some weeks now. The price, you'll never believe. Ten million!" "You joking?"

"I swear it!" "Holy shit! That's incredible Sylvo! Tell me all about it!" I did just what Uncle Barley asked, and I told him all about the mysterious man who approached me, and how Jones got all of us into this heist. I talked about the drill and the interview, Accardi, the vault, the underground lounge, the horse race. Speaking it all aloud at once really put things in perspective. This job was truly grand, and wild on every front. But Barley began with some talk that had me questioning my next steps. "Ten million! How in all the world are you gonna spend that, my lad!?" "Well, firstly, I'm gonna get out of this city, as you understand what a price my head would be worth. I'm gonna go somewhere nice, buy up all I can. Y'know, nice place, full of the nicest shit. It's going to be great; I'll never have to work again; I'll never have to do any of this shit ever again. I'll be the king of the world! And secondly, don't forget that I'm splitting that dough with the four fellows I'm working with." Uncle Barley stopped his persistent drinking. He looked me in the eyes in a disgusted manner. "Split the money?" he asked. "Well yea, we all worked on this together." "Have I taught you nothing, my boy? Who gives a crap about those fools! This is a dark world, and you gotta be willing to take from it before it takes from you! If I ever shared, I wouldn't be as successful as I am now. It's you and you alone in this city. You gotta fend for yourself, only, and always! So, are you gonna make your Uncle Barley proud and take what you deserve, or are you gonna sit around for one of those other guys to wisen up and do you dirty?" Uncle Barley left me with a good question, and I went back to the warehouse that night in great contemplation. Was my uncle right? I'd never had anyone's back, but David, Jones, Bobby, and Jeff had made me feel so...

so… I don't really know? I've never really had guys like them before. Y'know… But maybe Barley was right. I've always looked out for myself, so why should I change now? How do I know I can even trust these guys? What if this is all a front? What if David plans to sell us out to Accardi? What if Jeff decides to arrest us to get his old job back? What if Jones takes that money for himself, or what if Bobby is the one who takes it? I worried and fretted to no end. Questioning things, always being so suspicious, constantly asking what if? It's so much work, but that's the way Uncle Barley wired me, and for good reason. I gotta have every possibility sketched out in my mind so I can always be three steps ahead. I took my time to decide what to do. But then I had a moment of clarity. That French lady who somehow is a cop arrested me while I was sitting back on a couch, eating and relaxing. I've had my fair share of experience with the police, but this time was different. I knew that I could really see some bad lights if I was caught. When I was at the station, I saw what could happen to me, what could happen to my life if one tiny thing went wrong. I deserve all that I wish, and so why not fight for that? That's what I thought, and so on the first night we stayed at the curry restaurant, I enacted my ingenious plan. Firstly, I stole an item from each of my coworkers. I took Bobby's old employee card from that manufacturing place, which he still had in the bottom of his bag. I took Jeff's old police gun which he had secretly kept. I took David's wallet which he would always misplace, and thus not think twice of it. Finally, I took Jones' driver's license and headed out the door. I drove over to the hangar and made my way down the long tunnel to the underground lounge. I entered and hid each of the four items around the room, all in places my four comrades would never see, but would be quickly found in a thorough investigation. I hid Jeff's gun under one of the couches, David's wallet under a stool at the bar, and Bobby's employee card as well as Jones' driver's license under the large rug. I returned without a single spec of suspicion from my four coworkers. My plan was simple as could be. After the investigation, we would party hard the first night before we all left in the morning, at which time I would wait to steal all the divided bags of money and leave for the airport. I would, however, leave a little. Because when the police would show up after finding the carefully placed evidence I planted, they would find just enough stolen cash to lock up my four acquaintances. Even if they tried to rat me out, the four men would have no idea where I would be. It was genius, but I wasn't as sneaky as I thought. It was morning and we all set off for the day's work, the day being the one before the race. And much was needed to be done. David was the first to leave, then Bobby and Jones left with one of the trucks, leaving Jeff and I to travel in the other. While Jeff was taking an incredibly long time in the bathroom, I was having a smoke at one of the tables in the dining area. Suddenly, the restaurant owner, a good friend of Jones, came up to me. "Hey, Hasan," I said to the man I had gotten to know a little. He, however wasted no time to exclaim, "I saw you." "What?" I asked. Wide-eyed, and without a hint of attempt to whisper, he said, "I saw you go out last night. I was up late doing some cooking for a big catering order we had, and I heard one of the cars turn on. It was about an hour later when it returned, with you jumping out of it. Though you were idiotically loud outside, as soon as you stepped foot in my restaurant, you began tiptoeing like a cartoon cat. I know you were up to something, and Jones and I go back long time, so tell me what you were doing or I'll go to him." I nervously tossed my eyes over to the bathroom door which remained shut, then I looked back over and tried to play dumb. "Hasan, I—" "I'd prefer it if you'd call me Mr. Mitra." "Ah, ok. Very well, Mr. Mitra. Look, I don't know what you saw last night, but I was here the entire time, sleeping." "Don't try that with me. I know a liar when I see one, and I know a man when I see him, even in the darkest of hours." I paused and scratched my brain for a solution. "Ah!" I said. "I did go out briefly to get a late-night snack. I'm always hungry, you see." "You went to get a snack while you were sleeping next to a kitchen full of foods of all sorts?" There was no way around it, I thought. This clown knew what I'd done, or at least, what intentions I had. I looked back over to the bathroom door, which still was shut. I then pounced on the old Latino like a lion on its prey. I threw him against the wall with all my mighty strength, pulled out the knife I always carried in my back pocket, and swung the metal up, right next to the old guy's face. I whispered to him, wiping the blade against his skin, "Listen here, you old cocksucker, if you let out a peep of this to Jones, or any of the others, I will gut you like the squirmy fish you are! Do you understand?" The man nodded, and so I dropped him to the ground. Jeff walked out and asked what was going on, seeing the restaurant owner panting like a dog on the floor. I tried to speak quickly, but before I could, the man I had knocked down jumped to his feet, and in fright said with my powerful presence over his shoulder, "I just slipped on some milk I spilt. I am so clumsy at times." Jeff accepted this, ignored the situation, and waved me out to the truck. I nodded, followed, and returned the knife I held behind my back to my pocket. I believed I had gotten to the man. He seemed like a soft little dog, ready to roll over. So I didn't think twice about him the whole day, nor worried he would tell anyone. Then again, if he seems any bit weird tomorrow, might have to do something about it. It was an easy day, though filled with tough labor, nothing too much, and plus, we were only hours away, or should I say, I was only hours away from getting my money. Money I worked for my entire life, and now the universe was rewarding me. I questioned my decision to stab these guys in the back, but I remembered what Uncle Barley told me, and look at him now, in all his glory. This world ain't one to be kind in. Being kind to people is like bleeding next to a shark. I've got to fend for myself, because I'm the only one who I can trust, and the only one who truly cares about me. I kept this attitude the entirety of the day. But then there was that scene at the bar. I acted like a coward, and if the rest of my companions didn't have any suspicion of my loyalty before, they surely had some now. I did make a pretty incredible move getting away from that lady cop, but the others knew it was only so we could finish the job. I was a bit stunned at how quickly the others ran to Bobby's side, Jeff most of all. I mean, sure he's on our team, but he's colored, he must've gotten used to those kinds of beatdowns. I wouldn't have thought twice about it, but then David and Jones stood up, and I didn't want to look like a fool, so I stood up as well. When the brawl started, though, I leaped to cover. Why should I get involved? I didn't think I needed to watch my comrades' backs, though they surely had each other's. I was fine not helping, because I kept my attitude of looking out for myself, the very attitude I'd been raised on, lived on, survived on. But then something happened that shook me to my very core. I nearly died. A man ready to pull the trigger had his sight on the center of my back, and in an instant, I could've been a goner. But David shot the man, saving my life. Though it would be easier with five, the job at this point could be done with just four men, and I'd just showed that I had no intension of looking out for any of them. Yet David saved me, and for the first time in probably my whole life, I felt like I didn't have to do all the work. I felt that I could trust someone. We went home that night, and I couldn't sleep one bit. Though I was still drunk as a skunk, I sobered up quickly, and my thoughts went unending. I began to question what I was feeling. The very thing I had longed for my entire life had finally found me, friendship and trust. But I did not trust it, and I did not believe it. I jumped out of bed and snuck out to one of the trucks. I drove over to the hangar, raced down to the underground lounge, and grabbed all the evidence I had planted before. I can't quite put into words all the feelings I carried, but I knew that I didn't want to steal money from these people anymore. I don't know why I didn't, I love money, and I didn't feel guilty, or like I owed them. I simply, without understanding, did not want to hurt them. It was a peculiar feeling, one that made me feel all twisted inside but very good at the same time. I walked in, and when I did, the restaurant owner stood in front of me. I didn't know why he was awake, and he couldn't have known why I was, not truly, but there he was. He walked up to me and said, "I don't know what you are doing, but I could tell by your face you were doing something wrong last night, and I can tell by your face now that you did something right." Just like that, the old man walked off into the kitchen. It was a strange interaction, but somehow, in that moment, it made sense. I returned all the stolen pieces of evidence to where I found them and then retired to bed. I stayed up for a bit longer, replaying what the restaurant owner had said to me. It was like he put into words what I was feeling, and it made me feel confident in the way I was feeling. Whatever happened tomorrow during the big day, I knew my friends would have my back, and for the first time, I knew I would have theirs.

Chapter 6

The Heist

It was the day, the day the five men had been working toward for more than a month. Riches were almost in their clutches. But out of every step they had taken, through all the downs and obstacles they had faced, this final day was by far the hardest part of the job. The men rose early, before the sun came up. Sylvester, with a slight headache from the excessive drinking the night before, now put together the sniper, adjusting it to his liking and confirming its readiness. After he did such, he disassembled it and restuffed it in the long black bag. David got dressed in a very nice suit with his gun in his holster; meanwhile, Bobby was adjusting the diving suit to his liking. And Jones and Jeff were going over the plan at the coffee table in the back. David flicked up his wrist, showing his eyes a glimpse of the time. The shiny, gold watch read six o'clock, and as it was time for him to head out, he picked up his briefcase and headed over to the door. When he got to the door, he stopped and turned toward the rest of the group, who were all facing him.

Jones stood up and walked over to David. He first fixed the man's tie, then patted his shoulders like a proud father. "You ready for this?" he asked.

David took a short breath in and out, then said, "Yeah, I think so. I've got all I need and know everything I need to know. My part is covered, how about y'all?"

The rest nodded and replied with a confident "Yes," but before David could walk away, Jones began, "I just want to say that this has been a long few weeks. We've seen some good and we've seen some bad, but today is the last day, today is the day that will dictate the future of your lives. I trust you all have what you need to have, and I trust you all will do great. It has been a pleasure working with you. See you on the outside!"

One by one, each man said slowly with a smile, "See you on the outside," and just like that, the day of the heist began.

David left in the nice car, speeding off to the stadium. The whole way there, he could only think of his daughter. Through the traffic, the loud shouts of local New Yorkers and the honking of horns, David sat still and quiet in the car with an image of his little girl running around in a big open field. As she was giggling and playing in the field, a single tear fell down David's real face. And before he could wipe it off, he was at the stadium. He turned his face in an instant. He faded his smile into a small smirk, rubbed the tear off his face, nodded slightly in the air a few times before he grabbed his briefcase, hopped out of the car and walked inside like the proudest man you'd ever seen.

The morning was smooth for David. He talked to each and every guard about every little detail. He placed every person exactly where they were supposed to be, he went through the elevator with the technician to make sure it was working properly, he made sure the field was filled with just enough dirt, and he spoke to the horsekeeper to make sure each and every horse was as ready as could be. When he finished doing all this, it was about noon, right before they were to open the doors. In the breakroom, David stood in front of a grand audience of men who all worked for Accardi. He spoke loud and proud, making no mistake to be as clear and as strict as he could.

"Today is the biggest day of the year for Mr. Accardi and his company, thus it is the biggest day of your year. You have all been made aware of your posts and protocols. As we know, there are people from all over the country coming to this race, and we must do our best to be as strict as possible, while also being as polite as possible! And as you progress throughout your day, remember the three things we are here for. Number one is to protect Mr. Accardi. He should always be your number one concern. Second is the money. This means we must watch out for anyone who tries to pull a fast one, whether that be a small scam, taking from the gambling booths, or giving false tickets. Though we might need additional assistance sometimes, and I might direct you to a new station, we must make sure the vault in the lounge always has at least two guards by it. And third, we must protect the audience of the race. Is everything understood?"

The crowd nodded together as David continued, "Good! Now, you all know what to do, and I hope you all know what will happen, and what I will personally do to you if anything goes wrong. So be precise! And good luck! Now report to your stations! Doors open in exactly fifteen minutes!" The men all ran to their posts, and David in his dark black suit with his slicked-back hair looked down at his glimmering watch, taking a deep breath in.

Cars were lined up for miles on the road leading up to the stadium. Bobby, Jeff, and Jones sat in a row of chairs looking out to the traffic from the hangar. They all sat quietly, their tiny minds pondering. All the men could think about was the money they believed they would soon acquire, and what it meant for their entire lives. They sat there for about fifteen more minutes before they began preparing for their positions.

On the other side of town, cars were also honking and formed long lines, not because of the horse race, but because of the normal traffic the city held every day.

Lieutenant Stanza lay on a couch with a big ice pack resting on her head, right above the left eye. The American lieutenant, Rivers, walked in freely. As he looked down and got a glimpse of the big red spot on her head, he said jokingly, "Woah, what the hell happened to you?"

"I slipped!"

"Right, so following that guy didn't work out so well, did it?"

"What do you think?"

"I think I was right. Get anything other than that bruise?"

"Ugh, no, I've been here for four days and all with my boss' complete disapproval. And I have nothing to show for it. I mean, how hard is it to find a giant drill!?"

"Well, maybe it's underground, y'know? Like it's drilling down into the ground so you can't find it."

"No. I appreciate the thought, but no. The drill makes a huge thunder; anyone within a two-mile radius would be able to hear it."

"Well maybe it's out in an area where nobody is."

Stanza stood up and slowly walked over to the window without a word.

"What is it? You've figured something out, didn't you?"

"Is there anything around the Townsend stadium?"

"Um, no, it's just a bunch of land, I heard it was recently purchased by some big company, but I don't see how that relates to anything?"

Then it hit her. "That race! The horse race. I've heard about it, it's the event of the city, and people from all around your country are coming to it. Ha! Ça y est! We need to get to that stadium, now!"

"Ok, why?"

"Because it is about to be robbed!"

Both lieutenants and an army of officers sprung out the door to reach the stadium. At that stadium at that very moment, a bunch of janitors made busy cleaning every inch of the stadium, with its many guests making quite the messes. One of these janitors walked through the crowds to a staff staircase, dropping his mop on the ground. He ran up the stairs until he reached the security team's breakroom. The man entered the empty room, walking over to the trash bin nearby. This man scuffled through the bin's trash until he slowly lifted a long black bag stuffed at the bottom. This man was no janitor, but Sylvester with a fake mustache in janitor coveralls. And this bag was the same Sylvester stuffed the sniper in earlier that morning, which David had hidden in the trash bin. He then returned to the staircase and continued to go up.

It was truly a day for fine things. The cars and limousines that pulled into the stadium were of the finest kinds, only seeing Cadillacs, Chryslers, Bentleys and those types of cars that only the wealthiest and most powerful would have. The men all wore suits, dressed top to bottom in clean hats, proud mustaches, pockets full of cash, and shoes that shined like the sun. The ladies wore nice dresses, white, red, gold, blue, you name it; there were at least twenty women in it. Almost no children were present, and most certainly no common folk in sight. People from all around the country had traveled to this race. There were mob bosses, politicians, wealthy business owners, Hollywood stars, athletes, and dignitaries of all sorts, both foreign and domestic. And close to everyone there were either friends, business associates, or those otherwise working for Accardi.

It was one-fifteen, and the first of three races was about to commence. The gentlemen began to take their bets, and the women began to drink. How it would work was if anyone wanted to place a bet, they could walk up to the booths and pay a sum of money for a certain horse to win. Most people didn't bet for just one racer, most bet for at least four. The game was quite simple too: when the horn blew, the mechanical gates flung open and all ten horses and their riders would be released. The jockeys would ride the speeding horses around the track for three full laps, rather than the normal one, and the first to cross the finish line would be deemed the winner. There would then be a thirty-minute break period for people to use the restroom, purchase beverages, snacks, and of course place more bets for the following round. This system would be put in place for three rounds, with each round having a different set of horses and jockeys.

To obtain the most amount of money, the team would not execute the plan until the third round started. So, for the first round, everything blew by smoothly. Jones dropped off Bobby to where he needed to be while Jeff prepared the guns for the ambush. David stood in the top box with Mr. Accardi and other esteemed people from around the globe. David and three other men, Pasta, Doc, and Viggo, walked around the edges and outskirts of the box while Accardi drank and made conversation, both fun and serious with the twenty people in the luxury room. A clever man, Accardi was. He always won. Whatever he did, he won. For his entire life he went by without ever losing a game of chess. Not many believed it, but it was true, for Accardi always thought fifty moves ahead, anticipating every step his opponents may take. He applied this same strategy to life, which is why he was someone with such high power, and someone you definitely didn't want to cross. This is how his horse race always made so much profit. He would invite his wealthiest friends to the annual event and pamper them up to make large bets, of which only few would win.

It was David's job to keep eyes on all Accardi's men. The stadium had about a total of eighty guards, some who worked for Accardi, others hired for the event. Though there was much to be protected, their main objective would forever be to protect the big boss of who was hosting these games. The clock kept ticking, and the games went by. Everyone was almost fully prepared for their tasks, people of the audience kept betting and betting, putting more money into our friends' pockets, and best of all, no one suspected a thing. That was until David looked two feet to his right, seeing the French lieutenant, Stanza, and her friend, the American lieutenant, speaking to Accardi. David's eyes shut and his heart began pounding louder than the sound of the cheers of the audience. Sweat ran down his face faster than the horses on that track. He continued to stare at the woman who was speaking to Accardi, but when she began to glance out around the room, David quickly ran to the bathroom.

The shaking man knew Accardi would want to speak to him, but he couldn't go near the French woman, or she would reveal him. He hid in the bathroom, both hands resting on the edge of the sink, with his eyes locked into the endless barrel of his own irises through the spotless, crystal mirror in the men's room. He needed to get in touch with the others, but how could he? *What to do? What to do?* He kept asking this in his head over and over again. He thought and thought and stared aimlessly into the mirror in great worry.

David realized he must walk out of the room and pray the lieutenant wouldn't recognize him from the bar, or else they would start to get suspicious about where their head of security is. So he stood tall, wiped the sweat off his forehead, straightened his tie, combed his hair, ran his face with water and dried it with a small piece of cloth, then convinced himself the bar fight was too chaotic for the French woman to have gotten a good look at him. He took a deep breath in before marching out of the bathroom. He placed his hand on the door, pushed it open, and suddenly the room went cold, dark, quiet. Nothing was real, and nothing was there. David was so unbearably afraid that he nearly fainted. But right then, a light touch of a friendly hand on his shoulder brought him back to the real world.

"Where ya been at, Cockspy?" asked Doc. "Da boss been looking for ya."

"I was in the bathroom, I'll go to him now," David replied, walking over to his boss on the other end of the room.

"David!" shouted Accardi. "We were wondering where you were, my friend. David, these are members of the police force, and they're saying they have some discomforting news about our vault that they wish to discuss with us." David continued to look at Accardi who stood on his left, mustering the strength to face forward. He uncontrollably tilted his head and saw her, the female officer from the bar, Lieutenant Stanza. The two stared at each other for a brief moment, David's nerves coming undone and his eyes swelling red as meat.

"Hello, Mr. Cockspy, my name is Lieutenant Stanza, and if you do have a moment to spare, there really is something we would like to talk to you about. It is of the utmost urgency, and relevant to this event."

David's bones stood still, his heart slowed, and the heat cooled. He let out a smile and said, "Of course, why don't we all go discuss this in private. Would that be okay, Mr. Accardi?"

"Certainly," replied Accardi. The group exchanged smiles and walked outside. David's chest, meanwhile, was filled with relief. "What is it you two officers came to this race for?" Accardi asked with slight stress.

"Well, sir, we have reason to believe you are soon to be robbed," answered Stanza.

"Robbed?" David jumped in. "No, no, I am sorry, but our team has taken great and specific steps to ensure such a thing couldn't be achieved."

"Yes, we understand, but I don't think you understand the level of sophistication these men have."

"These gentlemen?" asked Accardi. "Do you have specific suspects in mind?"

"As a matter of fact, we do. A group of men recently stole a drill from my home country."

"A drill?"

"Yes, sir, a drill."

David began, "Hah! Listen here, Ms. Stanza, I am—"

"Lieutenant Stanza," interrupted the American lieutenant, Rivers.

"Right, sorry. Lieutenant Stanza, I am also deeply sorry about your stolen drill, but I am afraid your trip out here was a waste of time. There will be no such robbery today or ever in any place where I am in charge. So if you would please allow me to return to my job and Mr. Accardi to return to his guests, we would appreciate it."

Mr. Accardi appeared taken aback. "Do not speak for me, Mr. Cockspy. But I am afraid that you are wasting all of our time here, lieutenants, so why don't you go downstairs and take a seat yourselves, my treat. I would suggest you even make a bet or two. Now, if I may…"

"Mr. Accardi, this is serious. People very dangerous, who are probably already here, are about to rob this place and I have seen these animals give little thought to the people around them."

"Ma'am," said David, "I know you are not from around here, but we take pride in our security, and we shall not be threatened in any capacity by a theory of someone stealing a drill across the world and bringing it back here to rob us. I thank you for your warning, ma'am, but why don't you go home, make some pies and watch over the children as you should be while us men handle the very safe and heavily guarded vault."

"That's enough!" exclaimed Accardi. "Lieutenants, I apologize for my friend's absent manners, but what he speaks is the truth. I have a big event to get back to, and frankly, my time is being tossed out the window by you two right now, so please allow us to look out for ourselves, and if there is ever anything else you can help us with, perhaps make sure we truly need the help."

Accardi walked back to the luxury box and David followed. Stanza stood there with a face of rage before she stormed off away from the box and to the stairs, with Rivers behind her. As soon as Accardi placed his hand on the door handle to the box, he paused, and said quietly while facing David, "If anything unexpected happens today, Mr. Cockspy, I hope you understand that I will never stop hunting you down to kill you and cause you more harm than you can imagine. If that wasn't clear before."

David was left with a painful beat in his chest as he watched his boss slowly walk into the box. The next round had already commenced and it was about another half hour before the move would be made. And while David continued to be on duty with Accardi, Jeff and Jones, who were in the nearby hangar, got dressed in black outfits. They put on black sweaters and pants, black boots and black balaclavas. They proceeded to get into one of the trucks and head down the tunnel with their guns in the back.

Back at the stadium, both lieutenants went down to the entrance to greet more officers who had just arrived on Rivers' call. "Patrol the area, look for anything out of the ordinary," Stanza said, ignoring Accardi's prideful advice to leave. The many officers surrounding her did nothing but blink. The American lieutenant stepped forward then, yelling, "You heard her! Spread out, look for anything unusual!"

The officers fanned out that second, and Stanza slowly tilted her head to the other lieutenant. "I can stand up for myself," she said.

"I know, I'm just trying to help you out."

"Yea, well do me a favor and help me out by not undermining me."

While the two lieutenants continued to talk, the time swung by, and the third race was near commencement. On the roof of the oval-shaped stadium, Sylvester opened the long black bag and pulled out the sniper. He set up the bipod and adjusted the scope, laid down, and closed one eye.

David walked up closer and closer to the window. Step by step he pictured his daughter running and laughing. And as he wiped the sweat off his face and closed his eyes, taking a deep breath in, he looked up and straightened his tie, giving the signal. Hundreds of yards away, Sylvester, who was scoped in on David, received the signal. And as he wiped off his own sweat, he aimed the sniper perfectly above Accardi's shoulder. Everything went silent, and Sylvester pulled the trigger. Just like that, the final stage of the heist was in motion. The laughing, cheering, singing, and boasting turned to screams and cries as a bullet flew through the window of the luxury box, sweeping right past Accardi's head and making a hole in the back wall.

Accardi fell to the ground as Pasta, Viggo, and Doc jumped on top of him. Everyone screamed and started sprinting out of the luxury box as fast as they could. The lower crowds did the same when they heard the loud gunshot that echoed through the enormous stadium. David pulled out his bulky two-way radio and exclaimed, "Shots fired! Attempted killing in the box! All patrol on the northern side report to Accardi, immediately! All patrol on the southern side, evacuate the stadium! Somebody get the extra guards from the lounge to come up and help!"

As David repeated his announcements and cleared the path for Accardi's hasty exit, the men on the southern side directed all of the guests out, and those on the northern ran to their boss. It didn't take long for the screaming to reach every section of the audience. A storm of people rushed out of the stadium like stampeding bulls. Lieutenant Stanza, upon seeing this, shouted out to her fellow officers, "What's happening!?"

"Ma'am, shots have apparently been fired," shouted an officer in the chaotic crowd. Stanza's eyes widened and she, in an instant, bolted up to the luxury box where Accardi was, but it was no use, for all the masses flying the other direction made her like a lone leaf going against the wind. "Everyone up to that box!" she screamed to all the nearby officers with a pointing finger. While Sylvester packed up his sniper on the peaceful roof, Accardi was being walked out by more than twenty men, and the floors below were made of madness, everyone running in all directions. Further down, in the underground lounge, a lone guard came down the elevator to relay the news of upstairs. All but two of the guards left to help the chaos, going up the elevator and proceeding to escort the rabble out of the stadium.

The timing was perfect. As soon as the majority of the vault guards in the underground lounge rushed out and upstairs, two men in all black with covered faces jumped out of a secret trapdoor in the wall with guns raised. The two guards who were left in the room tried to hold up their tommy guns, but Jeff shouted, "Stop!" with his own tommy gun raised, and Jones' shotgun aimed directly at them. It was one minute later when those two guards were tied up with rope in the pair of chairs facing away from the vault. Jones used an industrial-grade drill to carve a hole into the vault door. Jeff shoved a stick of dynamite in it, and the two backed up, with Jones whispering "Boom" right when the vault door blasted open. Jeff and Jones slowly approached the smokey room, their eyes clinching in the gray dust, but then springing wide open when they looked into the silver box to see piles of cash, enough to build a little shack. They looked back at each other in disbelief, then charged into the vault, tossing their empty bags to the side.

Their plan was not unthinkable, however, for Lieutenant Stanza stopped her rushing to the box, thinking and wondering about the reason this happened. Lieutenant Rivers, who was right behind her and rushing to Accardi with her, shouted through the loud screams, "What is it?"

Stanza remained silent, but after a moment of heavy pondering, she got it. She looked at the American lieutenant and exclaimed, "The vault!" They quickly called all personnel to the elevator that went down to the underground lounge. It took them about six minutes to get there, and when they did, Stanza, Rivers, and about five other officers went into the elevator. They pulled out their firearms inside the slow-moving elevator, and at that very second, Jones and Jeff carried four bags, two in each hand, to the truck. When they heard the elevator coming down, they screamed at each other, tossed the four cash-filled bags through the trapdoor and made a run for it. They jumped into the truck with their money but had no time to close the door to the tunnel. The elevator came down, and the first thing Lieutenant Stanza saw was an open trapdoor in the wall, with a truck hastily turning around behind it.

As the many officers saw the same thing, they began shooting at the truck behind the wall, but Jones and Jeff had already fled up the tunnel. Jones drove for thirty seconds before he slammed on the brakes. He gave Jeff a nod, who then jumped out of the car that had seemingly stopped at a very specific point, and ran over to the wall of the tunnel where a small metal box lay. He ran so fast, he tripped and fell face-first into the rocky ground, but he stood up in an instant and continued over to the wired block. He unlatched a lock on it, then grabbed the handle atop the box, where he finally pushed down on it with all of his strength. As the many officers ran through the lounge to chase after the fleeing men, Stanza screamed out, "Wait, no!" seeing a wire in the far-away tunnel. But her call was too late, and five officers, including Rivers, went soaring through the air as an explosive blast around the trapdoor ignited.

Lieutenant Stanza began to scream in fury. She went up to Lieutenant Rivers, who now, along with the other officers, lay flat on the ground. "Are you ok?" she asked.

The American lieutenant grabbed Stanza by the wrist, pulling her closer in to whisper with an aching tone, "We'll be fine. Go get these sons of bitches!" And that second, with an exchange of respect, Stanza left up the elevator, leaving Rivers down in the lounge. Stanza ran out onto the upper floor where the other officers had just arrived. She hurriedly told them of what had happened and told everyone to leave the stadium immediately to chase after the two men in the truck. As all of the officers quickly escaped the stadium, running to their vehicles. Jeff and Jones too escaped from the collapsing tunnel, making a return to the hangar. Once Stanza was in a car, she drove off with zero idea of where she was going. The only thing she could see for miles away was a small structure, and that second, she spun the car around, speeding toward it, knowing it was where the two men would be.

Lieutenant Stanza, with a swarm of police cars behind her, came upon the abandoned-looking hangar. She was about a quarter of a mile away from it when suddenly, the truck she was looking for sped out from it. Stanza swerved in that direction, causing all the vehicles behind her to do the same. The truck, a mile ahead of Stanza and her army of officers, entered the crowded streets of the city. With all the heavy traffic, the truck slowed, but as Stanza approached, it turned to the sidewalk and sped around the many cars in the most reckless way.

Stanza, with a furious-looking face, did the same without thinking and followed the speeding truck to the end of the street, where they both took a sharp turn. The first two cop cars behind the lieutenant didn't see the turn coming, however, and crashed into each other when they came upon it. Though this caused a blockage on the road for the rest of the chasing police cars to continue, Stanza was still on the go and grew ever closer to the truck. Stanza's pursuit took her and her target through the city like two zigzagging bullets. The lieutenant soon found that the truck driver knew the city well, cleverly making his way to the parts of town he knew would be less built-up with traffic. The two came into a railroad yard filled with nothing but dirt and railway tracks. The truck suddenly stopped, seeing a coming train to the left. Stanza came upon her stopped target in an instant, and that same instant, the truck sped across the tracks like a bull charging at a muleta. With great suspense, Stanza watched the coming train approach as the truck went over the tracks. She shut her eyes in fear, then a moment later, reopened them, looked out her front windshield, and to her genuine relief, saw the truck on the other side of the tracks, having successfully avoided a collision with the train.

The truck continued on, and Stanza did the same on the other side. The two traveled down the moving train on either side until they came to its end, where four more cop cars sat, waiting. The truck rushed to the left as soon as it passed the tail of the train, speeding in front of Stanza on the other side. The lieutenant slammed on her brakes when her target returned to that side of the tracks and flew by right in front of her. She quickly turned and kept her speed on the truck, now with a fleet of police cars behind her. As the chase continued, it grew hastier. The truck kept speeding up, making quicker turns and taking riskier roads. But through it all, the cops held their distance. The many cars reached a small, one-way bridge, and the truck sped onto it. But the truck was going the wrong direction, and out of nowhere, a huge commercial truck showed up. Both trucks braked and swerved with little control to stop, but one of them, the one being involved in the chase, smashed through the rails of the bridge. Stanza and the many officers behind her held wide-open eyes as they saw the very truck they were chasing fall uncontrollably off the bridge and crash into the wide river below it.

Lieutenant Stanza pulled over and jumped out of her car upon hearing the thundering splash. She ran over to the edge, looked down, and saw the truck upside down, slowly sinking into the depths of the water. Right behind her, more cops ran up. Luckily, they had a pair of frogmen on hand that reported to the scene quickly. The lieutenant waited eagerly as they plunged into the river to retrieve the bodies and materials trapped inside the sunken truck. Bubbles went blowing up through the dark water. The divers below saw with their open eyes the big truck. They each grabbed one side of the big truck door and pulled it open.

Back above, the lieutenant stood over the water talking to some officers as to how the chase went down. Right then, the divers ascended from the water, dried off, and when Stanza rushed over to learn of what they'd seen and brought, she held an astonished-looking face. She did not see any bodies, nor any cash-filled bags, but only two men who looked at her in confusion. One of them said, "There was nothing there, ma'am. No bodies. No bags. Nothing at all." The lieutenant looked around, appearing confused and angered.

At Accardi's mansion, where David and all of his men had escorted him to, the host of the games that had just gone so wrong sat in silence. Monopoly went up to his boss and informed him that the vault had been robbed, and the firing was a diversion. Accardi looked at the men around him and shouted, "Where is Cockspy!?"

"Da bathroom, boss," Doc responded.

"Go fetch him!" Doc did just what Accardi said, but when he went into the bathroom, he saw no sign of David. Earlier, David had gone to the bathroom, but he did not plan on returning. He entered the vacant restroom and went straight to the window, which he then opened and followed to jump out of. He fell in the green grass and quickly picked up a brown jacket he had hidden in the bushes. The sight of light and the sound of victory lapped in his head as he proudly walked away. Across town, as police were covering every area of the stadium, people were still leaving. And one of those people was Sylvester. With a janitor's outfit and the sniper bag in the trash upstairs, Sylvester walked proudly, holding a smile on his face that showed he was tasting his victory.

And on the other, other side of town, Bobby and Jones ascended from the river, climbing out right to an empty side street, with Bobby wearing the diving suit, and Jones, a mask connected to the suit's bag of air. They walked further up to find the same type of truck involved in the earlier chase, driven by Jeff. The soaking pair jumped in through the back and gazed with glittering eyes at the bags filled with cash that sat in the vehicle. They sped off with the sight of victory in their faces. Jeff looked in the back and said with a big smile, "How'd id it go?"

"Perfect!" replied Jones. "As soon as I left the hangar in the other truck, all the cops followed me, letting you leave free as a bird from that same hangar a few minutes later. And Bobby came from the depths of the water to save me as soon as I crashed. He was right on time! He gave me the second mask so I could breathe, and we swam here."

All the men went back to the restaurant to celebrate their great victory. They all carried huge smiles and proud heads, for The Accardi Job was done, or so they thought.

When they all arrived, they wasted no time to begin partying. The record player began to sing, full glasses began to clink, and the table full of curry found itself empty within fifteen minutes. The men laughed, danced, sang, and all took turns sitting on the throne made of the bags filled with their newly acquired cash. The celebration was rejoiceful, every man in the room was drinking their hearts out, with a constant flow of laughter in the air. This was the day they felt in all their hearts would change their lives.

The men told stories, partied to no end, and went on a spree of telling their plans to spend their great wealth. Even the restaurant owner and the pair of workers came back to take a quick dance. The men had never been happier, and their hearts were never filled with so much joy. For David realized he could see his daughter again and win back his wife. Jeff stood proud, feeling success like never before. Bobby drank so much, he coughed up some of the chicken he ate, never being more optimistic about what he could do with his life. Sylvester felt the sickness of riches and greed in his palms that gave him nothing but an undeserving smile all night long.

Jones clinked his glass with a spoon and raised it up in the air to give a toast.

"Gentlemen, today we have accomplished something no man has ever done, eat five pounds of chicken!"

"Haha!" the men laughed.

Jones continued, "No-no, but seriously, one month ago I witnessed with my own eyes a band of pathetic miscreants who had no hope in their souls, and I gave them a choice. A choice that would bring them trouble, anxiety, and a whole lot of hard work! But after weeks of preparing and hard, hard work, going through all sorts of obstacles, we have here the greatest prize of all, and to my dear friends I say this, great work!" All the gentlemen clinked their glasses and tossed their next bunch of alcohol down their throats. They all went up to Jones, patting him and each other on the back. "Excuse me, fellas, but I need to relieve myself," Jones exclaimed as he departed to the back restroom. The other men gathered around the furniture and sat in it with their fat asses full of sin. They kept as they were, congratulating one another at their fine work.

"You had the craziest car chase I have ever heard of!"

"Maybe, but you worked with Accardi for a month, nothing crazier than that!"

"Who knew I was such a good shot, huh!?"

"Haha!"

The prideful compliments never saw an end. The men began to go back and forth of what they would do with their share of the money, and as the question had been asked time and time before, even earlier that night, no surprises came to light; that is before Lieutenant Stanza broke down the door with her gun facing out toward the four men.

"Hands in the air! Where I can see them! Now!"

Stanza shouted and shouted as the rest of the officers behind her walked in to handcuff the men, who's faces were red, jaws stuck to the ground, and eyes held open with denial. They exchanged frightful faces, all being actively handcuffed and stood up by the officers. The lieutenant, with a wide smile on her face, returned her gun to the holster and stepped over to the throne of bags. She unzipped one to find it half full of cash. Not full, but half full. She continued to open all of the bags, and the men were so bewildered when they saw the rest of them to hold nothing but cut-up newspapers, stacked up to look like money. The men looked at each other again, this time with even more confusion. The lieutenant stepped over and screamed, "Where is it!? Where is the rest of the money!?"

She stared into the eyes of the men as they all looked back at her with the utmost honesty and genuineness, whispering in shock, "We have no idea."

Six days later:

"All rise for the honorable Judge Molton," the guard shouted as Bobby, Sylvester, David, Jeff, Jimmy Green, who was their attorney, and the rest of the room stood up for the entering judge to take a seat. Wearing cheap suits and holding glum faces, the four men on trial sat at a long wooden table on the left side of the huge courtroom. On the other side was the prosecutor, Pasta, and two empty seats. The judge, in his big black robes and his grand, bald head, read aloud with a large, deep tone, "We are here today for the trial of one Robert Davinson, Sylvester Erellio, David Cockspy, and Jefferson Williams for the crimes of grand theft, resisting arrest, reckless driving, and attempted murder, all on multiple accounts. Mr. Wellsworth, I can see that there are a few empty seats on your side of the courtroom, are we expecting to see Mr. Accardi today?"

"Yes, sir, he is just running a bit late. He should be here shortly." Suddenly, the doors of the courtroom flung open, and two men walked in. David recognized one to be Accardi, but all four men recognized the other man: Jones. "Forgive me, Judge Molton," exclaimed Jones. "I am sorry for our unpunctuality, but I can assure you that nothing but respect will be seen by us in this here courtroom."

"Yes, and you are…?"

"Indeed, your honor, my name is Giovanni Jones Accardi, the CEO of Mericorn Incorporated," Jones said, tall and proud, with a strong Italian accent that he hadn't carried around the other men. "And this is my Chief Officer of Secuirty," he continued, pointing to the man beside him, who David believed to be Accardi.

"Very well, please take a seat," the judge exclaimed. The four men looked back and forth at each other, bewildered by the black Italian mafioso with an expensive, silk suit they once thought to be their friend. They all leaned over to their attorney, explaining the madness.

"What the!?"

"It's *him*!"

"That's the guy that brought us together!"

"The heist was his idea!"

"That is not Accardi! Is it?"

BAM! BAM! Judge Molton's gavel went, slamming down on the wood in front of him. "Mr. Green, please explain to the accused that speaking out of pocket at the indecent level they are will not be tolerated in my courtroom!"

"Yes, your honor, forgive us, but there has been a pretty large new development," Green responded, taking a stand.

"Yes, well that's why we're here, isn't it? To share all of the developments. So now if you don't mind sitting down and proceeding in the trial with respect and elegance much like the prosecution is doing." The judge gave a respectful smile toward Accardi.

The trial was not like anything Jimmy Green had ever seen. It was as if, no-no-no, it was in truth that the entirety of the courtroom had been bribed, blackmailed, or otherwise in on it from the beginning. No trial ever occurred six days after the arrest. It was unheard of and clearly had been pushed up by someone who was tired of waiting; however, the prosecution seemed as if it had months to plan, like they'd known this trial would happen long before the four men ever did. And when the prosecution called its first witness, things got stranger.

The first witness presented was a shot to the gut to Jeff—his old chief. Jeff's jaw stuck to the floor as he saw his old partner and friend take the stand and give a false testimony. He talked about how angry Jeff was when he was fired, and how he claimed he would hurt the system like it hurt him. Green tried to do a decent cross-examination, but the chief's story was airtight, and all of his questions had already been cleared up by the prosecution in a devastating way.

Who was the next witness, but Cleo the Cow, who claimed Sylvester sold him fake diamonds in a legitimate deal. Again, Green was left helpless. Then, Hasan Mitra, the owner of the curry restaurant came up. He told the court that he'd been threatened to hide these men, give them free food, and give them shelter. Sylvester, Bobby, Jeff, David, and Green held shocked, lifeless expressions with total chaos in their heads as they slowly realized that this was an unwinnable case, with false evidence being presented from every person that could've helped them. Who was next? the men thought. Who would be the next person to stab them in the back, and give a false testimony? The next person up was unknown to three of the men, but David recognized the old man to be the barber he saw Doc beat up a while back.

The barber, Liam Hart, showed some bruises from his beating, but instead of saying that Doc was the one who gave them to him, he pointed to David and claimed he was the one who beat him senseless when Accardi asked him to simply pick up a check. David shook his head repeatedly and told his cousin, Green, to do something. But what could Green do? Hart claimed that David beat him with the end of his pistol to incite more fear in his poor, old self, to avoid the question of why David's hands held no bruises themselves if he was the one who threw the punches. David was angry at the old man, and then he got even angrier when Doc went up to the stage, talking about how David would constantly express great trauma, anger, and fear from his time in the war. Green tried to talk about Doc's bruises on his hands during cross, to connect him to Liam Hart's beating, but he had a solid story about doing a construction project at home.

David's trauma from the war and his loony behavior was talked much about from the next few witnesses, all who worked for Accardi. These were Frank, Monopoly, Viggo, even Pasta, who said nothing but nodded to the question of if David relayed these behaviors. David nearly cried when he saw his friend's betrayal, the one who never spoke, and the one who meant the most to him. But David's sadness swapped for great confusion in an instant, when the next witness walked up.

With a knowledgeable smirk, Johnny stared at David. The stunned man did nothing but blink endlessly, refusing to believe he was looking at the guy he'd shot and killed, or perhaps just shot. Could it be? No, no David refused to believe it, and yet it was true. However, he began to think that when he shot Johnny those weeks ago, the man must've been wearing some sort of steel under his shirt. Something to catch that bullet, and perhaps all the blood came from some kind of clever concoction dealing with red sauce or paint.

Johnny told the court of how David shot him, and how the steel flask in his front pocket took the hit. He said that David then tried to finish the job but Accardi stepped in and stopped him. David, who watched and listened carefully, could not believe anything at the moment.

Next up was the pilot, Manier, who said that Jeff and Bobby held him at gunpoint to take them and the drill to America. Right after him, Jeremy came up, and being the one who helped them carry out that heist, he confirmed everything, explaining how he too was threatened, forced to help them. The men lost all faith, and their level of anger had never been higher. Every person they talked to on this job had turned on them, telling false versions of the truth. Versions that would convince the jury to find the four men guilty. After some of the fifty men from Harlem came up and once again, told false versions of the story, further incriminating the four men, Stanza went up.

"Lieutenant Stanza, when you told Mr. Accardi about the possible threat of the robbery, was the man next to him that man right there?" the prosecutor asked, pointing to David.

"Yes, it was."

"You are sure? You're certain it was not another white man with brown hair?"

"Yes, Mr. Wellsworth, I think I would be able to tell the difference if it were."

All the men panicked in disbelief when they heard this, knowing full well that nothing good was coming for them. The prosecution continued with their witness. "Lieutenant, can you please describe to the court what you saw when you first made the arrest?"

"Of course. The station received an anonymous tip of where these men would be, and after a rather reckless chase, which indeed put many innocent civilians at stake, we rushed over to the address. We then spoke with the owner of the restaurant. He said there were four men that had been threatening to kill him if he didn't let them stay in the back of his restaurant, as we had earlier that week found their original base of operations, which was a warehouse just outside the city. When we walked up to the door, we pulled out our guns, then naturally ran in and made the arrests. I walked over to retrieve the stolen money, only to find all the bags held were cut-up newspapers, positioned to look like money, with one half-full bag containing real cash. We managed to trace the serial numbers of the portion of cash we found and confirm that those were the same bills that were accounted for in the vault of the Mericorn-owned stadium."

"Thank you, Lieutenant Stanza," said the prosecutor.

The rest of the trial was brutal; witness after witness came up, telling nothing but lies. The defense didn't land a single shot, getting nothing from nobody. The prosecution had about twenty witnesses, and the defense had only four, being Sylvester, Bobby, Jeff, and David. These men went up and gave testimonies of what really happened. They told the whole truth, and nothing but the truth, probably for the first time in their lives. They talked of how Jones brought them together, and how Accardi's Chief Officer of Security posed as the big boss while Jones held a double face. But the words of the accused weren't enough for the jury of twelve, who most of which had likely already been paid off. The quick, rigged, unjust and unfair trial was nearing its end. The final witness was called to the stand, and the four men were screaming inside with fear. But all that fear, all that sadness, all those loose emotions came together in an instant, colliding to form a big ball of rage. For they all stared at the final witness, Giovanni Jones Accardi. He walked up with such elegance to the stand.

He wore the nicest brown suit you'd ever seen, with a blue undershirt, a much nicer pork pie hat carrying a lone feather on its side, a very expensive watch, and a long, thick, brown tie. When asked to tell the story of what happened, Giovanni Accardi, or as the men knew him, Jones, explained, "My Chief Officer of Security, who's sitting right over there now, came down with some severe medical issues. Being very close to our business' annual horse race, we needed a replacement. So we began hunting for a new head of security, and we found a man named David Cockspy. At the time, he appeared kind, respectful, and did everything to the fullest. And I cannot say how betrayed I felt upon learning this act of betrayal."

David's ears began whistling, his face turned red, his fists clenched, and his anger had been held in too long.

Accardi continued, "I felt so embarrassed and—"

"LIAR!" David shouted, jumping out of his chair. "LIAR! TELL THEM WHAT REALLY HAPPENED, JONES! YOU SPEAK OF BETRAYAL YOU MISERABLE LITTLE CUNT! FUCK YOU! I SERVED THIS COUNTRY IN THE SECOND GREAT WAR AND I THOUGHT I HAD SEEN EVIL BUT THIS IS TRICKERY! THIS IS DEVILRY! THIS IS MADNESS! HOW DARE YOU STAND THERE ACCUSING US OF THE VERY THING YOU PULLED US INTO! HOW DARE YOU!"

The scene of the court was all over the papers. And as Jones, or rather, Giovanni Accardi, sat back in his chair with the straightest face and deadlocked eyes, the many guards of the courtroom rushed on David. They tackled him to the ground, trying to de-escalate the situation, the judge banging his gavel, shouting, "Order! Order! Order in my court!" But David wouldn't stop screaming and cursing. He was carried out of the courtroom, and as Jones watched, he whispered to himself, "You can only see one's true colors when the lights go out." And just like that, the trial was concluded.

One day later:
"All rise for the honorable Judge Molton," the guard exclaimed as the judge walked up to the bench. He asked aloud with all present in the courtroom, "Has the jury reached a verdict?"

"Yes, your honor," replied the standing spokesman of the twelve deliberators. "the jury has come to a conclusive decision that in the case of Davinson, Cockspy, Erellio and Williams, the defense is… guilty on all accounts."

"Very well," replied the judge. "I hereby sentence David Cockspy, Sylvester Erellio, Jeff Williams, and Bobby Davinson to forty-five years in prison."

The four men, who sat in their seats, were frozen in terror and nearly shocked to death. Their brains turned inside out, and their hearts fell flat. They were walked out to a big white truck where they were then handcuffed. The truck carried the men slowly and they could feel every turn the vehicle made, until it slowed to a full stop. They wondered what was happening, for it was too soon for them to have arrived at the prison. But then they heard a sound, a sound of the truck unlatching and opening. They tilted their eyebrows upon seeing the suited dark Italian man that had brought them together.

The once Mysterious Man had revealed his full name, and as he climbed into the truck, emotions were tossed all around. The men felt everything—anger, betrayal, confusion, sadness, fear, and the desire to kill. Jones, or as most knew him, Accardi, lit a cigar and lay back in the far seat of the big white state truck.

He asked softly, "How's it going, boys?"

"What makes you think we won't strangle you where you sit?" David asked in a dark and sinister voice.

"Oh please, the only thing you could ever kill is your little brother," Jones said as David pounced from his seat. But his chained foot held him back, attached to the leg of the bench.

He fell to the ground and looked up at Jones. "Why?" he asked with fury in his eyes, getting up.

"You know, I was actually worried that y'all would figure it out, but here we are, a plan as perfect as can be."

"Figure what out?" Bobby asked, confused.

"God. You boys really have no clue."

"No clue as to what?" Sylvester jumped in.

"No clue as to why you're here, dear Sylvester. You see, here y'all were, making good choices and smart plays, thinking you had full control of the horse, but who do you think built the track? Who do you think trained the horses where to go and how to run? Jeff, you think your boss really just decided to fire one of his best guys? Ha! David, you really think you killed a man? No! Sylvester, you really think little Cleo would recognize fake diamonds? That dumbass couldn't tell the difference between his mom and a horse's ass! And little Bobby, so gullible you let a stranger in the back of a cop car convince you to rob the mob! You see, boys, I didn't just bring y'all together; I shaped this chapter of your lives. Every person you thought was conning for this job, well, they were really conning you. Every choice and decision you decided to make, that was just me making you feel like you had the wheel of the car, but no. I had the wheel the whole damn time, and every step was designed to get you here."

"So you…"

"Yep! It was me, anything you have done in the past nine months had been carefully stringed by me, Giovanni Jones Accardi!"

"But why?" Jeff asked. "Why us? Why this elaborate scheme?"

"Well, you see, I took a little break from business and needed a bit more cash flow, so what better way to make money than to steal from yourself? See, I stole from my very own company, so now insurance will be covering what was stolen."

"Of course, that's why you had your little actor have all those long meetings with the insurance agency, just to double your money," David said, soulless.

"Correct, my dear David, however, it wasn't exactly double. I had to leave some behind to get you to prison for the rest of your miserable lives. You see, there's an old saying, an eye for an eye, well, I'm not gonna kill you for what you did, but I am going to make you suffer."

"AND WHAT EXACTLY IS IT THAT WE DID!?" Bobby screamed.

Jones put down his cigar with no rush, and his face turned as he began to narrate his story.

"Some years ago," he began, "my great-grandfather came to this country. He built a life for him and his family, but that life was taken from him, so in order to be free of the wolves, he had to become a lion. And for nearly eighty years, my family has had a hand on this city as one of the greatest families in the country! But the business... the business isn't all it's cracked up to be, and it wasn't my taste of tea. Now I know what you're thinking, a black Accardi, that's nuts! Haha yeah well, it's a long story, my father enjoyed a bit of dark chocolate, if you know what I mean. Hahaha! Well, anyway, even with my lack of care for the business, as well as the color of my skin, I was brought up to be the next head of the family. But one day I met the most beautiful French woman. She was my everything.

"I remember the day I first met her. Her glistening blue eyes, her silky hair, and her... her smile." Jones teared up, but he continued. "We decided to get married, and when she got pregnant, nothing else mattered. It broke my father's heart, but I just didn't care about the business anymore. So I left the business, with nothing, no money, no friends, not even my father's blessing, but I had all I needed. A while passed, and my daughter was turning two. I had gotten this job down at a local butcher shop. We only had so much money, so we went from place to place, but at the time of my daughter's second birthday, we were in this small motel downtown." The dots began to click, and some of the men's brains began ticking as their faces began turning.

"I went out to get the cake. Like I said, we didn't have much money, but I was insistent on getting my little girl this big chocolate cake we had seen at a bakery nearby. She... she was so sweet, and... and... I would've done anything to make her happy, so I saved every penny to get her that cake for her big day. I couldn't wait to see the look on her face when I brought it home to her." Jones' face began to leak, and his mouth formed a small smile at the memory. "That night... that night..."

The men's eyes began widening.

"My wife and daughter were drawing upstairs; little did they know that below their room was another guest, another guest who suffered with trauma from the war, another guest who had recently lost a dear sibling in the war. Suffering severely from the illness, the man thought he would kill himself, and for some reason, he thought the best plan was to light himself on fire in a goddamn motel."

Jones' sad smile turned into a disgusted frown. "The man's name was David Cockspy, and he... and *you*," Jones explained, looking at David who held wide-open eyes with realization. "You lay in bed and threw a match on the floor where you had spilled some liquor. The room went ablaze, but as you closed your eyes, you came to your senses, perhaps thinking of your own daughter. Your epiphany to keep trying to live saved your life, and so you hopped out of bed, running out the room once you'd realized the fire couldn't be put out. You attempted suicide but decided not to go through with it, but that doesn't mean that lives were not taken that night. You see, my wife and daughter began coughing and smelling the smoke as the floor turned to ash and the walls turned to light.

"They ran to the fire extinguisher that luckily was held in their room, only for it to unluckily not work. But it wasn't luck, you see, for the man who sold the fire extinguishers to the motel was a small conman, who was just trying to make a quick buck. You sold false fire extinguishers to a wooden motel... *Sylvester.*"

Sylvester, whose jaw was dropped and who too was tearing up, listened attentively as Jones continued on. "My wife and daughter rushed to the door and tried everything, banging on it, screaming, clawing for their very lives, but the motel owner, Bobby Davinson, was too cheap to buy good materials, so my wife and daughter were locked in the room because of rusted locks." Bobby leaned back in horror as Jones continued his story with more and more rage.

"David, trying to fix the situation, ran to the owner, Bobby, who wasn't there at the time, but passed out on the floor of a nightclub a few blocks away. David tried to call the police and dialed the number as fast he could once he heard the terrifying screams of my wife and daughter. But there was a robbery uptown, and the only respondent in the vicinity who could've came and helped was a young, prideful cop, who heard the call on his radio but turned it off because he was enjoying the pleasures of lust too much to save a woman and her daughter. The cop would later get demoted but not fired or sent to prison. This cop with no sense of duty or heroism was Jeff."

Jeff and the others sat in terror and bewilderment. "I came home to find not a happy little girl drawing with her mother, but a bonfire the size of a mountain, five fire trucks, three police cars and an ambulance with two body bags in it. One big... and one little."

Jones' tone let the whole truck feel his pain, his suffering, and the four men could feel the screams of agony that night. Their mouths all frowned, their eyes all teared up and not a single word was said until Jones finished, "I returned to my family, to my business, and as I could not overcome my grief, I decided to take justice into my own hands when I found out that only one man was brought to prison for the death of my wife and daughter. And this man, who was David, was given a mere few years for his act! So I created a plan, an ingenious plan. I called in every favor I had and used every breath in my body to see that it would be finished. From having Cleo's daughter attack Sylvester to get him to take the job, to having my Chief Officer of Security, an aspiring actor, pose as me while I led the job, I got it done. You see, I own this city, and now, you all will go to prison for the rest of your lives. And since I know every man inside that place, I have made arrangements for them to make each of your lives as miserable as can be until the day you die, which, don't worry, won't be for a long, long, long time. I've made sure of that. You brought me the greatest pain I have ever had to endure, and now, I will bring the same to you. You thought all along that you were the masters behind The Accardi Job, but no, The Accardi Job was all about you."

Jones, still enraged and dropping tears, remembering, stood up and stepped out of the truck, staring one last time into the eyes of the speechless men he had fooled. And as he walked away, he said softly, "Don't fret David, I'll look after your daughter."

The truck doors closed, and the vehicle slowly pulled away. Jeff whispered to the frozen group, "How has this happened?"

Bobby, finally understanding what Jones wished for them to learn, looked at his friends and said, "We all thought we deserved a second chance, and that we were going to get it too, but second chances are for the good guys, and we have mistaken ourselves to be ones. We are greedy, foolish, undeserving, selfish men, and I think we all know that. Jones has brought justice for our mistakes."

The men said nothing more, for nothing more needed to be said. Their eyes filled with tears, and their hearts bounced around in chaos.

Jones stepped into his luxurious car where his driver, chief of security, friend and the man who impersonated him during the job, asked the one true Accardi, "Where to boss?"

Jones stared out into the clouds as he said softly, slowly and with hope, "The cemetery."

Finished with her case, Lieutenant Stanza packed up her bags at the hotel of which she was staying. She heard a knock on the door, and the American Lieutenant, with a cast around his arm, walked in. "Dan! You're okay!"

"Yes, yes I am, Elizabeth."

"Why do you say it like that?"

"Like what?"

"With a voice of disappointment."

The American lieutenant walked further into the room, sighed, and spoke, "I was at the trial."

"We got them! Deal's a deal. I already told your captain you did all the tough work."

"That's not what I meant."

"What did you mean then?"

"I heard your testimony, and I just want to know why you lied. We both met Accardi at the stadium, and that was a different Accardi at the trial. I was with you on this case every step since you got here. I know the facts. I know what happened. And that trial was rigged. I thought you were one to bring justice?"

"Justice? The law isn't justice; the law is the result of humanity believing it can control the world and prevent it from going ablaze. But it can't do that, can it? When I was a girl, my sister and I loved playing games. My mother didn't want us to go outside most days. We were too young to understand and too ignorant to listen. One night, my sister and I snuck out of the house to go play at the park. We had so much fun that night. The moon was brighter than the sun. We ran around, climbed on the trees, tried to catch frogs, and played what you call hide and seek. There was one round of hide and seek where I was the seeker. I looked around, and I kept screaming to my sister that I was going to find her super fast, and that she had no chance of winning. But after a second or two, I realized that I could not hear the sound of my own voice. My ears rang, and my legs began to shake. It was as if God was tearing up the world. It was so loud, like never-ending thunder. I didn't know what was going on, and I could hear nothing. I was so confused.

"I looked up to the sky to see what I thought were a flock of birds. One of the birds used the bathroom in the air, and I could see a clump of darkness falling in front of the stars. But it was not birds that I saw, nor was it their shit that fell from the sky. The ground was already thundering, but in an instant, it pulled me down, with the loudest noise I'd ever heard erupting from all around. I was sobbing, afraid, alone, and confused. I lay face down on the shaking dirt with my hands over my head. But then I remembered my sister, and so I used all my strength to stand up, just to be immediately sent back down with another shake of the very world. I'll never forget the sight of it all. The smoke, the flames, the screaming.

"All the houses around the park had their doors flung open by running families. There were screams, and I couldn't hear my voice again. I tried a few more times to get up, and when I finally did, I ran around the whole park looking for my sister. Each time the world shook, I would fall to the ground, and each time I would stand back up to see another puff of smoke the color of the sun. I checked by a log in the middle of the open field, and by the great power of the Lord I was able to find my sister, who was curled up inside the hollow wood with tears running down her small face. I didn't know what to do other than comfort my sister, so I crawled in with her, and we hugged till our hearing dissipated completely and sleep finally came to us. We awoke the next morning to a man with heavy boots, a blue cloth greatcoat and a képi atop his head. He tried to help us, but my sister and I ran away from him, screaming our mother and father's names. We tripped more than a dozen times on the rubble as we rushed home and were bleeding out of our knees by the time we finally ran up to our house, where we saw nothing, absolutely nothing.

"We stepped over the dusty rocks, with multiple officers chasing after us. My sister began to scream, and I began to sob when we saw the two charred skeletons embracing each other in a hug, with what flesh they had left melted together. The officers picked both of us up and carried our kicking, crying, screaming selves away from the place we once called home, as well as the people we once called our family. Was that justice? No! Justice is always absent, unless we make it ourselves."

"I'm sorry," the American lieutenant said, "but I know true anger when I see it, so I ask you, was what you did justice, or revenge for something those guys might've done?"

The man then walked out of the room, whispering, "Goodbye." "Goodbye," replied Stanza.

Jones' Recollection

I stood at the edge of that cliff on the cloudy afternoon, standing above the two graves that belong to my loves. Behind me was that big tree that seemed as if it's been there since the dawn of time. A single leaf blew off it and slowly fell through the air before being caught by Elizabeth. "It's done," I said. "They are going to suffer for the rest of their lives, all because of one little mistake." "You regret it?" Elizabeth asked me. "No." "What I did, I wouldn't have done anything like it for anyone else, for anything else. You loved my sister, possibly more than I did, and she loved you. She would always write to me, saying that one day, when the war was over, you would earn enough money to buy and rebuild the house we grew up in, and I would stay with your new family. She was the kindest person I ever knew. But something keeps popping up in my mind. This whole time, we thought we were delivering justice, but was it justice, or was it revenge?" "Neither. Both. Why does it matter? It's done. Things aren't always one thing. Those men are bad people, and they are being punished for their sins, their faults, their mistakes, that is justice. But the extent of what we did, that is just how the world works. It's dark, and one has to fight if they want a second chance; it doesn't just come naturally. Those men only got one chance, and they messed it up, so we took our justice, and we took our revenge." "I suppose so. What will you do now?" "For years I thought life was an endless parade of misery and tolerance, until I met your sister. After they both left me, I was fueled by grief and vengeance. Now I have no vengeance left in me, no love to continue with, except for whatever still remains in my fractured shell you might call a heart. I can't go back to the way I lived before them, and I cannot continue as I have." "It's always good to see you, Jones," Elizabeth told me, giving me a big hug. "I must ask, how did you get all that money out of there without them knowing?" she then asked, beginning to walk off. "Simple. Right before the big car chase which, gotta give it to you, hats off." "Thank you!" "Well, I replaced it when Jeff was having a cigarette; he does that a lot, at least, he used to." Elizabeth walked away and said, "Goodbye, my friend. I hope you find a new way to live." "Goodbye," I replied to my sister-in-law. I then turned back out to the edge of the cliff, where I took out the envelope in my right pocket. I opened it and pulled out the letter, which I read aloud, standing over the gray, polished gravestones of my family.

"My dear Ella,

I have played back the night we met over and over again in my head. You wore a beautiful white dress with pink and yellow flowers on it. I remember us sitting on the hill as we looked up at the stars. I remember the touch of your lips, and how soft they were, and how I felt when I first kissed you. I hadn't known life before I met you, and as I also replay the night you and Rosa left me, I keep thinking what could have gone differently. What if I was there? What if you jumped out the window? What if I had done this or you had done that? But I must live in the present. I have completed my job, and I now have this sense of closure. My dreams of you will never stop, but I have learned that maybe life isn't all that it appears. Maybe I can be happy again, maybe I can move on, maybe I can find love again. The old me wouldn't think much of that, but you showed me how to be hopeful, and you have taught me that I owe it to myself, to you, to our little girl, to try. I love you more than anything in this life, and that is one thing that will never change, but now that my vengeance is done, maybe it is time for me to start the next chapter, for The Accardi Job is finished."

57539224R00145